NO LONGER PROPERTY OF
SEATTLE PUBLIC LIBRARY

MOMMA: GONE

A Personal Story

Nina Foxx

Houston, Texas * Washington, D.C.

Momma Gone © 2014 by Nina Foxx
Brown Girls Publishing, LLC
www.browngirlspublishing.com

ISBN: 9781625174499

All rights reserved. No part of this book may be reproduced in any form or
by any means including electronic, mechanical or photocopying or stored
in a retrieval system without permission in writing from the publisher
except by a reviewer who may quote brief passages to be included in a
review.

First Brown Girls Publishing LLC trade printing

Manufactured and Printed in the United States of America

If you purchased this book without a cover, you should be aware
that this book is stolen property. It is reported as "unsold and
destroyed to the publisher, and neither the author nor the publisher has
received any payment for this "stripped" book.

In memory of my mother, Elvie Jackson, and for all families affected by cancer.

For Brian

ONE

*M*omma put me up on the jukebox. I could see everything from there, even all the people in the room.

"Sweetie is my little lady," she said. She steadied herself with one hand and pushed away from the bar with the other. Her skin was fair and the bluish veins showed through like she was much older than her thirty years. They all turned and looked and smiled at us with that plastered-on, woozy kind of smile. The smell that goes along with men in bars followed their heads as they turned and I could smell it, strong, leaping out at me. I heard Gramma call this "preserved-in-alcohol." I smiled because I knew I was supposed to, but I was a little scared. Butterflies swam in my stomach and I bounced my legs off the jukebox to help calm them down.

From where I was sitting, I could see over the top of everyone in the room. Momma and I were the only two ladies here. I guess the other ladies didn't need medicine, only men and Momma. Momma said that other ladies took their medicine at home, but Daddy didn't let her have hers there, so we went to get it. Sometimes, just like now, she took me with her. I really didn't understand it all; medicine is supposed to make you better, but Momma seemed to get sicker and sicker after she had it.

Freda Payne was singing "Bring the Boys Home."

Everyone had forgotten about me.

"Turn it up, Jeffrey. Turn it up." Momma closed her eyes slowly and opened them again. Her head moved to something deeper than just the rhythm of the song.

"Bring 'em back alive!" Freda said.

Whenever I heard this song I wondered who she was talking about. Momma liked it and she played it over and over at home. She played it so much and danced and cried out for June-Bug till Daddy threw the record player in the yard. I was sad when he did that; I couldn't play my Muffin Man song anymore. We tried to make the record player work again, but it was no good trying; it just wouldn't go. Daddy apologized to Momma and when I asked him why he did it, he said because that song made Momma sad and he couldn't stand to see her cry. Maybe that was why I didn't get beat like other kids on our block; I cried as soon as I got in trouble, so Daddy just left me alone.

I didn't know where June-Bug had gone, but I sure wished he would come back. They said he went someplace to fight folks. Momma and Freda wanted him back like I did.

"How come he can fight and I can't?" I asked the same question over and over but I never got an answer. It was almost like they thought I didn't understand how things worked, but I did. More than they wanted to say.

June-Bug was the best big brother a little sister could have. He bought me ice cream and took me everywhere he went, even to see karate movies. He had an Afro and people called him Red because he was the color of the Alabama Red dirt that Auntie called "bay-bay" dirt. She baked it in the ovens sometimes and ate it, too. I liked when she did stuff like that; folks in New York never baked no dirt, but folks in Alabama ain't ever seen too many folks like June-Bug neither.

I wanted an Afro like June-Bug but Momma said no Afro for me. We tried it in secret one time, but my hair wouldn't stand up. To tell the truth, his didn't stand up either, not really. His 'fro was always sort of flat on one side, but that was okay with me, he still looked cool.

"Elva, can that sweetie pie of yours dance?"

One man hollered at Momma although he didn't have to. He was standing right by her and the music wasn't really that loud. The fat man kept wiping the bar and Momma laughed. She put me on the floor at the same time.

"Dance, baby. You show 'em your stuff."

She almost spilled her drink on me and I felt sorta trapped with all the big smelly people around me, but I danced anyway. When Freda said to turn the ships around, I did one of my best spins I could. I put myself far away; I imagined I was a ballerina like on TV, but with more soul. I twirled and bopped as best I could, halfway listening to the music. I wanted to take dancing lessons but Momma said I was too young. I asked Daddy if I could and he said he didn't want "no buck-dancing niggers" in his house; he said I needed to concentrate on learning to read and write so I could make something of myself. I asked Gramma what buck dancing was. She told me to get away and to go play before she got her switch. Grown-ups were so confusing. I heard her ask Momma what they were teaching me up in the north.

Freda was finished now, and I stopped dancing and looked at Momma. Some man started to sing about loving somebody being wrong and he don't want to be right. I didn't understand that either because whenever I called Gramma she was always telling me to make sure I do right. This man was singing about doing wrong and everybody was singing along with him.

The song was over and everybody went back to smiling and grinning at me. The man with one leg behind the bar gave me a soda. I looked at Momma and she nodded to me that it was okay to take it. He popped the top for me with his can opener and I drank it directly from the can. It fizzled as it went down and I thought about the burn in my throat and followed it down to my tummy.

"Say, thank you, sweetie," Momma said. One piece of her hair had fallen into her face. She pushed it away.

She always called me Sweetie. I think some folks thought my name was Sweetie, but it wasn't. My name is Monica Denise Wooten. I am seven years old and I am going to start second grade in school.

I said thanks to the man in my small voice and Momma took my hand in her real soft one with the thin skin. He gave me a nickel and smiled at me with a wide-open grin. I could see that he was missing teeth, too. I looked behind the bar now and I stood behind Momma's leg and took a peek around her skirt. It scared me and was exciting all at the same time because I knew the man only had one leg. The other leg was a peg. Every time I asked, Momma said that Sugar took his leg.

I wondered who Sugar was and I also wanted to know why she needed an extra leg. They always laughed at me when I said that. Momma told me to remember not to ask Daddy that question. I guess I would have to explain to him why I was in a bar taking soda and money from a man with one leg and missing teeth.

It was bright outside and I blinked when we stepped into the light. I didn't know why they didn't turn on more lights in that place anyway.

It was kinda early and I knew we were going home now so Momma could go to sleep. She came home from work at the hospital in the morning before Daddy left for work. Momma is a nurse and she takes care of crazy people. At least that's what Daddy said.

We drove her to work at the hospital that locked its doors every night and she got a ride home with somebody else. We had to drive her there because somebody stole her car. It was a yellow car with stripes down the middle and my daddy gave it to her. She loved it even though it had a dent in the front from where the truck hit us. The truck really backed up onto us while we wasn't moving, but Momma said it hit us so I said it, too.

Anyway, the police found the car later and we went to see it. It didn't look like much of a car to me anymore. It didn't have no wheels or doors left. I looked in what was left of the trunk to see if my Peppermint Twist was still there, but it was gone. I knew it would be. Any thief with sense would want it; it was such a great toy. My favorite. It had a ring on the end of a string, with a ball attached to the end. Mine was all purple and pink and yellow. You put your leg into the ring and swung the string around and jumped over it with the other leg. Too bad that it was gone because I had almost learned how to do it, almost as good as the big girls.

I only got my legs wrapped up in the cord occasionally. It felt so good to put the ring around my skinny leg and look down as I swung it around and around. I hopped over it with my other leg almost perfectly, almost every time. But it was gone now, just like June-Bug. Maybe Daddy would get me another one.

Two

I stood on the corner with Momma. Not really, I stood there and she just sort of hung from the fence by the back of her shirt, like she was trying to sit down in a chair, only there wasn't no chair, her eyes half-closed and her mouth half-open. We stood, waiting for someone to come and help us get home because I was too short for Momma to lean on and she was too heavy for me to help her walk. I licked my lollipop and watched the people go by.

I wondered why they didn't look at us. We had to look funny, a little girl with bouncy curls and a red lollipop, and a momma hanging on the fence, but no one turned their head to look as they passed by, they just went by, sneaking peeks at us out of the corner of their eyes. Their stares made my cheeks burn. I knew that we were not ordinary. I yearned for ordinary every day.

Momma had too much medicine, I guess. James helped us this far; I could see our house from here and I could see the neighbors in the windows, too. No one came out of their house to help, but I knew they saw us. Folks around here saw everything.

I thought Momma was sleeping. Drool came out of the right corner of her mouth and rolled down her chin. James got tired of helping Momma so he went to see if Daddy was home so he could come and get us. James was weak, I had never seen him eat food, only drink the same medicine that Momma did, but I figured everybody eats something sometimes.

Time moved in slow motion, with Momma drooling and hanging from the fence, and people walking by secretly watching but not helping. It felt like we had been waiting a long time. Once we got home, I knew Momma and Daddy would fight and Momma would end up crying and she'd finally shout "Good-bye cruel world!" like she always did. That's the way it goes.

Every now and then she tried to get up off the fence, but her legs acted like jelly and they couldn't hold her weight and she flopped down like my Raggedy Ann doll. If her shirt wasn't caught on the fence she would've fallen on the ground.

Every time she woke up she asked, "You here, sweetie pie?" like she thought I might have gone somewhere. I knew that I had to stay with my momma no matter what. I didn't know how to cross the street.

Finally, Daddy and James were coming. I could feel Daddy's anger as he got closer. It rolled from his head and vibrated through the air like lightning rolls across the sky in the summer. Daddy stepped up and ran his hand through my hair but didn't say a word. Instead, he picked Momma up and cradled her like a baby. James made a move to help like he could, and he stumbled. My daddy sucked his teeth and pushed him away but still, no one said a word.

"Bye, Mr. James." I was the one to break the silence. I smiled at him and managed a very small wave. He didn't say anything but instead he licked his mustache, then rolled it between his fingers. He watched me and Daddy and Momma as we went across the street and up the steps and into our house.

Momma was awake now and I knew they were going to fight. I made my way up the stairs and to my room, but no door was going to keep out the noise, not really. I didn't even try to close it. At first, all I could hear was the bass in Daddy's voice, and although he was calm, his calmness was really covering his anger. He was good at doing that; the more upset he got, the smaller his voice was.

I couldn't hear the exact words, but I knew what they were saying; this wasn't the first time. Daddy wanted Momma to stay out of the bar with the men and the jukebox. Momma didn't think he understood. I could hear it before she said it.

"Goodbye, cruel world!" I could never tell exactly what she meant by this. Where was she going and why was the world so cruel?

Doors slammed and Momma stomped up the steps.

My little brother cried in the next room. He was very little and he cried all the time.

I listened from my room as Momma talked at Daddy who was still downstairs. She was crying now and I knew she was putting things in a bag.

"The girl can stay with you!" Whenever they fought she never called me Sweetie. Then, I was just "the girl." Momma was sniffling and talking at the same time. It was always the same.

"She likes you better anyway! I am taking my baby; you can't have him."

"Oh, Elva, be reasonable." Daddy was upstairs now and his voice was still calm.

I didn't even flinch as I listened. We went through this drill all the time, she wouldn't even say good-bye, I knew that. More stomping, more yelling, doors slamming; finally, I heard the car start up, Daddy's car. My momma and brother were in it. If she really didn't come back this time I would miss her, but not him. Never him. Seems like this all started when he came.

They weren't going nowhere but to the park. She took us both one time; it kinda depended on how she felt. They were going to go and park and sit until the cops told them to move or she got tired and then they would come back. There would be no sounds and everyone would act like nothing had happened and we would all drive her to work once again. I could hear the clock ticking for a long time and I finally fell asleep somehow. No one came to talk to me like parents talked to kids on TV, to tell me that it would be all right. I wondered if they really thought I couldn't hear them or that I didn't understand. I understood more than they would ever know. My Gramma said I was an old soul.

Daddy shook me awake and I realized that things had happened just as I thought they would and it was time to take Momma to work. We all moved silently to the car and no one said a word. Daddy turned on the radio and Momma rolled down the windows. We sang along, and for a few minutes, things were as normal as they could be.

THREE

*I*t was my first day of school and I was excited; Momma bought me a new dress that made me look like a sailor girl. It was blue with a big, wide square collar. She ironed it for hours and the skirt swung when I twirled around.

Momma hadn't had anything to drink in a long time because she was happy, but I knew that wouldn't last long. I went with her to the doctor yesterday and he told her that "it" was back. She almost made it, too. They said if she made it five years she would make it all the way. Momma cried when the doctor told her the news. I cried, too, but I was crying because Momma was. "It" was never explained to me, but I could tell by how sad my Momma got that "it" was real bad, worse than ice cream without the soda.

This morning I was already awake; I could hear Momma coming up the stairs, and instead of getting up, I closed my eyes and squeezed them shut. I pretended to be asleep. If my eyes were closed I knew she would kiss me awake and I couldn't wait to let her do it. I loved the smell of her hair as it flopped in my face during the kissing.

"Wake up, my sleepy-head! Do you know what today is?" Her voice was soft and I could tell without looking that she was smiling. I knew she could tell that I was really awake, but she enjoyed this wakey-wakey game we played as much as I did.

I kept my eyes closed even though I couldn't keep a straight face and started to grin like the Cheshire cat.

"Wakey, wakey, rise and shine!" Her singsong voice almost made an echo in my small bedroom. There was no need for me to answer because she was as excited as I was. I smiled with her as she talked to me and told me about how smart I was and how much fun second grade was going to be. She didn't need to reassure me, like on TV. I already knew I would like school. Momma helped me into my dress and fussed over me. She spent a long time ironing my no-iron dress and making sure my socks were frilly and matched just so. She even bought me a book bag, although I didn't think you'd need such a big book bag for second grade.

The school wasn't far, just up the block. I knew where it was and wanted to go by myself but Momma said she was going to take me anyway. I think she was more excited about going back to school than me, although I didn't think that was possible.

The happiness ended when we went downstairs. Everyone was silent while we ate breakfast. June-Bug didn't even fight me for my orange juice like he normally did. He came home from fighting folks three weeks ago. Everyone was glad about that around here; a lot of people that went to fight didn't seem to come home at all and folks were walking around wearing bracelets with those people's names on them, like that was going to bring them back. Momma told me that some of those folks were missing-in-action, like they just popped into somewhere else. Magic. Chills ran down my spine when she said that. She said they might even be prisoners-of-war.

I felt my stomach starting to get nervous as I played with my fried egg. I normally liked fried eggs, but this time the excitement of school and the silence in the room was squashing my hunger for food.

I think the doctor told Momma something real bad yesterday. She had been going to the doctor a lot and yesterday was one of those times. When she came home, she was crying and Daddy even came home from work early. He almost never did that. Even June-Bug cried. I don't think I'd ever seen him do that before. They called Gramma down South and all of my Momma's brothers and all of her sisters, too. No one told me anything and they all whispered in the phone for a long time. Hours.

I wasn't supposed to know what was wrong, although I could tell that something was. Every time I came into the room, they all got silent like they were now and tried to hide their tears behind their fakey smiles. And then it was over, like it never happened.

Momma eventually started fussing again over me starting school and then stayed in her room the rest of the night. Even with all the strangeness in the house the past couple of days, I could not wait to get dressed up and to go to school like normal kids. The girl next door wouldn't go until next year and she had been asking me every kind of question; she was sure that I knew everything because I was going to school and I had been answering every question. What I didn't know the answer to, I made up. She wasn't too smart because she believed everything I said. I made a game out of it just to see how far I could go.

All I heard in this room was the clink clink of silverware hitting the plates. My family was real good at trying to act normal when nothing was. You didn't have to be able to predict the future to know a storm was coming. I just wondered if it would be today.

FOUR

School was fun. I liked it a lot. We played first day games and went to the library. We all had to pick a book and then write about it. My teacher read to us, too. She was young and nice and I thought I was going to like her a lot. Momma picked me up from school and I talked all the way home.

"You should have been there, Momma. I read out loud in my best voice and the teacher made me read my assignment out loud in front of the whole class."

Momma seemed far away from the happiness she had this morning. "Did she?" she said. Her smile was thin and weak.

"Yes, she said it was the best one, out of all of them."

Momma nodded and smiled, but there was a faraway look in her otherwise beautiful eyes. She didn't speak or ask me any questions. She just listened. I could tell that she was still a little worried about whatever the doctor said.

We finally made it home and instead of asking me if I wanted to help her cook like she always did, Momma went to the kitchen by herself.

"Don't you want me to help you, Momma?"

I was surprised that she hadn't asked me so I figured she was preoccupied and I helped her out a little. She didn't answer me and started to pull the pots out of the pot closet.

Maybe we wouldn't cook together anymore now that I was in school again. She even forgot to turn on the radio like normal. I did it for her but she didn't seem to notice. If the radio wasn't on, dinner wouldn't taste good. That's the way it worked. Our singing along with the music and acting silly added a little something special to every recipe.

I stood behind Momma just in case she needed my help while she cooked; she always said that my help made the food just right. She reached out and turned the knob on the stove but nothing happened. The stove just made that click-click sound it sometimes made when the eye had no intention of lighting. Sort of like it was making fun of us and sucking its teeth or something. I smelled the gas almost immediately.

Momma had to step around me because I was a little slow getting out of the way. She still had not said anything at all to me, it was like she was in some kind of trance or operating on automatic. She reached for a match from on top of the brown aluminum dish chest. They were up there so we couldn't get them.

The matches were moved up high after I went to the kitchen one night to try and make a potion that was like Gramma's brew. I mixed everything liquid in the refrigerator together to try and get the color right. It tasted horrible. It didn't make any sense, it had looked like it should taste good.

In slow motion, Momma ran the match along the side of the dish cabinet and all at once, she paused as a flame hopped onto the end of the matchstick. The way matches light is magic. Flames just appeared at the end of a little stick.

Instead of holding the match to the eye of the stove to relight the pilot, Momma turned and stretched her slender arm up, toward the plastic kitchen curtains. She was so proud of those curtains when she put them up. I was frozen in place.

The little match flame transferred to the plastic curtains and I stood still, watching as the curtains were quickly taken over. They didn't burn like I thought they should, instead they melted.

Stop, drop, and roll, stop, drop and roll. The commercial screamed inside my head as I watched the curtains transfer the flame to the kitchen wall. I could taste the fear rising in my throat.

"Call 9-1-1, baby girl! Now!" Momma was speaking to me; the flame had snapped her back as if it transferred to her, too. I didn't remember the steps in between, but the phone was in my hand.

"My kitchen is on fire!" I couldn't hear anything the operator said because Momma grabbed me and I dropped the phone as we ran through the house. The rooms went by in slow motion. Dining room, living room, front room and without stopping, Momma scooped up my little brother and then, we were out the door.

We ran next door and Momma talked fast. Sirens screamed in the distance.

"Millie, I was cooking and some sparks set the kitchen curtains on fire."

"You all okay?" Millie looked from me to Momma and back to me. She was our neighbor and one of Momma's best friends. I didn't think I had ever seen her smile.

"You go, I will watch them," Millie said. I knew she meant me and my brother. Momma left us there with the neighbors and went outside to meet the fire trucks. The big red truck pulled up and I watched from the window. In less than an instant, the firemen swarmed over the house like the fire ants in Alabama swarmed over me when I stepped on their hill. They broke every window in the house, one by one, crash after crash. Water was poured in the windows.

"The fire is in the kitchen, Millie." None of the crashing came from the back of the house where the fire actually was.

"Shush, girl. They know what they doin'." Millie flashed her permanent gold teeth and flipped her curly wig. I opened my mouth to speak again but I decided not to, then closed it so hard my lips made a popping sound. Millie had a tendency to wash kids' mouth out with soap if they said stuff she didn't like. I had seen her do it. It still didn't make sense why they had to break all of the windows to me, but I wasn't going to say so, at least not to her. That soapy water was nasty, even worse than the refrigerator brew.

In twenty minutes, it was over. I didn't see Momma, but Daddy was coming up the walkway. The silence in Millie's house was crazy anyway.

"Hey, Millie. Thanks for watching them."

"No, problem." She always drew out her words like she was still down South and hadn't lived in New York for ten years.

"This is Detective Rapier." Daddy was talking about the man that came in with him. They all did like grown-ups do and shook hands. I had turned so that my back was now to the window and the detective-man came over to me.

"Hey, cutie."

"Only my daddy can call me that." I pursed my lips. Who was he anyway?

"It's okay, honey." My daddy's eyes were soft and watery and I walked to him. He hugged me and the detective-man got down on one knee. I knew he read in a book somewhere that he was supposed to get down on my level, or at least that's what I heard on TV.

"Honey? Can you tell me what happened?" I looked from him to Daddy and Daddy egged me on with his chin. I couldn't find any words. I realized that I was not too sure myself.

I was silent as I wondered what the right thing was to say and everybody sighed together.

"Little girl, *how* did the kitchen catch on fire?" The detective man asked me again, this time emphasizing the "How." The fear that was in my throat as I watched the flames lick our kitchen sat on my tongue, and I couldn't speak.

"Can you make her talk?" he said to my daddy.

"Sweetie, it's okay." My daddy's voice was soft. He put his hand on my shoulder. Millie left the room and went to her kitchen, but I knew she was listening behind the wall.

"Little girl, did your *mother* set the kitchen on fire?" The detective-man sounded stern now, like Daddy did sometimes. I didn't know what I was supposed to do. I looked from Daddy to the policeman and back to Daddy again to try and figure it out. I knew Daddy wanted me to tell the truth, but I was not sure what the truth was. The man tapped his pen on his policeman notepad.

I blew out my breath. *She lit the match.* I blew out my breath. *Not the kitchen.* I blew out my breath and finally, I talked.

"No." My voice was small as I searched Daddy's face. I could see his shoulders relax.

"Are you *sure*?" The detective-man's voice was louder now.

"It was an accident." I sounded confident. "The flame was too high."

The detective man stepped toward me, and daddy stepped in the middle, scooping me up, finally.

"You heard her, an accident."

I hugged him and he turned away from the detective-man.

"Can I ask her...?"

"No, no more questions." Daddy was stern, like when I got in trouble. "She is just a kid."

I put my head into Daddy's neck and he guided the man back out of Millie's door. He handed Daddy a piece of paper and we watched as he walked away.

⌾

The house was a mess. We were going to stay with Millie tonight, I could tell. Although the fire was small and in the back of our house, there was water from the front door to the back, upstairs and down. Everything smelled like smoke, even my new school clothes. I stood in the front room and looked around. The TV was broken. We only had one and it was the best TV ever. It sat on the floor in the corner. I guessed I couldn't watch *Emergency 911* or *Hawaii Five-0* anymore. They were my favorite, especially *Emergency 911*. Everyone was always saved.

I wanted to go to my room and get stuff, but Momma wouldn't let me.

"Wait right here." She made me wait on the steps with my little brother. He had no idea what was going on. We sat and waited while Momma and Daddy went inside and got stuff for us. As we sat there, the neighbors were still milling around outside, others were passing through the block. Some crossed the street and walked past. Some crossed the street and stood, whispering, looking over. Some bold ones were standing in the middle of the street, just looking, right into the front of our house, turning their necks around to see how much they could see. The firemen had thrown our things out into the front yard. Mattresses and things that they had broken apart. How could that have helped a kitchen fire?

Momma and Daddy finally came out of the house. I could tell that they were arguing but had gotten silent for us. Momma smiled at me and I stood.

"C'mon, sweeties. Let's go. You are going to stay with Millie tonight."

I knew we would. I walked in front and she carried my brother. We headed back next door. Daddy watched but didn't come as we went through our yard, now full of junk, through our squeaky gate and into Millie's gate, which doesn't creak at all. Millie opened the door again. She didn't speak.

"You mind?" Momma asked her.

She didn't answer, just tilted her head in a way that I knew said, "Just come in." She moved over so I could step through the door, and Momma put my brother on the floor behind me. She stayed outside.

"When it rains, it pours, huh?"

Momma was trying to sound like this was all no big deal. Millie still didn't answer, she just grunted. I went to the window and Momma waved at me, blowing kisses. I felt tears well up in my eyes, and she saw it because she told me not to cry. I looked at her through the window and watched the wind that had now picked up, and was dancing in her shoulder-length hair. She really was beautiful. Millie's hair was short and fake and it didn't even smell the same.

I wondered who was going to wake me up for school in the morning. Momma had to come and do it or I might not be able to get to school. Millie might not even know how to fry my eggs the right way.

Millie closed her door and Momma turned and walked down the walkway. Daddy was waiting in the car now, at the curb. Momma waved at me one last time and paused and put a stick of Juicy Fruit in her mouth, and although I couldn't hear her anymore, I heard the way she popped her gum in my head.

I couldn't do it like her. Momma said it was because I didn't have no holes in my teeth but I always tried.

She opened the car door and sat in the car. I counted the steps, just like she showed me. One, turn your back to the car, legs together. Two, gently place your bottom on the seat, legs outside. Three, rotate your legs into the car. She said that was how a lady entered a car. I couldn't help but smile as she got to three. She was such a lady. She closed the door and looked up, smiling back in my direction. She knew I was still in the window with my face pressed up against the glass.

The tears that had welled up in my eyes finally started to roll down my face on one side. At the same time, Daddy drove off and Millie put her hand on my shoulder.

I wanted to be strong. People said Momma was strong, and I wiped my tears with the back of my hand. I looked up at Millie and then followed her into her silent kitchen to wait for Momma and Daddy to come back and get me.

❧

We stayed at Millie's all weekend. When Momma finally came to get us, our house had been cleaned up some. Things were missing that could not be saved. I paused at the door until Momma nudged me on.

"Go ahead, now. It's okay."

I looked around the front room, realizing that what she said was true; all of the water was gone. The house still smelled like smoke though. I stepped into the room. The TV still had a hole.

"We will get a new one for you next week. When I get paid." She gave me one of her weak and thin smiles.

I walked through the house slowly, taking it all in. Although there was no water, everything still felt soggy. Front room, living room, dining room, and finally the kitchen.

I stood in the doorway and looked around. Everything was pretty much in its place. We even had brand new plastic curtains.

And then I saw it. The curtains seemed to be pointing to a spot, under the table. The fire burned a hole clear through the wall. I squinted, making my eyes small. I could still smell the fire there, almost like all the stink in the whole house was coming from that hole in the wall and the smell polluted the whole house. I guessed they couldn't fix that in a couple of days.

Momma had followed me through the house, like she was holding her breath or something. I tried to compose myself because I knew when I turned around she was going to try and read my face.

"This okay?" she asked.

I nodded my head without answering, a small nod. I was afraid that too much emotion might be bad. I didn't think what I thought really mattered but I wanted to make her happy. I searched her face for some reaction. She looked away from my eyes.

"Good, then." That's all she said about it. I really wished she would explain what was going on.

She sighed. "I have some news, Sweetie."

What now? I wondered.

"I am not going to work at night anymore." Momma paused, waiting for my reaction. I didn't say anything. "I got switched to the day shift instead. Do you know what that means?"

Instead of answering her, I just blinked, once, then twice. I knew that if I didn't answer her, she would answer anyway.

"It means that I will wake you up in the morning *and* put you to bed."

I inhaled and searched her face for clues to what I was supposed to say. I couldn't figure it out, so I just smiled a big, toothy smile. I was afraid to upset the balance of things. Momma hugged me, pulling me to her. The smile always worked. She still smelled the same, although everything was crazy. The smile musta been the right thing to do. I hugged her tight, until she finally pushed me back, holding onto me at arm's length.

"We have to find someone to watch you and your brother, though. A babysitter."

I said it slow in my head. Baayybeesitterrr. What did she mean? I go to school. I didn't need watching. I ain't a baby no more. She saw the look on my face as I went through the inventory in my head. I hoped it wasn't Frankie. She worked with Momma sometimes. She pinched my cheeks too hard.

"Don't worry, we will find someone nice."

Momma was back to reading my mind again. That ruled out Frankie. Hope it ain't Millie. There was never any music in her house. And Mrs. Massetti brought me gingerbread men. Maybe it could be her. She was the only white lady left in our neighborhood. Daddy said the rest flew away like a flock of birds.

Momma continued, "We'll figure all that out later. We need to go the store now." She took my hand and guided me toward the door. I watched as she got the stroller ready for Little Man and tried to remember if the jukebox place was next door to the store. I hoped we weren't stopping there today.

Momma looked at me, smiling her toothpaste-perfect smile.

"You okay, Sweetie?" She asked again, like she was afraid that I had somehow gotten broken overnight.

I smiled back and nodded a small nod at her again. I hoped the sitter didn't turn out to be Miss Jensen on the corner. She had two big kids, teenagers, like seventeen or something. She didn't come out of her house much, and the kids in the neighborhood said she was a witch and her house was a witch house. They said if you walked past it, you would get sucked in. So we ran past it. The paint on her house was even the darkest on the block.

I walked with Momma and Little Man down the street. She chattered away, like she was nervous or something, but I was not listening. Instead, I ran my hands down the bushes in front of the houses as we walked past them, or I clicked my fingers on the gates like I was Tom Sawyer, pretending my fingers were a stick.

In our neighborhood, all of the houses were almost the same. They took up the same space, had the same size yard. All of our houses looked to be row houses; they all went straight back. None of them spread out like the house on the *Brady Bunch*. No one in our neighborhood had an Alice. Every house did have a yard in front with a little grass, and maybe some flowers. If you walked through our block at the right time, almost everyone was standing outside, watering the grass and greeting people as they came home from work. Or watching, trying to get in folks' business.

In front of every house there was one tree, always painted white front mid-trunk down to the ground. The curbs were also painted white, except where the driveways were; those were yellow. Daddy helped our neighborhood group do that.

A lady was standing in her doorway with the yellow curb, talking to Momma. I didn't know who she was, I was not allowed around the corner by myself.

"You need a babysitter?" She was talking with a singsong in her voice; she was not from here.

Momma paused, then answered her. "Yes, ma'am. I do."

We walked closer to the lady's house. She had tall hedges that lined her walkway, taller than me. Her curbs were not painted like ours. I sat on her steps as Momma talked with her. I looked at my shoes and acted like I wasn't listening, but I was.

"I baby-sit. Such precious babies." She nodded in my direction, pointing with her chin.

Momma smiled and looked at me and Little Man. "These are my sweeties." She never called me by my name unless I was in trouble. "We work weird hours sometimes. I am a nurse. My husband is a cop."

"Dat's not a problem for me." The lady was older than my grandma. She wouldn't be able to play with me. I knew she would be the one. Momma was very comfortable already.

"Where are you from? I haven't seen you before." Momma still talked, asking questions. She moved the stroller back and forth, as if the movement would keep Little Man quiet.

Daddy's momma lived in our house before us. They said

she lived with us until she died, but I didn't remember her, just her legs, below her skirt. She knew everybody that lived around our neighborhood, at least that was what Daddy said. He said that her and his daddy were the first colored family to live here.

The lady kept talking. "We just moved in, two weeks ago. Would you like to come in?"

I sucked in my breath. Momma always told me not to go in strangers' houses. I looked at her to see what she wanted to do. I already knew.

"C'mon, Sweetie."

I stood up and she helped me up the stairs like I was a little girl. She felt me hesitate as I scowled at her.

"It's okay," she said.

I made my eyes small as I looked at her, but I went with her into the strange lady's house. It had red carpet and red walls. Her house was a row, too, and she had a plastic runner that led the way, all the way back to the kitchen, like the yellow brick road, except it was clear, so the red carpet showed through. All of the furniture had plastic on it, too. We walked down the runner toward the kitchen, and I tried to touch the walls as we went by; they were fuzzy with raised designs. Momma gave me her "you better not" look, and I returned my hands to my side quickly and looked at the floor.

The house smelled like fried chicken and museum mixed up together. There was no dust anywhere and everything was in its place. That meant there were no kids here. The lady offered me a chicken leg. I looked at Momma and she told me to go ahead, so I took the chicken leg and concentrated on eating it, blocking Momma and the woman out.

I ate my chicken leg slowly; it was very good. The lady talked and played with Little Man. Before long, they laughed together, too.

Betrayed.

I could tell from this laughter that she would be the one, the babysitter. Momma's laugh told me that she liked her. At least her fried chicken was good.

"Let's go, Sweetie." Momma stood up. "We still have to get to the store."

I held up my hands so Momma could wipe them for me. It was settled.

"So, I will bring them after we get back from our trip. In two weeks. That okay?"

The new babysitter nodded her head and kept smiling her smile with the perfect teeth. She bent down and put her face near mine. She smelled like Ben Gay like Gramma. Her face was wrinkled, but only on her forehead. She must have been real old. The rest of her face was smooth, caramel-colored. Her hair was curled under all the way around her head, down to her shoulders. It had speckles of gray running through it. I stepped back as she moved closer to me.

"We are going to have so much fun." She pinched my cheeks, both at the same time. *Ugh.* I just looked at her and held onto Momma's hand tighter. I had never heard anyone talk like her before. I still didn't know where she was from. We walked back down the runner-road and her and Momma were talking again. She walked in front of us and I noticed that her legs were so bowed that they almost formed an O. Her walk reminded me of a Weeble; she rocked first to one leg, then to the other, like they were connected at her feet and she was actually rolling from one to the other. I tried to mimic her but Momma still had my hand and she yanked me real hard to make me stop.

We waved good-bye at the door and as we walked away, Momma wasn't talking nervously anymore. She was relieved and she hummed a song under her breath.

FIVE

The teacher sent a note home yesterday. I didn't read it before I got home and I should have because now I was in trouble. She wanted Momma and Daddy to come to school to talk with her, about me. I didn't know what I did, but any time they had to go to school, it was bad. I heard Momma and Daddy arguing about it. He didn't want to take time off from work. His work was the most important thing to him.

Momma won the argument. She always did, but he had been silent all the way to the school. I didn't know what I did or what the teacher was going to say and my stomach had been flip-flopping since last night.

The red brick building looked lonely and deserted. It was after school and all the kids were gone. I wanted to be gone, at home instead of here, helping Momma get dinner ready. The teacher picked the worst time to ask them to come, too, we were just getting back to normal after the fire and adjusting to the new sitter. More bad news would just make things worse.

Momma took my hand and we walked a step behind Daddy. Her heels made a clicking sound as we went down the hallway. Daddy was still solemn. There was a lump in my throat as I ran the days through my mind, trying to figure out what the problem might be. I couldn't imagine what I could have done wrong in Miss Faust's class. Daddy told me that his mother whipped him in front of the class when she had to go to his school. I hoped Momma didn't let him do that to me.

My teacher was waiting, just inside the door to my classroom. She smiled at us, and the flowered skirt she wore fluttered a little as she turned around and came to shake hands with Momma and Daddy. Momma smiled, but Daddy still had no expression. Instead he looked at his watch. He said he would probably go back to work after this was over.

"Come sit down." The teacher motioned toward the small desks that we used during the day. Although I was scared, I wanted to laugh. Daddy was a big man, and he had to fold himself up like a piece of paper to fit.

"What is this about?" Daddy finally said.

Momma glared at him, then cleared her voice. "It's just that your note was almost cryptic. We couldn't tell why you needed to see us now. Has Denise been misbehaving?" my father asked, calling me by my middle name like he always did.

I held my breath.

The teacher laughed. "Nothing like that. I wanted to see you to talk about Monica's work."

"I thought she was doing fine." A look of worry flitted across Momma's face.

The teacher took some papers off of her desk, then turned around and handed them to Momma. It was my work, writing work, that we did earlier this week.

"We gave the students an assignment to tell us what they did this summer. This is Monica's. It really is exceptional for second grade. Take a look. If I didn't know better, I would think a fourth or fifth-grader wrote this."

I relaxed a little and then smiled at Miss Faust. I was not in trouble at all.

Momma's eyes scanned the page and then she handed it to Daddy.

He read it over, too, then passed it back to the teacher.

"So, I still don't understand why you called us here." His voice was still very calm, but I could tell that he was as glad as I was that I hadn't done anything wrong.

"She is very talented. In fact, I have never seen any other students do this well at her age." She paused.

Momma and Daddy were tense again. They weren't smiling anymore.

"Just how many colored students have you seen?" Momma asked. Her nose flared just a little.

It was the teacher's turn to be uncomfortable. She shifted her weight from one foot to the other.

"I don't think that came out correctly. What I meant to say was, your daughter writes very well. Exceptionally so. I want your permission to give her extra writing work, to prepare her for some of the citywide competitions. Technically, she is not too young, although we have never had anyone her age compete before. At least not from this school." She cleared her throat and her eyes moved around the room nervously.

Momma and Daddy looked at each other, but they didn't speak. The classroom clock ticked louder than I remembered it being and I looked at the floor so they couldn't see my smile. Finally, Daddy spoke. He put his hand on my shoulder and his fingers squeezed just a little bit.

"We are very aware that Monica is a talented child. And we don't have a problem with her being in a competition, if that is what she wants to do. But we only want her to do it because she is a talented writer. Not because she is your most talented *colored* writer."

"I can assure you that her skills are above most, if not all, of my students." She paused again and licked her lips. She handed them another piece of paper. "This is information about the program. Please consider it."

Momma and Daddy stood to leave. A wide smile stretched across Momma's face.

I knew she was proud of me.

They thanked the teacher and Momma took my hand again. We were almost to the door when the teacher called my name.

"Yes, Miss Faust?"

"This is for you." She walked over and handed me a book with a purple cloth cover. Her whole body smiled at me and I decided that I liked her.

I ran my fingers over the rough surface.

"I want you to have this journal, no matter what your parents decide. You can have a place to write your stories."

"Thank you."

No one said anything. We got back in the car, and this time, Daddy pushed an eight track into the player. It was not as tense as before. I sat in the middle of the back seat. He turned the key in the ignition and I looked up, our eyes met in the rearview mirror. There was a smile on his face for a change.

Six

The babysitter had no teeth. None. I saw her take them out and put them in a jar. We had been going to her for a week or so now, for a couple of hours a day. She tried to be really nice to us but she didn't talk to us much; she just watched TV and listened to music. Soap operas and talking radio shows were her favorite.

Her music was different than what we heard at home. She liked country music and calypso, songs with names like Delta Dawn. I learned all the words to her songs the first time I heard them because they sang the same thing over and over, something about a faded rose and meeting people and stuff.

We didn't do anything while we were at her house, just watched TV on her small set that sat on a little cart. I could always tell when it was almost time to go, the 4:30 movie ended and then somebody came to get us; for the last couple of days it had been Daddy. She bought us special chairs to sit on that we folded up and put away before Daddy came. It was okay with me, the plastic covers on her couch were uncomfortable anyway. The one time I did sit on them, they itched my legs and made the backs of my knees sweat.

The chairs were too big for Little Man; they were the kind with the cushioned seat and metal frame that folded really easily. I carried his for him and set it up. I was very careful as I helped him into his seat. If I sat him too far back the chair would fold just enough so he slid through the back. That happened the first day and he cried for a really long time.

The babysitter sat on the couch. Right on the plastic. It crunched when she went down. In the same spot every time. The couch was kinda low, so she hovered above her spot, took aim and then kinda let herself drop down into place. Her O-shaped legs didn't seem to turn or bend in any way that would make sitting down easier. The plastic crunched and complained when she made contact and I couldn't imagine that it was comfortable for her either.

We had to walk exactly on the runner. She taught us how to put our folding chairs down so that our feet hit the runner and not her blood red rug. If I did it wrong, she sucked her teeth at me. She made a really long, loud sound; I had never heard anyone suck their teeth like that before. She burped like that, too. Every day after dinner, she made a belch that shook the china in her hallway cabinet where it was set up for the display. It really was amazing. Every time she did it, my eyes got really wide; I knew I would get in trouble for sure if I belched like that.

Her grandson, Everett peeked into the room. He was dark, like milk chocolate, but in a funny kind of way. His skin looked like the African got all mixed up with the Indian. He had a strong redness to his skin, but not so red that they would call him "red-bone" down in Muscoda like they called June-Bug. He was so tall that he had to bend down to walk through from room to room. His head was roundish and he was clean-shaven, with almost no hair anywhere on his face. No eyebrows, no mustache, no beard, even the top of his head was completely bald. He had a dent running along the back of his head that seemed to reach all the way around to the front. He didn't talk at all, he just grinned. My skin crawled and I looked away. The baby sitter glared at him. Everett snorted, then headed up the stairs.

Even though the TV was on, I could hear the clock ticking away the minutes while we waited. I hated that clock. I was sure it wanted me to notice every minute of every hour that we sat on those chairs waiting for Daddy to come.

"Fold de chairs, gal." She had lost the perfect speech that had a hint of British accent to it.

Every day, at ten minutes to six, she said the same thing. I put both of them away, and then we'd stand in the front room, making sure to stay on the runner. I couldn't help but imagine that I was standing on the yellow brick road, surrounded by quicksand. If I stepped off I was positive that we would sink into that red rug. The only way it could get that color was from the blood of little kids like me, I was sure of that.

In the front room, we waited on the runner, careful not to touch a thing. Since Daddy started picking us up, he had almost always been there to get us on time. Even Little Man had been able to last through the wait. I usually held his hand real tight. I didn't want him to get into trouble for touching or breaking or leaving a fingerprint. The room was so clean we would leave a smudge if we breathed too hard.

At one minute to six, she began to smile. It was like she was getting warmed up so she could appear happy when the doorbell rang. When it did ring, she opened it and Daddy never came in. She handed our bags out the door and smiled and the exchange between them was always the same.

"How were they today?"

"Oh, fine man. Fine, like likkle angels." Her sing-songy voice was animated. She called everyone "man."

"Okay then, see you tomorrow."

And we walked out the door and got into the car.

Every day, Daddy drove us home in silence. I guessed that was because Momma had been sick again. He didn't even play any music in the car or sing songs with us like he sometimes did. He just drove. I was silent, too. The air was very heavy in the car and I could tell that he was thinking.

As soon as we got to the house, Daddy went to his room. There were always people at our house now. Daddy didn't say a word; he just left us and they took over. My Auntie Jay, my momma's sister, had been there most often, and today was no exception. She was in the kitchen when we arrived. She didn't play music when she cooked or asked me to help or anything like Momma did. She just smiled at us with a painted-on smile the way grown-ups sometimes did. I did the same to her, stopping my smile as soon as she wasn't looking. I didn't think she even noticed. Sometimes I even stuck out my tongue at her.

After dinner, Auntie Jay gave us a bath. She didn't do like Momma did. She didn't bathe me and Little Man together. She didn't think it was proper, but she let me watch.

When Momma thought we were all clean, she would let the water out of the tub and turn on the faucet again. She would wet the rag, first with warm, and then with cold water, squeezing it out over us in between. This was my favorite part of the bath. I didn't feel squeaky clean unless she did it. The first day Auntie Jay gave us a bath, I tried to tell her how to do it the way Momma did.

"You 'spose to squeeze water on us, Auntie Jay."

"Oh," she said. It was like she had caught the silent bug, like everyone else around us. She continued to ignore me, washing Little Man extra hard.

"That's what Momma does." I pressed my lips together, hard, making them poke out.

"Hmpph. Well, I am not her." She didn't even look up.

I tried to do it myself, but it wasn't the same, it didn't feel the same. I made a big mess in the bathroom and got in trouble. I always felt like I was going to be the smelly kid in school because my bath had not been finished the right way since.

Auntie Jay always gave Little Man his bath first, and he cried the whole way through. When she left the room, I stuck my hand into the water once, to check it, the way Momma showed me how to do, with the inside of my wrist. It was way too hot. No wonder he cried.

I didn't say anything, but I stood in the door and watched while she bathed him. Auntie Jay talked to him like she was trying to calm him down, but she wasn't always saying nice things. She thought no one can hear her, but I could. I heard her tell him that it was his fault that Momma was sick. I didn't know how that could be at all.

After our bath, Auntie Jay put us to bed. She did it all wrong again. She didn't read us a bedtime story or anything. I knew that Little man was used to Momma reading to us, so I tried to read to him like she did. When I thought she couldn't hear anymore, I got a book and looked at the pictures, trying to remember the story as much as possible. What I didn't remember, I made up, reading Little Man to sleep.

By morning, Auntie Jay was gone. Instead, we had a lady in a white uniform. We had been having a different one almost every other day. This one had panty hose that were too white. They looked funny on her brown legs. I was already awake, waiting in bed. She came into the room with one of those phony smiles that I had been seeing a lot of lately. Her platform white shoes squished when she walked and her dress was too tight.

"Would you like some breakfast, honey?" She batted her false eyelashes at me. I bet she didn't even know that my momma called me Sweetie, not Honey. I gave her one of her own false smiles back.

"Um-umh." Momma hated when I said um umh, but I said it anyway. She wasn't here to hear it.

"Eggs, okay?" I didn't answer because I was going to get eggs anyway.

We went downstairs and the house was quiet, even June-Bug was already gone. The air was heavy in the house all the time now, like it was fat. It was so thick I couldn't breathe. I slid into my chair at the table.

Little Man could almost climb up into his own chair now. He was almost too big for his high chair. She didn't let him try. She just plopped him down into his chair so hard that I knew it must hurt.

In no time at all, she brought a plate full of eggs, done all wrong. They were scrambled, not fried. And they were soft. The only thing worse than scrambled eggs is soft eggs. I hated them because they looked like brains to me.

"I need a fried egg," I said, pushing my plate away. The lady put one hand on her hip. "Momma makes me fried eggs."

I felt the tears lumping up in my throat. Didn't she know how things go? I didn't understand why they sent her if she didn't.

She sighed. "Today we are having scrambled. Don't you want to try something new?"

"No." I liked things the same old way they were before. I wanted to tell her that, but I didn't. Instead, I swallowed my tears and pushed the plate full of eggs away. She didn't try to make me eat them. Instead she sat down near Little Man and helped him smear food all over his face. I excused myself and got myself dressed. I didn't think she would help me anyway.

I had to prepare myself for school; I didn't mean get dressed, I meant get ready. When I walked up with this lady in white holding my hand, I knew the other kids would tease me.

The lady didn't talk to me on the way to school. She walked too fast and her thighs rubbed together, making that swishing sound. She ignored me as I tried to slow her down. Maybe if we walked slowly enough, everyone would go into the school building before we got there and no one would see me with Miss White Legs.

I counted every crack on the way. There are 632 cracks on the five blocks from our house to the school. I didn't step on a single one. Momma and I counted them together. Momma had enough things to worry about without having to worry about a broken back, too.

We didn't walk slow enough because everyone was still outside, lining up on the sidewalk. I swore that everyone was turning around to look at us as we walked up to the school. They all stopped what they were doing and I could feel a whisper go through the crowd.

"Are you sick, Sweetie?" A girl in my class was the only one that talked.

"No, dummy." I looked at my feet. I was tired of answering questions.

Miss White Legs got the attention of my teacher, Miss Faust, and dropped my hand. I bet she wouldn't be the one picking me up, but maybe. That was a good thing, I think. I hoped I would never have to see her again. Because of her, I knew I would have to explain about twenty times that no, I was not sick, no, her name isn't Alice or Hazel, my mother was in the hospital, you idiot. It would keep on until the teacher told us to be quiet, glaring at me like it was my fault or something, like *I* had done something wrong.

She turned and left fast, like childhood was a disease you could catch. She kind of scurried, the way the class hamster did, and I joined everyone else and waited for the questions to begin.

Miss Faust came over and put her arm around my shoulders, guiding me away from the other kids. I felt a little relieved to not have to talk to them. I didn't feel like it right now.

"Is everything okay, Sweetie?" she asked.

I nodded, looking at my shoes. Part of me was glad that she had asked, but I didn't want to talk about it with her any more than I did the other kids. Tears stung my eyes. I sniffled to fight them back and then looked over my shoulder. A few kids sneered at us, but I walked with her into the building anyway.

Seven

Momma came home from the hospital while I was at school. She looked a little pale to me and I felt like I should tiptoe and be quiet.

"How do you like my hair, Sweetie?"

Her hair was short and cut into a style that curled right below her ears.

"Why'd you do that?" I asked and scratched my nose. We all liked her with her other hair. I did anyway. There was nothing left for me to smell.

"The medicine from the doctor was making it fall out so I cut it first."

I didn't know what to say to that so I closed my mouth. I heard about stuff like that happening on TV, except this was real life. Other than the short hair, things were trying to fake their way back to normal.

Momma was going to cook dinner; she had even turned on the music again in the kitchen. I stood outside the kitchen door (I was afraid to go in), and watched as Momma swayed back and forth while singing along about drowning in a sea of love. Drowning in a sea of strange silence was more like it.

She talked in between the verses.

"We are going to see Auntie Jay tomorrow."

I been down one time.

Auntie Jay lived in the city, in the tallest building there was. At least it seemed like that to me.

"We need to take her some things. Clothes." She talked *at* me, almost like she expected me to have some comment, but I didn't have anything to say.

I been down two times.

"Hers burnt up in the fire. It's the least I can do."

"Was her pilot out?" I asked.

Momma looked at me, tilting her head to the side. "No, someone smoked in bed. But she is okay."

Now I'm drowning in the sea of love.

⚮

Auntie Jay's building has a million stories in it, I'm sure. She lives on the sixth floor in a part of the city where all of the buildings seem stuck together. I pressed my nose up against the car window and watched them as they went by. There were big buildings next to small ones next to ones that had been burnt out and gutted. These always smelled like smoke to me no matter how long ago they burned. As close as they were, it's no wonder that if one caught on fire the whole city didn't go up, like in the song Daddy sang about the great Chicago fire and that Old Woman with the cow in her shed.

We had to walk up six flights of stairs to get to Auntie Jay's. That was a lot of steps. There was no elevator. The building was musty and smelled faintly of smoke, like our kitchen. There was no bell either. Momma knocked on the door.

"Who?" Auntie Jay yelled from behind her big door.

"Elva and Sweetie." Momma answered her as loud as Auntie Jay yelled. She sang through the peephole.

Why didn't she do one or the other? Why didn't she look before she asked? Isn't that what the peephole was there for? She was glad to see us. I could hear her hands move across the four deadbolts on her door.

Momma and her sister hugged a long time with us standing in the doorway. They looked alike, only Momma was prettier, but with shorter hair now. They used to have the same hair. And Auntie Jay was missing teeth. I heard Gramma say that some man knocked them out when she was younger, but when I looked at her I couldn't help but think about a witch. They always seemed to be missing teeth, too.

Auntie Jay finally stepped away and let us in and I looked past her, looking for some signs of her fire. I didn't see any, but I smelled the smoke, just like the smoke I still smelled in our kitchen.

"Elva, I was so scared, girl." She was the big sister.

"Girl, I know. We just went through this, remember?" They called each other girl and were talking like I was not there. Auntie Jay screwed her face around.

"Somebody went to sleep with a cigarette, downstairs on the second floor. I could smell the smoke. It was so black in here it woke me up." She finally saw me. "Hey, Sweetie," she said.

My eyes were wide; I wanted to know what she did when she woke up in the room full of smoke.

"Elva, what's wrong with her? Didn't you teach her to talk when folks speak to her?"

"You ain't give her a chance. Say hello, Sweetie."

I looked down at my shoes and studied the scuffed-up toes.

"Hello, Auntie Jay."

She continued. "Well, I 'membered the commercial, and I crawled to the winda, to the fire 'scape." Auntie Jay guided us over to the fire escape. She flipped open the window. "I climbed--"

I couldn't hear her anymore, but I watched as she stepped out of the window and went down the fire escape to a lower roof. She was yelling so we could hear.

"I just waited here until they said it was okay!"

And then Momma and me watched as she climbed back up.

Momma put her hand on her cheek. "Where you hurt?" She finally got a chance to talk.

"Naw, girl. Not really. I just got a little burnt on my be-hind."

And Auntie Jay dropped her pants and mooned us. Right in the middle of the room.

Momma gasped. "I thought you said it was just smoke in here! Did you put something on that, Jay?" The hand on her cheek moved to cover her mouth.

"This here isn't from the fire. It is from the radiator. I leaned on it in my nightdress whilst I was tryin' ta get the winda open."

"Thank God for that!" Momma said. "Do you have anything here to put on it? Some salve? What did the doctor say? It looks terrible. You don't want it to get infected."

"I'll be all right, Elva," Auntie Jay pulled up her pants. She changed the subject.

"I see you brought Li'l Man." We had been in her house for a good while now and she finally noticed him.

Momma sucked in her breath. I might have been small but I knew what tension felt like, and right then it felt like the tension between my momma and Auntie Jay was growing, getting thick like the smoke was in our house that day. I knew that they were going to get all involved and talk like I wasn't there.

"Yeah, ain't he just growing?" Momma asked. She smiled and rubbed her hand through his hair that was just as long as mine. I don't think she expected an answer, but Auntie Jay answered anyway.

"I don't want to talk about him, Elva," she said. "You know how I feel." Jay turned away from Momma, but not before I saw the frown on her face. She spit her snuff into her spit can.

Momma sucked her teeth. "Tch. How can we not talk about it? He is here now. The past is the past, Jay. He is my son."

"You know you damn near traded your life for him, don't ya?" Auntie Jay raised her voice and I suddenly had to go to the bathroom.

I started to do the bathroom dance. I didn't want to hear them. Momma saw me.

"You gotta go pottie, Sweetie?" she asked.

Even though I was in school now she still said pottie. I could have fussed, but instead I just nodded my head. My eyes were round. I might not make it. The bathroom in Auntie Jay's house was not even in her house. It was down the hall. There was only one on each floor that four apartments had to share. It scared me to go, but I couldn't hold it anymore.

They continued to talk about Little Man. I half listened as their voices faded away, all the way down the hall. I stood outside the bathroom door, listening for a minute, but then I couldn't stand it no more and I knocked on the door. When I was sure there was no one inside, I went in, did my business, and started to wash my hands in the porcelain sink that was no longer white. I decided against it because the sink was probably dirtier than my hands were anyway. I didn't think any cleaner in the world could take off the dirt on that sink.

Gramma's house didn't have any running water and we actually had to go outside to use the outhouse there. There was no sink in the outhouse, but I decided that this bathroom, indoors, with running water and a sink was worse than having to brave the elements on any given day or pee-peeing in a chamber pot at night. And an empty chamber pot was the worst, everyone could always hear you pee.

By the time I got back to Auntie Jay's house, Momma was going out the door, still talking. "For the last time, let's not talk about it," she was saying to Auntie Jay.

I stopped and stood and looked at her. She saw me, telling me to come on. Auntie Jay slammed her door behind us.

Momma was silent on the walk down the steps. I was not too worried about it; they had this discussion every time we came over. Instead I concentrated on trying to make myself busy as we walked down the seemingly endless spiral of stairs and got into our car. She didn't turn on the radio on the ride home, like she wanted to hear herself think better.

We stopped at a light and she glanced over her shoulder at us. Little Man was already asleep.

I cleared my throat. "Momma?"

She smiled a little before she answered me. "Yes, Sweetie."

"Why does Auntie Jay hate Little Man?"

"She doesn't hate Little Man."

"Then why does she act like it all the time. She is mean to him and things."

"She doesn't hate him. She is just angry about things, that's all. She doesn't know how to say what she feels. It's hard for her. Not her fault."

I thought about that for a minute. Gramma always said that a person was responsible for their own actions, so I didn't understand how Auntie Jay wasn't responsible for hers. "But it isn't Little Man's fault either."

Momma glanced at me again in the rearview mirror. "You are right, Sweetie. I suppose it's not." She reached over and turned on the radio. I still didn't understand what Auntie was angry about, but Momma turning on the music meant she wasn't going to tell me. I willed myself to join Little Man and I fell asleep too.

EIGHT

*M*omma hadn't talked to Auntie Jay for three weeks and she was sad the whole time. Then she went back into the hospital again. We were going to visit her today; another lady in a white uniform was here, and her dress was too tight, too, just like the lady before her.

We stayed at the sitter's house last night, and this morning, instead of getting dressed for school, me and Little Man got to wear our Sunday clothes because we were going to the hospital with Daddy. This was the first time we ever got to go to the hospital, so I was a little scared. I was really happy about the visit, though, and I wanted everything to be perfect. I wanted to hug Momma and tell her about school and ask her what she thought I could take for show and tell.

The hospital that Momma was in was big and had a tall fence around it. The fence was so tall that it was even over my daddy's head. It was on the other side of town, by our doctor's office. Every time we went over there Momma would tell me that this was where James Brown lived, she liked him a lot. I couldn't understand anything he was saying in his songs. I didn't know if this was true or not, that he lived in the house where they said he did. I couldn't imagine why he would live here, in New York with us, instead of in Motown or Hollywood, where all the other stars lived. The house she said he lived in was big and pretty, though, with no fence in front, just a hedge, but I didn't think that was too good. What would Momma have leaned on if we were waiting in front of that house? She would have just fallen through the hedge.

I didn't think Momma would not tell me the truth on purpose, but I knew that she had been trying to keep things from me. Her and Daddy had been whispering and if they were on the phone they stopped talking when I came into the room, but I could still tell that things were happening. This trip to the hospital had confirmed that. "We're here, kids." Daddy talked to us like Momma usually did. His voice was soft and higher than normal. We didn't answer him, instead, I stared at the fence and Little Man just stood there, grinning like he always did. He really looked like a little man now; he got his first haircut the other day. Now people would stop calling him a she instead of a he. Before he wore his hair in long braids, like mine. He was almost pretty and people sometimes thought we were both girls.

The nurse lady was still with us. "You go with her," Daddy said, almost like he was afraid to give her a name, like that would make her real. He went into the hospital and left us outside. We each held one of the lady's hands and went where she led us. She held onto our hands so hard I thought that all the blood was gone out of mine. She must have thought we were going to run away from her or something.

We stood under a window and looked where the nurse looked.

"Can I go with my daddy?" I asked.

"No," she said, smiling her plastic smile. "There are no children allowed."

This was stupid. Why even let me come at all if I was not going to be able to hug my mother or anything?

At that moment, as I was debating whether or not I was going to cry, the nurse talked again. "Look, there's your momma. Wave." The nurse dropped my hand but not Little Man's. She picked him up so he could see better.

I couldn't believe it. I drew in my breath, looking at the window that the nurse was pointing at. About four windows up, there she was. Her hair was gone, but my momma was in the window, waving and blowing kisses and I could tell she was talking but she was too far up to hear. I jumped up and down and waved both hands.

"Momma! Momma!" I shouted, waving at her frantically. I was happy, but tears rolled down my face anyway, making prisms that made the sunlight cloud my vision. "There's my momma."

People walking by smiled at us, but I didn't care. Daddy was in the window too, but he was behind Momma. We waved for a couple more minutes, and then they moved away from the window and we couldn't see them anymore. I kept looking up, until the back of my neck hurt, waiting for them to come back so I could see again. The nurse took my hand again.

"That's it, honey." Her voice was soft.

I started to cry again, but this time I was mad.

"Don't cry," she said, trying to pull me to her, with only one hand, because she was still holding onto Little Man. He had become interested in a nearby butterfly and was pulling toward it. What did she know about it? Probably nothing. She would cry too if she were me.

She was fidgeting and getting nervous. She kept looking toward the hospital door, like she was looking for my daddy, hoping he hurried back down. I sucked my tears back in, looked at my Sunday shoes, realizing that the white polish was thin on the toes, but I continued to hold her hand. Momma would have fixed that polish. I wanted Daddy to hurry too, but for a different reason. I didn't want her to keep looking at me with that poor-girl-mother-in-the-hospital look in her eyes.

Daddy finally came back downstairs where we were.

"Mommy sends her love," Daddy said. "She was so happy to see you." He had finally arrived and was still talking in his soft voice.

"But I didn't get to . . ."

"I know." He rubbed my back. The tears were coming to my eyes again and I wiped them away with the back of my hand. I didn't want him to see me cry; lately it felt like he was always on the brink of crying himself. The nurse dropped my hand and I held it out so Daddy could take it instead. He picked up Little Man and we headed back to the car. Our visit was done and I didn't even get to smell her hair.

NINE

Four-thirty came and went, and that clock ticked louder than ever, mocking me. The baby-sitter was very quiet today, not even making her burping noises. When she talked on the phone she kept going into the next room and whispering. I felt like I did when it was almost the end of summer and everyone, even the animals, seemed to sit around and wait for the heat to be over.

We put our chairs away as usual and began our wait by the door. Little Man had started to be very fidgety lately and I had to put my hand on the top of his shoulder and hold on with all my might to keep him from stepping off the plastic runner onto the red rug or rubbing his fingers along the raised wallpaper.

The sitter opened the door today and stood there, waiting. I could smell the dampness of outside; the rain had made the new spring grass wet and its scent floated through the air. New things would grow soon.

Her grin was more forced than normal, and instead of Daddy appearing at the screen door, this time it was Momma. The sitter stepped away and let Momma come through the door. She didn't speak, but I do not think she cared. Momma almost pushed her way in and I was standing still from shock.

I thought she was still in the hospital. She did seem to spend almost as much time in as out now and all my days were getting confused.

She gathered both me and Little Man together and put her arms around both of us at the same time. I closed my eyes and I hugged her back. We all rocked together just a little. My tears welled up. She hugged us like she had never hugged us before and maybe never would again. Finally, she let us go and stepped back, taking my chin between her thumb and forefinger.

"Things okay, Sweetie?" She paused, waiting for my answer.

What does okay mean? What is the right answer? What could I say that would not put things back the way they were before Old Lady Momma put a match to our kitchen curtains? I couldn't even remember a time when I didn't go to the corner bar with her.

The baby-sitter cleared her throat and the tears that came to my eyes before slid down my cheek. I nodded instead of asking any questions. Momma released my chin and rubbed my head. I wondered what she thought of my curls the way the sitter had them tied up in multicolored ribbons.

They still did not speak. She guided us out the door and into the car where Daddy was waiting. Would she tell me how long this would last?

There was no music in the car, so I knew that Momma's unexpected homecoming did not signal a return to normalcy. Daddy did not say hello to us. He started the car and we headed away from home, to the city. They didn't bother to tell us where we are going. We rode in silence.

Before long, I began to see tall buildings and for a minute I wondered if we were going uptown, to Auntie Jay's. Maybe she and Momma had made up once again. It didn't matter if they had. Little Man had learned to cry every time Auntie Jay came around whether she was scalding him with hot water or not.

I had learned to eat cold cereal for breakfast instead of perfectly fried eggs done just so.

We stopped on a busy street. I didn't smell the familiar ghosts of fire that haunted Auntie Jay's neighborhood. We were in a loading zone. Daddy was dropping us off. Momma leaned over and kissed him.

"You call me whenever the bus stops." Daddy's forehead was filled with worry lines. He didn't move. He was not coming.

"I will. You sure you don't want to go with us?" Momma exited her door and came around to open ours.

"No, you know how I feel about that place. The country is not for me. They just took the laughing barrels off the streets down there." Daddy didn't look at us as he talked.

"Let's go, kids." Momma ushered us out of the car. I had heard Daddy talk about the laughing barrels before. I thought they were barrels that laughed, but he told me that I was wrong. Laughing barrels were not funny at all. He said that black people were not allowed to show their teeth on the street down South, a long time ago. You were supposed to stick your head into the barrels if you had to laugh. I thought that was very funny, but Momma said he made it up.

I waited a minute for Daddy to say something, to change his mind. He just looked out of the front window of the car with both hands on the steering wheel. The only sound he made was a single sniff.

We hopped out of the car and Momma grabbed our hands, one of us on each side. We had to run to catch up. There were people going in a thousand different directions and not one of them seemed to be looking down or paying attention to anyone else around them, especially us.

We made our way through the crowd and into the massive building. What was a mess outside was chaos inside. There were crowds of people, some standing, some sitting even where there were no chairs. It smelled hot, like steam.

Momma made her way to a ticket window and dropped our hands. She talked to someone and told them, "Muscoda, please," and pushed money through the slot in the window.

"How long?" She glanced down to check that we were still there. I would not have moved anyway; my legs were like jelly and they were shaking so hard my whole body was shaking too.

"Twenty-four hours?" She repeated what the invisible person in the window had told her and shrugged her shoulders. We were going on a trip.

TEN

A magic bus was taking us to see my Gramma. I couldn't tell how long we had been on it, but I had gotten tired of playing with my dolls to pass the time. After a while the roads all looked the same. I no longer wanted to play punch car with Momma, so instead I just slept hoping that when I woke up we would have arrived.

The towns meshed together as they went by the bus window in a blur of color. Big buildings and busy streets no longer filled the cities, but now there were dusty roads lined with small square shacks. We no longer got off at every stop, we just stayed on the bus and ate the many snacks and sandwiches that Momma had in her secret bag. My stomach hurt like the sides were touching each other. I longed for hot food. Little Man pulled off his socks and shoes and played with his toes. Momma attempted to read but more often than not she alternated between staring out the window and wiping tears from her eyes before they got a chance to fall down her face. That didn't make a whole lot of sense; even I know that it sometimes felt better to just cry. I guess that even mommas got sad too.

We all slept a lot, so much that the days and nights blended together. I had no idea how many nights we had been riding. The bus had been stopping on and off and people kept coming and going. Momma had kept her bag in the seat most of the way and no one ever asked her to move it. They knew that she had been crying as soon as they looked at her; her tears and her puffy red eyes seemed to make everyone avoid us.

The insides of my stomach were surely touching by now and the smell from the bathroom was making my tummy hurt. I sniffed and whined a little to myself as the bus pulled into another station. Momma grabbed her bag before the bus even stopped. I couldn't tell where we were because it was dark. The cricket sounds ran together in the night until they sounded like a roar.

"Let's go." She gathered all of our things and rose from her seat. We had been sitting so long that my knees were stiff. I felt like the Tin Man.

We didn't answer, we just followed, making our way to the front of the otherwise silent bus. No one else moved. A lot of the other passengers were sleeping. They shifted in their seats as we passed by, avoiding the possibility of a casual touch, as if we might leave a small piece of the cloud of sadness that was around us with them. I tried to look out the window and see something familiar, but the dim light was hiding everything in its shadows.

The bus station was deserted except for one lonely car. We watched as the bus pulled off, leaving our bags and us by the side of the road. We stood in our place with our small bags sitting in the dust like the people did on television, listening to the crickets make their crick-crick sound in a place so quiet, it sounded like they were echoing and talking right to us.

The one car was a cab. The cab driver wiped the drool from the side of his mouth as we stood near the side of the car. He must have been sleeping, waiting for our bus.

Even Little Man's eyes were wide open in anticipation. We climbed into the back of the car. It was old and smelled like tobacco and the cracked leather seats scratched the underside of my legs. Momma gave the stale-smelling driver our Gramma's address. I knew it by heart; Momma used to help me write her one letter a week.

There were almost no streetlights in Muscoda. I strained to see where we were going using the light thrown by the headlights of the cab. There was no moon. It didn't shine here. I didn't see much and the shadows played tricks on my eyes. I kept imagining monsters in the darkness as I smelled the country smells of grass and vegetables and animals through the open windows of the cab.

We rode in silence. I almost asked the cab driver to turn on his radio, but then I remembered that the music we liked was only on in the daytime. Down South, the good radio stations were on AM and Momma told me they closed down at dusk. I didn't know if we were in the middle of the night or early in the morning. I knew I should have been sleepy, but the excitement and strangeness of this unexpected trip to Gramma's was holding me awake now. If I slept I might miss something important.

Gramma's house was a little ways from the bus station, almost out in the country. I heard Gramma talk about the other side of town, the West side, as the side where the people with money lived. Her side didn't have fancy houses, most of them were wood and one-story, nothing like the two-story houses with aluminum on the sides like back home. There were no streetlights here or sidewalks with painted curbs. No sidewalks at all. Just houses. And everybody grew something. Even Gramma.

Gramma said she had a small place, but to me, it was a farm. She grew corn and okra and tomatoes and all sorts of things. There were always animals all over the place, mostly chicken and pigs.

We waited in the cab with the driver and Momma got out. She found a stick and used it to push the oleander out of the way. She fished for the secret key that Gramma kept in the yard. She kept it tied in an old hankie, along with some rocks for weight. Gramma said she put it in the oleander 'cause every country person knows that oleander is poison. They would have to really want the key to get it. Momma must've really wanted it.

It took her a few minutes to find the key without getting too entangled in the bushes. She finally got it, and motioned for us to get out of the car. I helped Little Man out and we all stepped up onto the porch. The driver waited for us to walk up the three steps and then pulled off into the night. The darkness wrapped itself around us and the crickets suddenly sounded much louder to me than they did before. I used to love this southern porch, so unlike our unfancy brick stoop at home, but now the crickets and the darkness made me feel unwelcome.

Momma fumbled with the key and a small pen type flashlight she pulled from her purse. She finally opened the door and put her finger to our lips, shushing us. We crept into Gramma's house, into the front room. Then, we sat in the dark like thieves taking things away until morning.

ELEVEN

*V*oices and smells woke me up. I knew immediately that we arrived at Gramma's on a Sunday. She was in the kitchen, clanging pots while she talked to Momma. Smells of rice and country bacon and cornbread mixed with the aroma of percolating coffee and floated through the air. Gramma cooked her own version of brunch on Sundays before heading to church.

Gramma noticed right away that I was awake.

"Sweetie, come on over here and give your grandmomma some sugar," she said. She extended her arms in my direction from the kitchen. I smiled and looked down at my feet as I stood up from the vinyl couch. My neck was stiff, and I wiggled it from side to side.

"Don't you be trying to act like you a-shy. C'mere, girl."

Gramma sometimes added an extra letter to words in the beginning in a way I thought was funny, but never laughed. I reached my Gramma in a few steps, and I planted my face in the middle of her white apron. It smelled of old-fashioned starch, from the box not the can, and was wrapped around the waist of my semi-plump grandma, over her church clothes.

"Stand back," she said. "Lemme get a good look at you."

Momma stood off to the side, not speaking yet. I knew that she was going to talk about how much I had grown since the last time she had seen me, even if I haven't. Gramma held me at arm's length, examining me. Her face was smooth and unwrinkled, but it was wet with tears. She hugged me again, bending down more this time, and I noticed that I had gotten taller. I looked around her and saw that things were still the same in her old kitchen, down to the jars of preserves on the shelf and the green tomatoes that she put in the window to ripen.

Momma finally spoke up. "You hungry, Sweetie?"

I nodded. Her voice was strained, practiced. I knew that meant they had been talking about whatever was going on with Momma, what the doctor told her.

"Well, baby," Gramma said, "why don't you run out yonder to the chicken coop and grab me some eggs to cook for you before your brother wakes up."

I looked into their faces, one at a time, and it was obvious they were doing the thing that grownups do when they were not quite finished talking about something they did not want you to hear about. She probably had eggs in the icebox, but I didn't argue. I had to go to the bathroom anyway, and the outhouse was near the chicken coop.

Gramma patted me on my butt as I turned. I passed the round washing machine that must have been ten years old, and headed out the back door. It slammed behind me and I stepped out onto the steps. They had been replaced by concrete steps since the last time we visited. I stood there for a minute, kicked them one time and breathed in the corn smells all around me. Momma and Gramma were waiting for me to get far enough away so I couldn't hear their voices through the open window. Only the ears of corn would hear what they had to say, but I already knew how bad it was; it hung over our heads every day, changing and aging everyone around, even me.

Instead of going back in, I sat on the back steps and waited for them to call me. I watched the stinkbugs move across the yard until I forgot I had to pee and hoped I didn't see a snake. I tried to hear them but couldn't. I picked up a nearby stick to draw in the dirt, but I never got to write more than my name.

Instead of calling me, Gramma came out and slowly sat down on the steps with me. I was surprised that she did and remembered that she struggled to get up from the couch which was higher than the tallest step. The thought of her stuck out on the back steps with me made me smile.

"Hey, baby." Gramma rubbed my back with her hand and I looked over at her, still smiling. "How you doing?"

I got the feeling that I was not supposed to answer, so I just shrugged my shoulders. It didn't matter; I realized that I was not feeling anything but empty. Gramma kept talking.

"These are strange times, ain't it? No one has talked to you about anything, have they?"

I shook my head.

"Well, Sweetie, sometimes grown folk don't know what to say, so they don't say anything. But you are my big girl, and you are going to have to be strong." Gramma moved her hand from my back to my knee. "It is going to get worse, you know."

I could feel my tears coming and I blinked to hold them back. I couldn't imagine worse than the secrets or the hospitals or the unexpected fires.

"When I was a girl, my daddy was gone and my momma worked for other people, all day and sometimes all night. They did that so we could survive. I was the only girl out of seven kids. I had to cook, clean, take care of everybody. I had to learn how to be strong, just like you are going to have to do."

I nodded. Gramma had told me the story before. I wondered if I was really going to have to learn how to cook.

"You are going to have to be strong too, Sweetie. You are going to have to be the big girl I know you are, especially for your daddy. He is lost already, and feeling is so much harder for men. Y'all gonna have to be patient with him. Think you can do that?"

This was the first time that anyone had asked me anything, but I still felt as if Gramma had not told me a thing. No one had given me a choice and I felt like I was outside my life looking in, like television. Instead of answering her, I nodded and felt like this was the end of something, but I couldn't figure out what.

Gramma tried to stand up from the concrete steps and laughed to herself. "Don't forget the eggs," she said. "You might want to take that stick with you in case that old rooster gets in your way." She paused. "You ain't afraid, are you?"

I shook my head no and then wiped my nose. I was not afraid of the chickens and I knew she knew that. Somehow, I felt like her question had more to it than I understood, but I didn't know what else I was supposed to be afraid of. She turned to go back into the house, and I stood up to head toward the chicken coop.

TWELVE

We were on the bus longer than we were in Muscoda. Momma said we had to leave because I had to go back to school soon. I wasn't too happy about that. I knew I was going to have a new teacher and none of the third grade teachers seemed very nice at all, not like Miss Faust was. She made me feel like I was very good at something, even if I was having a bad day and she wasn't mad at me when I didn't win that writing competition. Instead she asked me if I had done my best, and when I told her I had, she smiled and said she was proud then and that I should be too. I was gonna miss her.

I had a stomachache this morning but Granny Hambay-el made me get up anyway. (That is what we call her now.) Little Man is going to school with me this year. He moved so slow getting dressed that I thought we would miss the bus. I let him sag behind me on purpose so that maybe we would miss it and tomorrow could be the first day instead. It didn't work. It was there, waiting for us when we got to the bus stop, same as always. The bus driver grinned and opened the door for us to climb on. A few kids looked up but no one spoke or looked glad to see us. Little Man was scared. I could tell from the way he was holding my hand real hard. We found a seat together in the back of the bus.

Just as I thought, my new teacher was not friendly at all. She called us all by our last name and Miss or Mr., so I am Miss Wooten. From the way she said it, I could tell that there was no way that she was ever going to call me Sweetie. It didn't seem like she was even interested in learning our first names at all. Miss Faust not only knew everybody's first name, she knew special things about us like what we liked to eat or what our favorite color was and things.

I smiled at the new teacher thinking she might smile back but she just looked at me with eyes so hard they hurt. This was not going to be a good year.

Although my teacher had changed, everything else had stayed the same. The kids were still as unfriendly as they ever were. At recess, no one said anything to me at all. I sat on the stone wall at the playground with Little Man and watched all the other kids choose sides for Rongoleavio and Skully. No one picked us although I know that it looked like I wanted to be picked.

Recess was almost over and the other kids were still yelling "Ringoleavio, one, two, three," loud and strong. Most of them were sweaty and those that weren't had probably hit me or Little Man with their skully cap once or twice. Recess was the time of day I hated almost as much as riding the bus in the afternoon. Today's recess seemed to be the longest ever. I couldn't wait for it to be too cold for them to play outside. That way I wouldn't have to wait for them to choose me because no one would be playing any games at all.

"Monica." Miss Faust called me from across the playground. She marched toward me. Her face was tan from the summer and she was smiling. All the other kids seemed to stop what they were doing to watch her come. Teachers usually stayed near the building if they were the yard monitors or they didn't come outside for recess at all.

"How was your summer?"

I wasn't sure how to answer her question. I wasn't even sure if there was a right answer, if she really wanted to know about my days at Granny Hambay-el's house or visiting Momma in the hospital. I shrugged. "Fine."

That seemed to make her happy. She smiled a little harder at me.

Just then my new teacher came over, Mrs. Cohen. Her lips were drawn into a thin line. She stopped right in front of us and I could tell that she was not happy.

"Is there a problem?" she asked. "I hope Miss Wooten has not been misbehaving."

"No, she is an angel. I was just asking her about her summer, that's all. Have you discovered Monica's fine writing talent yet? She really is quite exceptional."

They talked about me like I was not there and just for a minute, I felt like I did at home. The kids around me were only acting as if they had returned to their games. I could see that some of them were giggling, making fun of me standing there with the two teachers near me. I felt heavy, like I wanted to sink into the wall instead of staying perched on top of it.

"Really? She hasn't shown me anything yet," Miss Cohen said. "There is nothing special about any of these kids. I don't believe in singling children out, Miss Faust. It's not a good practice. They need to face their realities from a very young age. It prepares them better for life. You will understand that when you get more experience."

Miss Faust looked surprised. Her mouth dropped open for a minute and then she closed it again very fast.

"We should talk about this inside," she said. "Monica, I hope you will write in that book I gave you every day."

I looked away from her. The only thing I had done with that book so far was draw pictures.

"Sometimes getting things down on paper really helps you to make sense of them." They turned to walk back toward the building.

I had a tight feeling in the pit of my stomach. I wanted to tell her that my Momma was sick and that my Gramma told me things I didn't understand, but I couldn't do it. I couldn't tell anyone. I didn't want to be different. I wanted to be strong, like Gramma said, but I didn't know how to do that either. There were some things I would always have to keep inside.

THIRTEEN

*M*omma had been in the hospital for three weeks. We were only home for two days before she had to go back in. We had been staying overnight at the sitter's house ever since. We had been going straight to school from there.

This morning we got to go home instead of going to school, but it was still a school day. When we got up, the sitter told me that there was a lady waiting downstairs to take us home instead. She didn't even have to say; I knew that the woman was another one of those baby nurses. We had been seeing a lot of them lately.

It was usually noisy in the sitter's house in the morning; the noise always woke me up. Everybody in the house seemed to wake up before it got light outside. And they all talked loud and screamed at each other, all at the same time. This morning was different, though. They weren't even playing the radio on talk radio or that AM station that they liked to listen to.

We slept upstairs. I slept in her granddaughter's room, on a cot. Her granddaughter, Elizabeth, was grown but she had just moved in here, I think. She talked just as funny as her mother. She had just come from wherever they were from to live here, too. She was supposed to have a son, but I didn't know where he was. He didn't come with her. They said she was going to send for him later.

It was always too cold in my room at the sitter's house, but I was afraid to say anything. Every time I talked, the sitter sucked her teeth so hard I was afraid she was going to suck them into the back of her head. I knew that they were not hers because I saw her put them in a glass, so I knew that they could move.

There was a fan in the window in our room, directly across from my cot. Elizabeth slept with it on all night, like this was the hottest place she had ever lived. I knew that this was not true, she told me that they did not have winter where they were from. She got up really early, before it got light outside, but she left the fan on all day long.

I only had a sheet to cover up with, so I could never get warm, I tried to sleep on my front, with my arms underneath me, but it didn't help.

Little Man slept down the hall, down the red rug that was the same as the one downstairs but with no runner, in the room with the sitter's grandson. He slept on a cot too. The grandson, Everett, seemed old. Just like Elizabeth and everything else in the house. I didn't know how old, but he went to clubs at night with people the sitter didn't like; I heard her call them loose women. They argued about it all the time. Everett was the only one that got to sleep late on Saturdays. Everyone else seemed to get up at the crack of dawn. She called him slovenly, a new word for me. I never heard anyone called that before. I had to look it up in the dictionary at school. Why couldn't she just say lazy and sloppy if that is what she meant?

She was mad at him this morning. She banged on his door real loud, yelling at him about the way he treated some woman that came to the house last night. She left crying and then he argued with Granny Hambay-el about it.

The sitter marched us down the stairs, and right to the front room, with an open hand on each of our shoulders. She squeezed mine a little too hard and it hurt me; I tried to pull away, but her grip was too tight. I knew I would probably have a bruise there later. I could feel it forming already.

The baby nurse was young. She was sitting in the front room waiting for us. Her arms were crossed across her chest like she was trying to protect herself from something. I wanted to tell her that it wouldn't work, but then the baby-sitter would say I was an upstart, another word she had taught me.

"Here they are," the sitter said. Her voice was sing-songy because of the lilt in it and she had on that plastered-on smile I had seen her use on Daddy.

The nurse didn't answer or say hello to us or anything. She just stood up and walked to the door, expecting us to follow. She must have been new; it was almost like she didn't know that she had to hold our hands. Sometimes I felt like we were taking care of them, not the other way around.

We walked all the way home without talking, but I was excited. We hadn't seen Daddy in the morning in a long time. Maybe I could even have my fried egg the right way today. The sitter never gave us eggs. Our breakfast had been the same there the whole time, farina, toast and one slice of American cheese. No pancakes, no eggs. And tea with milk, which she said was good for us.

The nurse let us go up the stairs first, and the door opened almost by itself. Daddy was in the front room, sitting in the recliner chair, but he was not reclined. He didn't look relaxed at all. And Momma's brother was here!

"Uncle Cedric..." My voice came out in a shout. I was so happy to see him, he was my favorite uncle.

"Hey, baby," he answered.

His voice was flat instead of happy the way it usually was. He didn't pick me up or hug me like he normally did. He didn't ask me, "What's cooking?" like he was supposed to. He just rubbed my head instead and I frowned. A sinking feeling came to the bottom of my stomach. Things were not the way they should be.

Daddy sat all the way to the front of the chair, with his head in his hands. The clock ticked louder than normal. Daddy didn't even look up at me.

Uncle Cedric guided me to Daddy with the same hand he patted me with.

"She's gone." Daddy was crying.

Real tears were streaming down his face and running into his mouth.

"Gone?" I asked. "Who? Gone where?"

Instead of answering me, he said it again. It was almost like he was not aware that we were there with him.

"She's gone." He cried harder, sobbing now, his shoulders moving up and down with each sound that came out of his mouth.

I had never seen my daddy cry before. He came close when he took us to the hospital, but he was crying actual tears, like Little Man did.

I looked at Uncle Cedric, and he looked away. The clock ticked louder. There was no air in the room. Little Man tried to force his way into Daddy's lap, and Daddy ignored him.

They were talking about Momma.

I looked from Daddy to Uncle Cedric, and no one said anything else to me. I felt a lump start, first in my stomach, slowing rising. That usually meant I was going to cry, but not this time. The lump stopped at the back of my throat, choking me. The tears didn't fall. Instead they were stuck in my throat, stretching me up as they tried to get out, like I was growing automatically. This must have been what Gramma was talking about. I had a doll whose hair grew like that when you pressed her back. Only instead of making my hair grow, the tears were growing me up and growing the space between me and everyone else in the room, like the trick room in that Alice in Wonderland book I read. I felt so far away from everyone it was almost like I was in the room by myself.

The nurse, who was standing in the door this whole time, finally came in, without talking. She stepped around me and picked up Little Man, who was still trying to get in Daddy's lap. He was squirming so much, she had a hard time hiking him up on her hip. He was too big to be carried now anyway.

She put her hand in the middle of my back and half guided, half pushed me into the living room, away from Daddy, still sitting and sobbing in his chair. No one said anything else, at least not to me.

There was a mirror in front of where I stopped, almost at the bottom of the stairs. I just stood in front of it in the house that was now silent except for Daddy's tears. Momma used to stand in that mirror and put on her lipstick every day, on her way out the door.

I didn't really understand where people go when they are "gone," but I knew that this was bad. In the mirror, I could see the seeds of those tears in the corners of my eye, but I couldn't see the lump in my throat that was still choking me, making me part my lips so a little extra air could get in. I could believe that Momma left me but not her little man. She would never leave him.

I stepped closer to the mirror to examine my tears, trying to make them come out, but they didn't seem to want to move. My eyes seemed to watch me as I moved my head from side to side. I couldn't feel anything but the lump that grew bigger by the minute. The nurse tended to Little Man, who fussed because he still wanted his daddy. He didn't understand. No one was paying attention to me.

<hr>

There were lots of people downstairs, I could hear them talking. I sat in my bed for a while, and I heard them coming and going, although everyone seemed to be talking low.

I went to the top of the steps so I could hear better. I used to stand there and listen to Momma and Daddy talk, back where they couldn't see me. Now I wanted to hear the people downstairs.

No one had said anything to me yet; not really, but I knew what was going on. I didn't know what was going to happen to me and Little Man. I didn't know who was going to take care of us. Daddy had to go to work so I didn't think he could do it. He can't even comb my hair, that much I did know. He and Momma used to joke about him not wanting to learn to do my hair.

I could see the folks downstairs from where I was sitting, right through the banister. I didn't recognize most of them. Most of the ladies that were coming in brought food of all kinds. Everyone talked in whispers as if they were afraid that if they talked too loud they might discover what everybody already knew was true.

I could only make out a few words, every now and them.

"Shame....mumble, mumble, mumble."

"Two kids, mumble, mumble."

"Mumble, mumble so young."

Daddy was still sitting in that chair where he was when we came home this morning. Every now and then I saw someone go in and try to talk to him, but he hadn't moved much. He wasn't crying anymore and he looked more like his old self. Uncle Cedric still stood by him.

Uncle Cedric moved up here to the big city with Momma. He lived in the big tall buildings like Auntie Jay with his wife and his three sons, except their building had an elevator. The oldest is the same age as me.

Uncle Cedric finally saw me, sitting there on the top step.

"Hey, Sweetie," he said. He still didn't ask me what's cooking, so I knew that things had not changed from this morning. She was still *gone*.

I didn't feel like answering him. He came up the thirteen steps in our house and scooped me up, taking me down to the bottom. But I didn't want to be carried, I wanted to know what was going on.

Another woman I didn't know walked into the room when Uncle Cedric came up the stairs to get me.

"Poor baby," she said, reaching for me. "What is she going to do?"

She talked to Uncle Cedric like I wasn't there and couldn't possibly understand what was going on. I still didn't say anything. The woman looked at Uncle Cedric like he actually had the answer.

"Oooh," she said. "She is speechless. This type thing can be very harmful to a child, you know. I would see about it. I once heard--"

"That's enough. She's fine. We'll all be fine." Uncle Cedric cut her off. "It's okay if she doesn't want to talk right now. Would you?"

He put the lady's hand in between his own and guided her away from me, toward the kitchen and the food. I peeked around the corner and I saw many more people in the living room and back into the kitchen than I thought were here.

They were sitting, standing everywhere. And they all talked in that horrible hushed voice.

A couple of people turned their heads toward me when I moved. They gave me that look, the same look that the lady Uncle Cedric led away did. They stopped what they were doing and just stared. A few shook their heads. I stopped moving right where I was, with one foot in front of the other, like I was playing freeze tag, hoping that the same way my moving made them look, my stopping would make them stop. But it didn't, and I felt like I was branded, like the cows down South. I felt like it was written on my forehead, "Momma: Gone."

The front door swung open in a noisy way. Everyone turned to look there instead of at me. I was relieved, but they all glared because whoever opened the door was not being quiet at all.

June-Bug walked in, letting the door slam behind him with a bang. His 'fro looked cool and he walked across the room like Shaft in the movie he snuck me into. I could almost hear the music in my head. He didn't talk to Daddy or Uncle Cedric. Instead he walked straight to me.

"What are you doing here, Sweetie?" He squeezed his eyebrows together. "You shouldn't be down here like this. How come no one combed your hair, girl?" My big brother talked a mile a minute. He looked around the room, at all the people sitting, when he spoke like he was accusing them more than asking me. They seemed to move back, as if his glance had pushed them. June-Bug knew that Momma would have wanted my hair just so, nothing like it was. I touched my now mushed-up curls and I shrugged my shoulders in response.

For a minute, everyone in the room stopped again, but this time they stared at June-Bug and they were not smiling, they looked annoyed.

He looked right back at them with a look that asked, "What are you looking at?" so loud that everyone heard it, even if his lips didn't move an inch. They all turned around and resumed their whispering and eating, stealing a glance every now and then. Daddy was still sitting in his chair.

"C'mon, let's go," June-Bug said. He grabbed my hand and led me up the stairs, guiding me. "We got to do something with that head."

The mirror at the bottom of the steps was covered with a sheet now. June-Bug passed by and the wind he made moved the sheet a little. He reached up and straightened it. I was helpless, but I followed him. I was grateful that someone had noticed me. For anything.

FOURTEEN

June-Bug told me that Momma had died and gone to heaven to live with the angels. The two of us now had to take care of each other and Little Man. June-Bug said that Daddy was going to do what daddies did best - work.

Our house had been going nonstop since we came home four days ago and they told us the news. People had been coming and going and talking and eating. Almost every one of them had claimed to be my cousin or something like that. I had no idea who most of them were. It seemed like folks came out the woodwork to get a meal and a glance at the strange children with no mother.

The strangers stood in groups around the house. Every few minutes one small group or another dropped their heads and broke into a prayer. They prayed like they did in Gramma's church down South, except they whispered, like they didn't want no one to hear. They prayed about God's will and for our future and other things that I couldn't get.

I couldn't always hear what they were saying, but I recognized the motions of praying just the same. It sounded like mumble, mumble, mumble, and then one member of the prayer group broke into "Yes, Jesus," or "Thank you, Lord." Every now and then I heard one of the praying groups say,

"Elva" or "precious babies." I couldn't tell if they were praying to bring my momma back or praying for her wherever she was now.

I hadn't talked to anyone but June-Bug. There had been no reason to. I hadn't even said much to him either other than to ask to go to the bathroom. The only person I wanted to talk to was Momma, and I was mad at Daddy because he never told me that this would happen. No one did. But I hadn't cried either. For some reason, I couldn't. The tears were still stuck in my throat. I tried to drink water and do everything else that usually worked to make tears go away, but they just sat there, blocking my throat. Sometimes it was worse than others and I felt like I might choke but nothing seemed to help. I couldn't help but wonder if choking might be better, if it might somehow help the confusion I felt.

We got dressed up like we were going to church. June-Bug said we were going to ride in a car like a limousine, like the television stars did. Little Man and me were the only ones wearing white. Everyone else was dressed up in black or brown, which was real strange because it was springtime, the time when all the flowers bloomed. Momma used to dress me in bright colors and things all the time during spring. She said springtime was the time of new life and that she wanted me to be as pretty as a new flower too.

June-Bug talked at me about nothing, like he was trying to distract me from what was really going on. He helped me do everything, even put on my shoes, even if I didn't need him too. He rambled on about everything that popped into his head. He did it so much that I started to ignore him, just tuning him out so I could think.

"It's time, Sweetie," June-Bug said. He took my hand when I was done being dressed and led me downstairs to where Daddy was waiting. Daddy was still sad, but he still had not talked to me about what happened. I think he was in shock, like people are on TV when something bad happens. He had been real busy, making arrangements and talking to all kinds of people that had been coming and going. And Little Man sat on Daddy's lap every chance he got.

Little Man still had no clue about what had happened. He probably thought this was a party or something because of all the food. He kept playing with all the strangers that were at the house. They all thought he looked real cute in his tiny little suit. I saw him playing with Daddy's tie, and Daddy ignoring him, talking to yet another stranger. Every now and then he would reach up and take his tie from Little Man, trying to smooth it back down. It didn't work. Little Man would pick it right back up again.

Finally, Daddy finished talking. He took Little Man and June-Bug held my hand and we went outside to get in the car. It was big and long and black, just like June-Bug said it would be. The car was big enough for us all to get into at the same time, in the back seat. Little Man and I sat on funny seats that popped up from the floor, facing June-Bug and Daddy.

We went to a funeral home. There were a lot of them in our neighborhood, but I had never actually been inside one before. Momma used to say that they were all owned by the same folks who owned the liquor stores. "They let you drink yourself to death and then they bury you, too," she would say.

When we got there, more people I didn't know were milling around outside. The only person I recognized was Miss Faust, and I looked away from her when she looked at me. We paused at the door, and for a minute I could see that there were people inside already too. They were all dressed in dark colors same as the people at the house.

A whisper went through the room and everyone seemed to turn around and look at us, standing there in the doorway. I felt naked for a minute, then just as quickly as they turned around to look, they turned back around again as if they were reminded that it was rude to stare.

All the chairs in the room were set up on either side of the door, facing forward. There was a podium or something at the front of the room, like church, and another woman that I didn't know played soft music. She also wore black and swayed along with her music.

The music was not like anything we would ever play at home. It didn't even have any words. Some people did seem to be humming along, and every now and then the woman playing it closed her eyes. People looked down at their shoes or stared out in front of them.

A big white box sat at the front of the room. It was long and half of it was open. A little podium was off to the side, with lots of flowers all around. Most of them were daisies, Momma's favorite.

I sat in the front row, with Daddy, June-Bug and Little Man. Uncle Cedric sat right behind us with his family. I knew that June-Bug talked to Gramma, but she was not here. She was still down South and couldn't come. She said she didn't want to get on no airplane, being that they fell from the sky and all. I think that she and Momma said their good-byes while we were there. I wish Momma had said good-bye to me too.

My feet didn't quite touch the ground as I sat in my chair. I kept looking down so I wouldn't have to look at anyone, and my neck burned as I felt people's eyes on me, staring. You would think I was glowing or something in my white dress.

I sat between Daddy and June-Bug, and every now and then one of them reached over and patted me somewhere, my leg, my arm, my head, or they asked me if I was okay, which was a silly question. I nodded at them that I was okay anyway, silly or not. I was not sure how I was supposed to be or to feel.

Finally, the music stopped, and a man started to speak, just like the minister in Gramma's church. I didn't listen to any words. I just sat and thought, hoping that this whole thing would be over soon.

People in the room were crying. There was sniffling all around me. They all sounded like they were really trying to hold their tears inside, so their tears could be stuck in their throats, like mine. When I looked up, I could see a few people dabbing their eyes with tissues and handkerchiefs. The woman at the piano sang "Amazing Grace," one of Momma's favorite songs. She got to the part about saving a wretch and

I couldn't help but wonder if Grace was so amazing why she didn't save Momma. She opened her mouth really wide while she sang and I saw all of her teeth.

After a while, June-Bug started to cry too. Tears rolled down his cheeks and his bawling was worse than I had ever seen even Little Man do. Even Daddy was sniffling again. I could tell he was really fighting to hold back, but once in a while a tear escaped anyway and rolled down his face, curling around his chin. Once Daddy started crying, Little Man wouldn't be far behind. I refused to look at them and instead I looked at the floor. I still couldn't cry. The tears that had stuck in my throat had now made me numb. I was afraid that if I cried then I would forget, and I wanted to remember her always.

Suddenly we all stood up, and June-Bug took my hand. He kept tugging me along, and we walked toward the white box in the front of the room. A murmur went through the people in the room again.

We approached the box, and went right up to it. Momma was inside, in her white dress. She was beautiful and smiling and looked just fine. But her eyes were closed. Daddy and June-Bug were crying again. June-Bug leaned over to me, and I thought he was going to kiss me on my cheek, but instead he whispered in my ear.

"Give Momma a kiss, Sweetie," he said. His voice was full of hesitation.

I paused a minute, not sure what to do. I wanted to give her a kiss, but only if I could smell her hair like I used to and only if she could kiss me back. I started to take half a step forward, and just as I did someone shouted out from the crowd.

"Wait a minute! Wait, just a minute!"

The owner of the voice was a woman, heavy-set, not too tall. She came toward us, walking and talking fast with a fiery, deep voice.

"These babies shouldn't be doing that. I have no idea what you are thinking, Junius, or maybe you are just not thinking at all. Y'all folks is crazy!" She shouted over the silence that had fallen in the room.

Her voice made me stop. Her words sounded funny, like the folks from Muscoda.

She got to the front of the room and I could see she had a mustache. The silence gave way to a whisper, heading toward a low roar. Everyone was joining in with this lady. I had never heard anyone call Daddy Junius before. The outburst from this woman started everyone in the room to talking, even Daddy. He handed Little Man to June-Bug and took a step back to face the woman.

"Stay out of this, Willie," he said. "I know what I am doing." Daddy's voice had that low-controlled sound to it again. Normally I would expect to see anger in his face, but instead all I could say was that he was tired. He dabbed the sweat appearing on his forehead with his free hand.

"Apparently not," she answered. "Apparently you done lost your fool mind. Life goes on. These kids should remember their momma alive. Not lying in some box. They shouldn't even be here."

"I know what I am doing," Daddy said again. "These are my kids." I felt him pull me toward him.

"Not for long if you keep making decisions like this. I told you that you couldn't handle these kids. I just thought it would take a little longer for the truth to come to light."

The lady with the mustache pointed her finger at Daddy and they went at it like there was no one else around.

The people in the crowd were restless. I could tell that some of them agreed with her.

June-Bug grabbed my hand again, real tight this time. Daddy was still arguing with the woman as June-Bug began to lead me out of the room.

"C'mon, Sweetie." He jerked on my hand so hard I stumbled, walking so fast that I almost couldn't keep up. Little Man was still being carried. He started to yell and kick.

"Daaaddy," he cried.

June-Bug ignored him and kept walking toward the door. People were so busy concentrating on Daddy they didn't even see us moving. This was what Momma would have called "grown-folks business." I was just relieved that we didn't have to kiss Momma.

We walked outside, to the sidewalk, where it was relatively quiet compared to the ruckus that had been started inside. June-Bug let my hand go.

"I'm sorry, Sweetie. Grown-ups can be so silly sometimes," he said, smoothing out my dress. He wiped his nose with the back of his hand at the same time. I knew Momma would have hated that and probably would have yelled at June-Bug to use a tissue. I didn't answer him but I didn't understand why he was apologizing. He didn't do anything. But I was sure glad that lady stopped us.

On TV when people die they always say they are cold. I didn't think I would have liked feeling coldness from Momma at all. My stomach growled and I shivered, suddenly having the feeling that coldness was going to be a familiar feeling from now on.

FIFTEEN

We had not slept at home since Momma died. She had been gone for two years, and Little Man and I were still sleeping on our cots, in separate corners at the sitter's house. I still couldn't believe that she was gone. Sometimes I told myself that she had taken a necessary trip and would come back one day, I even imagined seeing her sometimes out of the corner of my eye, like she was sitting back watching over us.

We were still calling the sitter, Granny Hambay-el, but she was nothing like my grandmother at all. There was rarely anything warm about her, she didn't have those grandma type smells that made you feel safe and welcomed. She dyed her silver hair a dull-lifeless black and she didn't bend the rules for anyone in her house, least of all Little Man and me. She ruled with an iron fist and everyone in her house still got up just as early as they did before Momma died, just 'cause she said so.

Today was Tuesday, but it felt just like every other day. The window fan was still in the window, blocking the sunshine, making me cold. They were downstairs talking loud, and the radio was playing "The Coldest Days of My Life." They listened to FM some mornings now, and I could hear the

Chi-Lites loud and clear. In the past two years, it seemed like more people had come through this house than through the Underground Railroad, every one of them having a slightly different musical taste. The music I heard here did not make me feel the same as it did back in Momma's kitchen, or even the times I remembered being in the bar with Momma. It didn't add warmth and it wasn't the special ingredient in anybody's cooking. Most of the time they still listened to AM and the bass was missing, making me feel like I was eating Daddy's stew without the pepper.

Daddy put pepper, lots of it, into everything he cooked, which wasn't a lot. Sometimes I thought that pepper was the only spice he used. His favorites were chili and chicken and dumplings. I loved them both, although I thought his chili should be called hotty instead. Sometimes it was so hot, all I could taste was the pepper, but I loved it just the same.

I tried to act like I was still sleeping, but I knew that the sitter would be busting into the room soon. She woke me up first, then Little Man, usually finding some reason to yell at one or the other of us.

Right on cue, the door slammed downstairs as the sitter's daughter left for work. She worked in a factory, sewing clothes for a big department store. She made clothes for everyone in the house too, often sewing way into the night. Everett even made a sewing room for her, downstairs. Granny Hambay-el still yelled at him about the late hours he kept. Other than sleeping, he always seemed to be fixing or building something around the house. Not too long after we came, he set up a makeshift wall, right down the middle of the dining room. The wall didn't go all the way to the ceiling, so everyone could hear her sewing all night. The whirring of her machine often put me to sleep.

Now, instead of a dining room where the other row houses in the neighborhood had one, they had two rooms, divided by the wall. One is a hall, and the other is her sewing room, which we were never allowed into. They even moved the plastic runner over to make sure that it was in place in the new hall, covering up as much as possible of the blood red rug that we were still not allowed to walk on. I let the whirr of her machine act as my lullaby, I even imagined words to the rhythm sometimes.

I heard the sitter coming. It was hard to miss her, her steps were heavy and her distinctive walk lumbered as she rolled from one leg to the other. She stuck her head in the room. My cot was right near the door.

"Get up, gal," she said. "You gwine sleep all day? It's time for you to get ready for school."

Her voice was just as sing-songy as it was two years ago, and she still didn't complete her words, leaving off r's and running everything together. We had learned to understand her. Sometimes we even sounded like her, so much that Daddy frowned at us when we talked.

She didn't wait for my answer, she immediately continued on down the hall, to wake up Little Man. I got up to start our daily routine, stripping the sheets from my cot. I folded the sheets so I could store them in the bottom of my makeshift closet. We didn't make our beds here, instead we took them apart every day.

"Dyamn boy!" I heard her yelling at Little Man. "When is this gwine stop? Get up! Get up right now!"

I heard a thud as Little Man fell, stumbling as he tried to get away from her. Without even seeing, I knew she had a belt in her hand. She began to mumble, still upset, but her voice had gotten lower. She always mumbled to herself after she yelled at us, like she was scolding herself too. I could no longer make out what she was saying. I wanted to stick my head outside my room and look, but I didn't dare for fear that she might start to yell at me too or hit me with that belt.

Little Man came down the hall, hurrying and crying, crying and hurrying. He passed my door and I looked up; he was naked and he was carrying his bedding, in front of him, in his arms. He used it as barrier, covering up his private parts.

Without asking, I knew that his sheets were wet again. He had been wetting his bed since Momma died. Daddy had been taking him to specialist after specialist, but no one seemed able to figure it out.

The sitter was right behind him and she was still talking at him.

"Itinkyoudothisonpurpose!" Her words ran together even more when she was angry. "You don' need no doctor! All you need is this belt cross your backside!" Her brow was furrowed together in deep rows and she sucked her teeth long and hard.

Little Man was running to get away from her, tripping on the ends of his sheets. He scurried past my room and went down the steps, almost falling. He had to go through the kitchen, down into the basement, to the washroom. She made him wash the sheets himself. She didn't want to touch them. She wouldn't follow him all the way downstairs, her legs would keep her from moving too fast down the steps and she wouldn't be able to keep up.

I began to fold up my cot. I didn't want to see him come back upstairs. I didn't want to see him with no clothes on again. He would be without his sheets this time to protect himself.

I didn't really have a closet here. They had hung a pole in the corner of the room, near the foot of my cot, for me to hang my things. It was not hard to get dressed, I had five outfits for school, one for each day of the week, with one pair of shoes and one pair of sneakers. Daddy was not too big on shopping.

I took down my Tuesday outfit, quickly pulling it on. It was not special or spectacular, it just was. I didn't even look in the mirror. It wasn't necessary. No one picked out my clothes the way Momma used to. They were not even ironed. I didn't get to wear pretty dresses or the latest fashions like the other girls at school. These were just clothes.

Little Man passed by my door. The sitter was back, too.

"You ready, gal?" she yelled from her room, next to mine.

My stomach rumbled, but I knew that I couldn't eat until my hair had been combed. I didn't answer, instead I grabbed the comb and brush and my bag of ribbons and went to her room. I stood in the doorway and waited for her to tell me to come in. I hated this part of the morning more than anything. She looked up at me after a minute.

"What you standing dere for? Come on in 'ere," she said. The sitter almost never pronounced the letter h.

She sat on the bed, waiting, looking annoyed at me for being. Her room was absolutely spotless and was amazing to me. There was no dust anywhere. Her bed, already made, was spread with a bedspread that matched the red rug. Her curtains matched too. The walls were pink. Staring, I got the same feeling I got every morning that I had fallen into a room that had been splashed with blood. This was one of the few places in the house where there was no plastic runner. I stopped being afraid of being sucked into the rug a long time ago. One day I woke up and realized I must have already been pulled down into its abyss, I just hadn't realized it.

Her dresser was spotless, too. She didn't have little bottles all over, like Momma did, filled with perfumes and other things that adult women used. Instead she had one small glass tray, in the middle, with four small bottles on it. These were no pretty perfume bottles, instead these were medicine vials refilled with her own brand of medicine, whatever she liked this week, purchased from some place that sells what she called herbs and roots or grown in her yard.

I was supposed to sit on the floor while she combed my hair, just like with Momma and Gramma. Only she didn't talk or tell me stories while she did it. Most of the time she was silent, except to yell at me. She used her knees to clasp my head and hold me in place, so I couldn't move or squirm even if I wanted to. I imagined she was barking to make the time pass faster, sometimes imagining the evils that I knew she must keep in her closet, behind the locked door.

I got the same hairstyle every day, no creativity here. I missed the Shirley Temple curls that Momma used to do. Those were long gone. Or the rows of braids Gramma gave me. I stopped wishing for all that after about six months here. The sitter didn't do any of that.

"Tchh." She sucked her teeth. "You nu should not take pride in yu hair, you know. Dat's bad luck. You need concentrate on what is on de inside anyway." Instead, she gave me three pigtails, two in the back and one on top. On special occasions the three got split into three each, and instead of being braided, they got twisted.

I sat between her legs and tried to focus on the vials on the dresser. I felt her hands moving my head around more like I was a Barbie doll than a real person. When she wanted me to move she pulled on my pigtails like they were dog leads. If I moved too much she might hit me with the comb, right on top of my head. I sat there, in fear, crouching as far down as I dared.

I dreaded the ribbons. All the girls at school got ribbons in their hair, including me. The only difference I could see between them and me was that theirs always matched their pretty clothes that they had picked out on their shopping trips with their mothers. There were no shopping trips for me; I had only heard of stories of the new shopping mall. Instead, I got whatever the sitter felt like that day. It seemed she just never liked matching, but instead she took whatever came right out of my ribbon bag. Sometimes, they didn't even match. I was not even sure she understood what it meant for things to match each other. She obviously didn't understand what it meant to me. I wasn't sure she wanted to understand me at all.

I held the ribbon bag clenched in my fist so hard that the color was leaving my palms. It was almost like my fist was clenched around my breath too. She was almost finished with the braiding. I automatically held the ribbon bag up.

She didn't even look at it, she reached her hand into the bag, her crooked fingers grasping at the ribbons. In the mirror I could see that she was choosing three ribbons with one grab. Three different ones that didn't coordinate with my dress, just like yesterday.

I knew I should try to hold in my disappointment, but I sighed before I could stop myself.

"Wha's wrong wit you?" she asked. The challenge in her voice leapt at me like a schoolyard bully. She jerked my head.

"Nothing."

She sucked her teeth again, dragging out the sound like she normally did.

The way the sitter sucked her teeth must be famous. She should be in the Guinness Book of World Records. I was positive she dragged the sound out a full thirty seconds.

"No ting what?"

"Nothing, ma'am." I answered quickly, not wanting to add challenge to our daily routine more than necessary.

"Damn American chil'ren. No manners." She went back to fixing my hair. She pulled on my ponytails a little harder.

We went through this every day. I couldn't figure out if she didn't care or didn't pay attention. This whole process took about fifteen minutes if I sat really still. Today was no different; Granny Hambay-El tugged and pulled at my head; sucking her teeth every few minutes. Sometimes I thought she was mad at me because she had to do it. It felt like she was holding on to me tighter than the teeth were glued to the cup in the Polident commercials.

Finally she was done. Relief spread through me as she released the iron grip she had on my head. The last thing she did every day, and today too, was to push my head away with her hand.

"Thank you, Granny Hambay-El." I felt like my ears were inflating back to their normal shape. She sucked her teeth again, this time only for a short time.

"I keep tellin' yunu not ta say tanks for ya hair."

"Oh. Yes, ma'am." I forgot, thank you is almost automatic.

"It is bad luck, you know."

I stood up and straightened up my Tuesday clothes. Granny Hambay-El did the same. I let her walk toward the door first. Little Man was dressed and he was standing outside her door too. It was his turn to have his head beaten. I felt sorry for him a little. He didn't have as much hair to cushion him as I did.

His hair combing ritual was shorter, but I thought it was far worse than mine. Granny Hambay-El didn't say anything to him, but watching her do this every day I was sure that she must've been still angry at him whether his sheets were wet or not. Like everyone else, she seemed to be angry at him for just *being*. I watched her as she took the wooden brush in one hand and his head in her other. He didn't sit on the floor like I did. Instead, they both stood.

I could see in his face that he was trying hard not to squirm as she cupped his chin in her hand, squeezing just a little too tight. She raised her hand to brush his close-cropped hair and Little Man closed his eyes. Granny Hambay-El began to brush his hair and I watched. Just like normal, she brushed it forward, the brush making a dull, popping sound every time she made contact with his head. He had learned not to flinch. Little Man and I both held our breath. She took exactly nine strokes, three on each side of his head and three in the middle.

Finally she released his head. Little Man had made it all the way through without crying this time. He cried a ton more than I did; those tears that got stuck in my throat were still there today, not allowing tears or any emotion to pass by them and show up on my face. They kept me from feeling most things. It is time for breakfast.

Sixteen

*L*ittle Man rode the school bus home with me, but now, we didn't sit together. Everyone sat on the bus according to grade and age, so I sat in the back. I could see him sitting up front, with the little kids. Neither one of us talked to anyone on the bus. Mostly we just held our breath, and hoped to get though the ride.

The other kids laughed and talked around us; they were all glad that school was over. I had been holding my breath for what seemed like forever. I didn't want to talk to anyone else. Every time I tried to talk with someone, they usually ended up making fun of us for one reason or another.

We were almost to our stop, we were always just about the last kids that got let off the bus. We lived farthest from school. Looking out the window, I was starting to see the familiar scenery that signaled the end of our school day, the familiar houses of our neighborhood. All row houses, like ours. The green one with white shutters. The pink ones with the plastic flamingos in the yard that Daddy said were tacky.

Suddenly, the kids in the front started to talk all at once. My heart sank to the bottom of my stomach; I could sense that whatever was going on had something to do with Little Man. Paying attention now, I could see that one of the bigger kids, Darryl, had moved to the front of the bus. No one except the bus monitor was supposed to be up and walking around when the bus was moving. I could tell without even hearing what he was saying that he was teasing Little Man. This was a weekly ritual.

I sighed and stood up while the bus was moving, although I knew that I was not supposed to. Just as I reached the front, the bus stopped. This was where we got off. Little Man stood as I neared his seat and started out the door. Darryl stood up to follow him, pushing his way in front of me, right behind Little Man. The hairs on the back of my neck rose. This could only mean trouble; this was not where Darryl lived.

Darryl started down the steps ahead of me, but then moved aside to let me pass, stopping on the bottom step, but just barely. I had to turn sideways to make it through. I came so close to brushing up against him, I could feel his breath in my face. A challenge. He moved over a little to let me step outside the bus behind Little Man.

I glanced up and noticed that the bus driver was looking on, but not saying anything. I knew he should be telling Darryl to sit down. Instead he smiled at me like he was teasing me too. I almost believed that he wanted us to fight. His smile mocked me just as Darryl was taunting Little Man.

Darryl twisted his mouth up, opening it to speak. He was about to form ugly words. Gramma always said that God don't like ugly and I knew that he will get his for whatever he was about to say, eventually. But Little Man would be upset now, right then, and I felt my anger rising. I didn't want to wait for eventually, and I didn't want anyone messing with my little brother for no good reason. He was my responsibility now.

Without thinking, I reached up and grabbed Darryl by the shirt collar, snatching him off the bus in one motion. He was bigger than I was, but the bus driver's mocking smile had empowered me, giving me strength. I knew I should have stopped myself, but before I realized it, it was too late. I hit Darryl, in the face, in the back, anywhere I could. I didn't give him time to fight back.

Little Man paused a minute, and then dropped his book bag. At the same time I dropped Darryl, right into the gutter, and he almost slid under the bus.

I punched.

Little Man kicked.

Darryl screamed.

Little Man and I didn't even need to speak to each other.

We could almost hear each other's thoughts like the telepathic characters on *Star Trek*. They were both loud and clear; we wanted to put a hurting on Darryl. The few kids that were left on the bus were yelling, egging us on, but not cheering for us.

We were their entertainment.

"Fight, fight!" they screamed through their windows. Their unruly chorus quickly became a chant. What was fun to them was serious business to Little Man and me.

Darryl was taking the beating for every person that had teased us this week, this month, and the past two years.

Daddy's words echoed in my head as if he were speaking them right next to me. I went home crying last time, after people at school picked on us.

"Make 'em think you are crazy," he told me. "Then they will leave you alone. You just grab hold of one of 'em, and slam their heads up against the nearest thing you can."

I didn't know if he believed I would ever do it when he told me to, but I heard his words like he was standing right next to me, speaking at me in his most stern voice. I visualized what he told me to do, and that vision guided me now.

Finally, I was pulled away from Darryl. The bus driver had seen enough and actually gotten up from his seat, and he had me by my collar. He was a big man in both directions, both tall and round, and he seemed to cover almost the entire door of the bus. I don't think I had ever seen him stand up before. He didn't even have to get all the way out of the bus to reach us.

"That's enough, now," he said. His voice sounded serious but there was still a twinkle in his eye.

He pulled me back from Darryl, scratches now covered his face and uncovered arms. My arms were still swinging, like a windmill, going round and round but hitting nothing. "You quiet kids are always the worst."

He laughed as he talked.

Darryl was whimpering like a little kid. He didn't seem so big and bad now, not like he did a moment before when he was teasing Little Man.

I looked down at my hand, still holding on to the shirt pocket that was no longer attached to his shirt. Little Man had stopped hitting Darryl too. Darryl stood up, and there was a scratch on his face. It was red and long and stretched diagonally from underneath the outer corner of his right eye to just below his jaw. It was beginning to seep blood.

I didn't remember scratching him, and I was surprised at how bad it looked. He reached up, touching his face, and I, at the same time, looked at my hands, checking underneath my fingernails for skin that I knew must be there because it sure wasn't on Darryl's face anymore. The kids on the bus seemed to all gasp at once, then became silent. For them the excitement was over.

Darryl climbed back onto the bus, and the bus driver followed him, closing the door. Little Man and I turned away and walked. We went back to being our normal, silent selves, as if nothing had happened. Neither one of us would tell, even when Darryl's mother called our house, as we knew she would. For a few minutes, we both felt as if we had been temporarily vindicated by the scar that we had etched into Darryl's face, as if it was, in some way, a representation of pain we felt daily. He would only have to live with his for a couple of weeks. Our scars were a permanent part of our life.

SEVENTEEN

Six blocks later, I rang the bell at the sitter's house. She opened the door and stepped aside to let us in, without talking. We knew the routine. We both walked, with me in front, on the clear runner, still afraid to step off onto the rug because we knew it would make her upset. I carefully put my school bag at the space that had been designated for it, at the bottom of the steps, and continued on toward the back of the house, where the folding chairs were stored for us.

These were the very same chairs that we sat on when we first starting coming to the babysitter's.

Granny Hambay-el headed toward the kitchen, where the pressure cooker was hissing, as always. She used it every day. Before we started coming here, I didn't even know what a pressure cooker was. I pulled out my TV tray, setting it up in front of me so I could do my homework. My stomach growled, telling me I was hungry, but I never looked forward to dinner.

Little Man and I sat in the living room, with no TV, and did our homework. Fifteen minutes passed, and Little Man tried to get my attention.

"What do you think it is today?" he whispered. This was the first time he had talked to me since we got off the bus.

"Not sure," I answered. "I just hope it ain't liver."

I hated liver, especially the way the baby-sitter made it. Momma used to make liver and onions and the liver was soft; it actually tasted good. I would stand in the kitchen and watch her beat the liver with the mallet to make it tender. She would strip off the outer thing, the thing that holds the liver together, to make it easy for us to chew.

The sitter's liver is nothing like Momma's. The first time she gave it to us, I almost couldn't recognize it. It was tough and leathery and hard to chew, and she didn't cook it with any onions at all. The worst part was that she sat in the kitchen with us and watched us eat. It took us an hour and a half to finish. An hour and a half!

Most of her food was yucky like that. The fish still looked like fish, scales and all. Bones, too. She served grits at dinner sometimes, cold and lumpy, nothing recognizable. Nothing like Gramma's. Her mashed potatoes were lumpy, too. The only good thing was her chicken. And her cakes.

The sitter only celebrated church holidays, like Easter and Christmas, not holidays like Halloween and other good holidays.

"American foolishness," she said.

On her holidays, she baked like nothing I had ever seen or tasted before. Gramma baked, but the sitter's baking was totally different. She made all types of things from where she was from, and most of them were good. Easter she made bun-things with crosses on them, and Christmas she brought out black cake that she made at Thanksgiving and soaked in rum for a month. Then we didn't mind eating, 'cause then we got dessert.

She called us from the other room.

"Sweetie! Little Man," she said. "Come 'ere to the table."

We looked at each other as we got up and headed toward the kitchen. Little Man pursed his lips real hard, pressing them together until they almost disappeared. He was hoping that she made chicken just the same as I was. We both knew that was the best we could hope for since we were nowhere near a church holiday.

Our plates were already on the table waiting for us when we got there. A strong odor grabbed my nose. Oxtail stew. Little Man looked at me, and I at him, neither one of us quite sure what to make of it. Couldn't we just have some plain old-fashioned chicken soup? Or gumbo? Something that we recognized as food and not as the animal it came from? My stomach churned.

Granny Hambay-el cleared her throat. We knew what she meant. We both clasped our hands, lowering our heads slightly. It was my turn to say the grace.

"God is good, God is great. Let us thank him for the food."

She stood in the kitchen doorway, feet spread wide, hands on her hips.

"Any minute," Little Man joined in, saying it with me. I had to sound convincing. If it did, then she would leave and let us eat our food alone. She would go into the other room and watch television.

"Very good." Her face was twisted into its normal scowl. She looked from me to Little Man but chose not to fight the "Any minute."

My bowl was filled to the top with lumpy brown stew. I sensed her hesitation in the doorway, and I looked up and smiled at her, my "I am darling" smile. My spoon was resting on the bowl and I placed my hand on it, looking up and smiling bigger at her in the same instant.

I wanted her to be really comfortable. I tried to get that "mmm, mmm, good" look on my face like on the TV commercials.

I put one spoonful of the stew into my mouth.

She narrowed her eyes at me. Her long black eyelashes fluttered just a little.

My smile did its job. The sitter turned around and began her foot-to-foot roll, landing heavily on each foot as she made her way to the living room. Little Man and I held our breath until we heard her familiar plop and whine of the air escaping from the plastic covers as she sat on the sofa.

I picked my paper napkin up and held it up to my mouth, spitting the stew into it. It was now four o'clock. We looked at each other and back at our plates. We both knew that we had to be careful and quiet. We couldn't finish our food too early. If we did, she would know something was up.

We sat at the table, watching the clock, occasionally clicking our spoons on the sides of our plates, but we didn't eat. We raised and lowered our glasses and made sure they made a thud when they hit the table. It had to appear that we were occasionally taking a drink. At 4:20, I pointed to him, and then to the refrigerator, giving him the signal to get ready.

I was always the captain, the one giving the orders, in these delicate operations. Little Man stood up very quietly. He tried his best not to move his chair as he left the table and moved over to the refrigerator. He didn't want it to make noise as it scraped the linoleum floor.

I mouthed a three count, no sound escaping from my lips. "One, two, three."

Little Man stood in front of the green side-by-side refrigerator, with his hand on the door. I coughed loudly, acting as if I was choking. At the same time, Little Man pulled the door open, and pressed the button that made the light come on, turning it back off before it could be noticed. We both paused, holding our breath again.

"You okay in dere?" the baby sitter yelled.

From where I was sitting, I could see Little Man's chest rising and falling. He was breathing hard.

"Yes, ma'am. Something just went down the wrong way," I answered loudly, making sure she could hear me.

We waited.

We didn't hear the plastic rustle. Little Man acted quickly, grabbing some slices of plain, old American cheese. He looked at me, and I could see beads of sweat forming on his forehead in spite of the temperature inside the refrigerator.

I coughed again.

He closed the door and slid back in his seat. Mission complete, like on TV.

Little Man passed me a slice of cheese. We both kept our hands underneath the plastic tablecloth to muffle the sounds of the over wrap as we remove it from the cheese.

We stuffed them into our mouths simultaneously. The clock ticked loudly. 4:25 PM.

I stood up first, taking my almost still full bowl over to the trashcan. I checked inside, and was relieved to find that there was other trash in the bag already. It was easier to work with a bag that already had something in it. We had learned that there was a science to this.

The sitter was always telling us that birds of a feather flock together. This was even true for garbage too. It had a tendency to mesh together, which was always better for concealing things.

I dumped the contents of my bowl down into the bag, taking care to scrape the bowl. Little Man followed me, doing the same. He scraped his down into the side. I took both of our napkins and placed them on top, strategically, to try and conceal the food we hadn't eaten. I put our bowls in the sink and we both smiled.

Just then a sound behind me made my heart jump into my mouth. I turned around and Everett was standing behind us. My heartbeat thundered in my ears. He had just come in from outside, and he stood, watching us and leaning against the door jamb. He folded his arms in front of him, chewing on the toothpick that was dangling from his lips.

I was frozen in front of the trash and he looked in my eyes, his eyebrows raised. He was mocking us, weighing what he was going to do. His eyes moved from us to the garbage and back to us, and then he grinned.

A chill ran through me. Little Man sniffled, and I put my hand on his shoulder.

Neither one of us said a word as Everett walked slowly through the kitchen. I did not dare look away from his gaze. I knew that we were caught, but I didn't want him to think we had done anything other than what we were supposed to.

Our stomachs grumbled together, but I didn't give hunger or Everett and a second thought. Better grumbly than sick.

Eighteen

Our house still had a knocker instead of a doorbell, and Daddy answered the door as soon as we knocked. He opened the door, sweeping us inside. He was glad to see us too. Daddy hugged me first and then Little Man. He wrapped his arms around each of us, lifting me off my feet a little.

"Hey, Sweetie," he said. "Have you guys been good Indians?"

He asked us the same thing every time. My feet dangled as he rubbed his jaw against my face. I could feel the little beard that had grown on him since he shaved this morning.

I squirmed and laughed. "Yep. You're itchy, Daddy." As usual, I complained, but his hugs and scruffy face felt good to me.

I stole a glance past him, checking to see if everything was the same here. Past the front room, it all looked the same as far as I could tell. Everything was still dusty and there were piles of magazines and newspapers all over. I knew that some of them were over two years old. The air smelled stale, still scented with a hint of smoke. Daddy never seemed to throw anything away.

Not much had changed in our house since Momma died; I knew that if I went up those stairs, things would be much the same in the bedrooms too. Sometimes I thought that a part of me was still sitting on the bottom of those stairs, just like the day when I saw Daddy cry. When we were home, we never went up there unless Daddy asked us to or we had to go to the bathroom. There was no need to.

I knew that in the room that used to be Momma's and Daddy's, Momma's clothes were hanging in the closet, and even the dresser was the way Momma left it. All of the pretty bottles filled with perfume were still there, covered with dust, just the way she left them. I used to play with those bottles and act like I was all grown up. No one touched them now, like not touching them would make things the way they used to be.

Little Man sat down to turn on the television, his body more relaxed than I had seen him in a while. We were both glad to be back in our house, no matter what. We knew we were now free to do whatever we wanted. We could even walk wherever we wanted without feeling like we would be sucked down into the Land of the Lost if we stepped off of a yellow-brick-road-plastic runner. No one yelled at us here and Daddy let us watch whatever we wanted on television.

"Did you two have a good day?" Daddy asked.

Little Man and I looked at each other. Little Man spoke before I had a chance to.

"She made us eat liver." He twisted up his face. "It was yucky and hard and I couldn't swallow it."

"Really. Liver is good for you. It will make you strong." Daddy had a half smile on his face. He didn't understand what Little Man meant.

"Daddy, it really was bad. I never had anything like it. I think her food makes Little Man sick. Why can't we come home with a key like some of the other kids do? We will be good, I promise."

Daddy's face became serious. "I know this is hard for you, but it is hard for me too. I would like nothing other than you be home, in your own house every day. But you are too young for that and I am doing the best that I can. I have to work to provide for you or we won't have a house for you to come home to." He paused and rubbed his hand across the top of Little Man's head. He lowered his voice. "And I don't think it is a good idea for you to say things like that, Sweetie. People may take it the wrong way. Mrs. Hambay-El is a good woman who means well. You might not understand all the time, but if anyone hears you say things like that, they might want to use that as ammunition, you know what I mean? They might want to take you guys away from me and send you to live with relatives or worse. You two are all I have. We have each other, okay?"

I felt a little afraid as I stared at Daddy. His words were saying that he didn't want us to go away, but he looked confused, like he wasn't too sure himself. I didn't want anyone to take us anywhere.

"Don't you guys want to go outside?" Daddy asked.

"No, Daddy," we answered together. Although Granny Hambay-El didn't let us go outside to play much, we didn't want to do that here. Kids would tease us. Either they would find my hair or clothes funny or they would find a way to make fun of how we lived calling us babies or something.

He looked upset, as if he didn't understand why we would want to just stay inside. "I really think you should. It will be dark soon and fresh air will be good for you."

"But-"

"No buts! You go. For a little while. Kids should have friends where they live." Daddy was firm. He rubbed Little Man on the head. We marched toward the door, walking as slow as possible and dragging our feet on the rug. It was unvacuumed and unlike the baby-sitter's house, there were bits and pieces of life all over it, like real people lived in it.

Outside, we stood on the red brick stoop and looked around the yard. It used to be filled with grass and flowers. Momma had a green thumb and grew everything, even stuff she didn't want to. There used to be grass, flowers and roses. I remembered that the grass was so thick that when Daddy threw the record player outside, it sank a little. The records that he threw out with it that day were partially hidden by the grass and I had to dig for them to get them back.

The only thing left in the yard now were roses. They grew like crazy, especially the red ones. It was almost as if they still had some of Momma's energy left in them. Amazing, considering I didn't believe they even got watered anymore.

We were well into fall and it was a little cold at night and Daddy worked a lot. He didn't work in the yard like Momma used to and there were still several blooms left on the roses. No one, not even June-Bug, watered any of the plants anymore. It was strange watching the roses mixed with the big maple leaves that were turning into their fall colors, like people wearing bathing suits in the snow.

I liked to watch people and I would often sit in the window and watch them from inside. Little Man and I watched the other kids now from the steps. They were running up and down the sidewalk, engaged in a game that I recognized from the way they ran as hide and seek. Even though I couldn't remember the last time I played it, I knew how it went. They were looking for Millie's daughter, Jamila.

Jamila was almost two years younger than I was and she always cheated at games, and I was sure she had done it again. Amy was "it" and she came running close to our gate. She was the shortest kid on our block; although she was in the third grade her head was barely taller than the fence.

"Hey, Amy."

Amy would not tease us, she was often the target of neighborhood jokes herself. I would have preferred to be inside the house reading a book, but I attempted a smile.

"Hey! Seen Jamila? She hides so well I can almost never find her and it is getting dark!" Amy was huffing and puffing, out of breath from running. Her chest moved up and down so hard I could see it from where I was sitting.

"Nope."

She continued on her search. I knew Jamila had probably gone inside. She did it every time and I knew that Amy would continue to look for her until her mother made her come inside for the evening. She was also not the smartest kid on our block. I think Jamila enjoyed being mean to Amy, and I knew tomorrow they would make fun of Amy again. They teased her too, and sometimes I felt sorry for her because she didn't even realize that the other kids were doing it.

The public bus stop was down the street, two blocks toward the school where I went to kindergarten. I saw a bus go by, having already dropped off its passengers. Six people got off the bus and headed this way. I recognized June-Bug's tall, leggy walk among them before I could even see his face. I couldn't help smiling. His hair wasn't so big anymore, but it was still cool. I couldn't tell if it had gotten smaller or if I had gotten bigger. The other kids saw him too. They stopped their game and ran to meet him at the corner. Little Man and I both stood up, watching. He was nice to all of them, but I could tell by the way he looked over their heads that he was looking for us.

We waited patiently and he finally made it to our house.

"What's up, folks?" June-Bug grinned a big grin, showing his missing teeth. Daddy said that cigarettes made them fall out but I think they were really knocked out in his secret life.

We weren't supposed to answer.

He rubbed his knuckles into the tops of our heads.

"Gotta get that head under control, Sweetie." He referred to my hairdo, which I knew was more bushy than he liked.

My smile faded away. I felt the impression of his knuckles on top of my head; he reminded me how much I hated my hair and my mismatched ribbons.

June-Bug had girlfriends all the time, pretty girlfriends. All of their hair was as cool as his. I knew that Granny Hambay-El would never make mine look that way.

Almost as if he could tell my feelings were hurt, June-Bug rubbed my head again, softer this time.

"It's okay, we'll fix it," he said.

I sniffled a little. I knew he would. He often did my hair at night when we were home and let me practice so that one day soon I would be able to do it myself.

June-Bug walked up our small walk toward the house and Little Man and I followed close behind. He opened the door and stepped into the dark house, which reminded me of a cave. We were right behind him. The house smelled stale to me now. I heard him sigh as he looked around at the piles of stuff that had been the same for months.

"I'm home!" he yelled into the house.

Daddy didn't answer. We continued to follow behind June-Bug like puppies, in our order, waiting. It was always June-Bug first, then me, then Little Man.

I wanted June-Bug to play with us. He sometimes grabbed me by my feet and held me upside down until I begged him to stop, or he tickled Little Man until he cried. Those times were some of the best parts about when we were all home together.

He did not feel. Instead the way he walked told me that he was generally disgusted, which was not good. June-Bug went into the kitchen and I stood in the door, not entering. I tried not to go into the kitchen if I could avoid it. The sink was almost always full of dishes nowadays. They only got washed when necessary or when a female relative visited.

As I stood in the door, the hole that was still in the kitchen wall jumped out at me. Daddy put a table in front of it, like he was trying to hide it, but I saw it immediately. Even if I didn't see it, the burned smell was there just the same. It assaulted my nose. I was the only one that still smelled it. I knew that because I asked Daddy to fix the smell one day and he looked at me like I was crazy.

"I don't know what you mean, Sweetie," he said. I never mentioned it again, even though I still could smell old fire everywhere. See it even, remembering the fire and the plastic curtains as if it were yesterday.

June-Bug opened the refrigerator and stood in front of it. Even without being able to see inside, I knew that it was pretty empty. Daddy didn't go grocery shopping often. He cooked only occasionally, and then it was always the same things, either fire engine chili or chicken and dumplings. Most of the time he ate at work or visited people to eat.

My brother paused a minute and then grunted, closing the refrigerator door with a bang. I stepped out of the way as he turned to head out of the kitchen, resuming my place in followdom behind him. We went upstairs, Little Man using both his feet and his hands to scramble up the steps behind us.

Daddy was upstairs in his room, with the door partially open. Music was coming from the room. Momma used to play music all over the house; now the only place we heard it, was coming from Daddy's room. Daddy had a massive record collection in there, hiding in the closet, along with the rest of Momma's things. He sometimes played music for me, always the old songs, on those rare occasion when we were home when he asked us to come upstairs with him. He said all his old records would be valuable someday, some already were.

We were not allowed to touch any of them, under any circumstances. I didn't think he had bought anything new in a long time; he said the old songs were the best anyway. Diana Ross and the Supremes were singing, "*Someday we'll be together.*"

June-Bug pushed the door the rest of the way open and we could all see Daddy lying on the bed, in just his pants and his T-shirt. He was on his back with his thick tan-colored arms under his head, using his hands for a pillow. He was wearing a brown leather gun holster, the kind that could hide a gun under a suit jacket. The way he lay there, it looked like it was strangling him. He appeared to be just looking at the ceiling, but I knew that this was his thought position. June-Bug cleared his throat.

"Hey." June-Bug never said the word hello. He always found creative ways to greet people. "When you goin' git you some new music, *old man?*"

June-Bug never called Daddy "daddy" either. He called him old man or pops or by his first name. Daddy hated when he did that. I tried to call him Junius too one time. Daddy's look was so mean it scared the desire to call him anything else but Daddy right from between my lips.

Daddy turned his head toward us. His face was stern and for a minute I saw anger dance across his brow.

"And when you going to mind your own business and get a job? I'm tired of supporting your lazy behind. And you know that new music ain't for nothing no way."

His voice was low in the Daddy kind of way, but I could spot the annoyance. We must have disturbed his thinking. I was not surprised, June-Bug and Daddy always talked to each other like this.

"You know I try. Every day." June-Bug sucked his teeth. His nose flared. He crossed his hands over his chest, like a shield, but he stood his ground as if preparing for a battle. I crossed my arms too.

"I don't seem to have any problems staying employed."

"Well, I ain't you, am I?" June-Bug raised his eyebrows, waiting. Little Man and I stepped back.

"No, you got that right. You are obviously not. I can't believe you even came out of your momma, you know that, son? God rest her soul." His words flew at June-Bug like bullets.

Time stopped. Little Man and I looked at each other. I couldn't believe Daddy could be so mean to June-Bug and so nice to us.

"When you gonna clean this place up? Life goes on, you know."

I was relieved because June-Bug had changed the subject, but I could see from the look on Daddy's face that a fight was coming. Daddy stood up from the bed. He came around and stood just inside the door. The Supremes were still singing behind him.

"When are you going to mind your own business, boy? What I do in here is my own business, and you need to keep your nose out of it." I could feel the anger coming from him.

It was pushing me back so hard I wanted to run and hide somewhere, but Daddy's voice was still low.

June-Bug turned away, heading toward his own room. Little Man and I stood in the middle of the upstairs landing and felt it transform into a boxing ring. We stood stock still, caught in the middle, ready to duck a stray punch at any time.

"Thank God I'm not you," June-Bug mumbled, but I heard him clear as day. Involuntarily, I stepped back. Daddy stepped outside his door.

"What did you say? I know you didn't!" His nostrils were opening up, like all of his anger was trying to flow out through them. "I feed you, clothe you, put up with you coming in all hours of the night with all breed of women and this is the thanks I get! You ain't even mine! Don't you dare talk to me like that!" Daddy yelled like I never heard him yell before. He clenched his fists and held them down by his side. I was frozen in place.

June-Bug turned around, looking down at us like he suddenly remembered that we were there.

"Junius," he said. "That's enough, the kids."

Daddy continued, "You are so ungrateful! You can't even hold a job! You think you deserve to be a freeloader because you went to Vietnam? You didn't even see any action, you coward! I'm a veteran too, of two wars, real ones and you don't see me doing any of that."

"Okay, that's enough," he said again. June-Bug's voice was as low as Daddy's. He was staring at us.

"I could never have fathered a child like you! You are a bad influence on my son!"

"No, you couldn'ta had no part in making me, now could you? You obviously don't want me here, maybe I should leave."

My mouth dropped open. What were they talking about! June-Bug couldn't leave. Who would look out for me? For Little Man?

Daddy continued, the anger in him seeping through his pores and out into the air. "Maybe you should take your tired behind back down South with all them other tired southern folks! Back to the laughing barrels and the KKK!"

The air on the landing was still as everyone paused for a second. I think my heart had even stopped beating. What did Daddy mean? June-Bug couldn't leave. He combed my hair. Taught me things. And how could Daddy not be everybody's daddy? He always was before.

Suddenly, Little Man started to wheeze. His hands flew up to his throat and his arms flailed around like he was trying to yank out whatever was clogging up his throat. He started to cry as his breath got raspy and shallow. He fell to the floor and in that split second he took on a blue tinge.

June-Bug was the one who sprang to action. "You see, Junius? You've upset them! They didn't need to know all that. You the one always talking about grown folks' business. Get his inhaler." June-Bug knelt down where Little Man was now laying. "It's okay, Little Man." He rubbed the top of his head, trying to comfort him.

The landing had enlarged for me again, and I felt removed from them all. The lump in my throat that had been there for two years was still there. I had almost forgotten it. I was so used to it now I knew it had no hope of moving. It reminded me it was there every now and then, and now was one of those times.

Daddy reached into his room, producing the inhaler for Little Man. He handed it to June-Bug. Asthma attacks were almost run of the mill for us since Momma died.

"What do you mean? They're kids. They have no idea what is going on, what I go through!" Daddy's chest heaved up and down.

June-Bug held the inhaler up to Little Man's mouth and pushed it.

"What about what they go through? They understand much more than you think. They are kids, but they are not stupid. Especially Sweetie." June-Bug pushed the inhaler again and Little Man's breath seemed to come easier. Daddy looked at me. I knew my eyes were big. I blinked.

"Sweetie," he said. He was back to talking in his usual calm voice. "Go turn on the TV and put a blanket on the sofa for Little Man. He is going to have to rest for a while."

June-Bug looked at me too. Little Man was breathing okay now but he was still crying. He would be okay. It used to be much worse. This was the first time in a long time that he had had an attack that didn't send us to the hospital.

I headed down the steps, leaving them on the landing, glad to leave them behind. I wanted to put the physical distance between us that my brain already had. I knew that June-Bug was going to leave us too. I could feel it.

Nineteen

This was the longest school day ever. I thought the teacher was talking about American History or something. I wasn't sure, I wasn't really paying attention. I hadn't for a while. School was not fun for me anymore, I just went to get out of Granny Hambay-el's house. I didn't think there was any part of it I really enjoyed, not even lunch. None of the other kids talked to me, and I didn't care. I wasn't sure if I wanted them to, anyway. School was just somewhere else to be.

The second hand on the clock had mesmerized me. I stared at it for almost two hours. It was a good thing that the teacher almost always stood right in front of it. She probably thought I was paying attention to what she was saying, but I was daydreaming again, and I couldn't even have told her what she was talking about if she asked.

"James Pearsey." The girl next to me squeaked a response to the teacher's question.

I let out a big sigh. I wasn't paying attention, but I knew that the answer was Crispus Attacks. Died in 1770. They treated me like I was the oddball, but I bet that not one of them knew the answer to that question.

The teacher corrected her. I was right. Again.

The bell rang and she closed her books. The students began to shuffle and hopped to their feet. The noise level in the classroom went up and I snapped fully back to the here and now.

"Monica,» the teacher called my name.

I looked up, but didn't speak.

"See Ms. Faust before you go to recess, okay?"

"But—"

"It'll wait."

I searched her face for a clue to why I had to see Ms. Faust. I'd seen her around since third grade, but she never seemed to know what to say to me.

I nodded, then gathered my books. I didn't have to look far to find her. By the time I got my things together, she was waiting right outside the classroom door.

Ms. Faust was prettier than she was before, her face fuller. She smiled at me, but didn't speak right away. I could tell she was waiting for the other students to get far enough away so they couldn't hear what we said. Her shoes clicked on the tile floor as we walked together down the hallway.

Finally, she broke our awkward silence. "How have you been, Monica?"

I cleared my throat. "Fine."

"Really? I have been keeping up with your progress."

I didn't say anything.

We paused in front of the principal's office. I chewed on my lip just a little and looked at the floor.

"Did you do your hair yourself?" she asked.

My face burned. Once again, my parts were not straight

and my ribbons didn't match each other or my clothes. I felt her eyes examining it, taking it all in. I shook my head.

"I see," she said. "Your hairstyle is interesting."

I didn't answer again. I could tell that she was now uncomfortable. She pulled papers from behind her back.

"Do you know why I wanted to see you?"

I shook my head no.

"Well, do you recognize this paper? This is an essay your teacher asked you to complete last week."

I glanced at the papers in her hands. I did recognize it as mine. The page was bleeding with red correction marks.

"Is something wrong with it?"

"Not really. In fact, it is very good." She paused. "But it isn't what the teacher asked you to write about at all. And it is quite obvious to me that you did not put any time nor effort into it. It is filled with errors, things that I know you know. Things you knew back in second grade. I was very surprised when I read it." She lowered her voice. "I know you think that when you left my class you were rid of me and that I wouldn't continue to care. But I do and I am not about to let you just fall through the cracks because of other things that may be making it harder for you to concentrate."

I looked down at the floor again.

"And your teacher tells me that all of your work is like this and that you barely seem to pay attention in class. Is there a problem you want to tell me about?"

I shook my head no. I used to really like being in Miss Faust's class. She made me feel that doing my best would get me somewhere. I used to like coming to school too.

She paused. I felt her eyes probing me. I looked back at her, my face hard and expressionless. There was nothing wrong with me that she or anything else could fix.

Her voice became more serious. "I run the resource classroom now, Monica, and I want you to come to me three times a week in the afternoons. You will have to miss recess for a bit, but I think I can help you. We all want to make sure that you live up to your potential."

"But there is nothing wrong with me."

"Come with me now so I can introduce you to the class." She guided me to another classroom a few doors away. "I didn't say there was anything wrong with you. Nor did anyone else. We just think you can do better than you have been. I know you can." She put her hand on my shoulder.

I drew back from her touch. I didn't want to be helped or fixed by Miss Faust or anyone else.

She pulled her lips into a fine line.

I didn't want to go to her classroom. All the dumb kids went there. The hopeless ones that they wanted to get out of the regular classrooms so that the other kids wouldn't bother them.

We stopped at the doorway and several kids were there waiting. They looked up.

I was not like them.

Jamila failed everything every year.

Greta was tapping her finger on a yellow pad. Little Man read better than she did and she was in the fourth grade.

I was not like them.

"You come here tomorrow instead of going to recess, just like I said. We'll try this for a while. Just until you get yourself back where we know you can be, okay?"

She didn't really care what I answered. It wouldn't matter. And I would be teased more than ever now, but I didn't think I had a choice.

TWENTY

*O*n Saturdays, no one had to wake me up. Today, like every other Saturday, I woke up early and lay on my bed, waiting for the sitter to tell us we could go home. Daddy usually called very early. We got to go home and do whatever we wanted. I could watch Saturday morning cartoons if I wanted to without sitting on folding chairs. Little Man played with his toys or had his GI Joe attack my Barbie town house. For a few hours we came close to normal.

Daddy was waiting for us when we got there. As I stepped into the house, I immediately noticed something different. Usually Daddy was waiting for us in his underwear pajamas and I would tease him because Granny Hambay-el insisted that I couldn't sleep in my underwear. Today he was fully dressed, shoes and all, with no scruff around his face. He was clean and his Old Spice smell tickled my nose when he hugged me. And everything he had on matched.

"Hey, kids. I have a surprise for you." Daddy smiled at us. I was cautious; I had learned to be wary of surprises.

"But I want to watch Scooby Doo." Little Man was whiny and still cranky from his morning wet-bed-sheet routine. He grabbed the belt this morning when Granny Hambay-el tried to hit him. I almost laughed because he looked like he was holding on for dear life. She was so mad she yelled and cursed at him more than usual as she whipped the strap around with him on the end. Her cries of "Dyam you, no! You dyam American children!" were so loud that she even woke her heathen grandson. I cheered privately for Little Man even as she sucked her teeth during breakfast, mumbling that he was an "upstart bwoy." She finally gave up on his beating and Little Man did not shed a tear. He was dry-eyed for a change, like he found a new determination.

"Scooby Doo can wait. We are going for a ride." Daddy ushered us back out the door and into the car.

I was silent, but I smiled. Car rides were fun with Daddy. I hoped we were going to the mall but I knew it was too early for that. Sometimes we all went and window-shopped, not buying anything but playing all of the mall games that Daddy knew.

Daddy knew lots of car games and songs too. We didn't count cars or anything like that, instead we sang together, mostly army chants and sailor songs. My favorite was the steam roller song. Daddy usually sang it extra loud, his deep, baritone voice resonating through the car. I always tried to mimic him, making my voice as deep as possible, but it just didn't come out the same. No one sang it as good as he did, not even June-Bug. I sang the song for Gramma on the phone, but she didn't seem to appreciate the words very much, especially when I sang the "baby's" or the part about being a dump truck and dumping my load all over you. I could hear her fussing at Daddy through the phone about what he was teaching me.

This time, we didn't sing or listen to any of Daddy's favorite eight-track tapes. Instead Daddy talked without any punctuation like Granny Hambay-el, his voice a little higher than normal. Everybody has a normal voice, a normal walk, and Daddy was definitely not talking in his. Instead, he was nervous and I wondered where we were going. I didn't ask, though. The last time I heard him sound this way was when Momma was sick.

"You two remember what we talked about before?"

Little Man and I looked at each other.

I shrugged.

"About us being a family?"

I only heard every few words he was saying. Instead I focused my attention on the neighborhood we were rolling through. Some of the yards had plants that were sprouting and I admired the yards that looked manicured already although it was only early spring.

Daddy cleared his throat very loudly. "Maybe I ought to try and find you a new mommy." He laughed nervously as he talked.

His words reached out and took hold of my attention. Our eyes met in the rearview mirror. I felt like I did when I was punched in the stomach.

Was he making a joke? I wondered. People were not replaceable.

We finally stopped in a neighborhood where the houses were all joined together, with no yards and a very small patch of grass, smaller than the houses where we lived. They also had big stoops with twice as many steps as our house. The cars were all parked on the street, nose to nose, like they were playing follow the leader, instead of in driveways. I didn't recognize this place. I had never been here before.

"Here we are." Daddy's voice broke into my thoughts as he maneuvered the car into a parking space. He turned the car off and we waited, hoping he would explain to us for a change.

Daddy turned around in his seat almost fully. The inside of the car was calm. Little Man and I were both expectant. Little Man broke the silence first.

"Where we going?" He always had to know the details, even if knowing them wouldn't make one bit of difference.

"Well…" Daddy searched for words. He wet his lips. "We are going to see a lady. You will remember her."

"What lady?" I asked. Daddy went to visit people a lot. Relatives usually. He ate at their houses but we usually ate at the sitter's.

"You guys might remember her. Remember Auntie Frances?" He paused, staring at me. A car whooshed by us and I felt our car shake. I wanted to turn around and check if I could see the wind like on the Roadrunner cartoon but I didn't.

Little Man said nothing.

I did remember Auntie Frances, but instead of talking, I blinked again. We hadn't seen her since Momma died.

Daddy continued. "Well, you remember, don't you, Sweetie? She was Momma's friend. I want you guys to be nice. Polite. Say please and thank you, okay?" His voice was shrill, a little high-pitched and faster than normal.

I wondered why he was uncomfortable. I wondered what he wasn't telling me.

We nodded. We always did. Daddy removed his seat belt and started to get out of the car. We did the same, waiting for him to come around and let us out too.

We got out of the car and I looked up at the house with the big stoop.

Auntie Frances. Skin the color of caramel, round hips. Her lips were thick and her face covered with so many freckles I wanted to connect the dots.

Momma's friend.

Most of Momma's friends hung around a little while after the funeral, but she didn't bother. She used to work with Momma and sometimes she would visit, bringing cookies and gifts to us all the time. She had a big, hearty laugh and when she came, everybody, including Daddy, would laugh with her.

Daddy stood behind us on the stoop and reached over Little Man and me and rang the doorbell. The door swung wide fast, like it had been snatched open. Auntie Frances had tears in her eyes.

"Look at how big Elva's babies have gotten." She spoke haltingly, each word its own sentence as she reached down and stroked my cheek. She smelled sweet, like she took a bath in her perfume, and the smell made my nose tickle. Then she did it. She grabbed my cheek between her massive thumb and forefinger and pinched. She moved her hand back and forth, and my head had no choice but to follow the vise grip her hand held me in. I felt a permanent bruise coming on.

Daddy saved me. "Are you going to let us in, woman?" His voice was familiar, like they had been friends a long while. Happy sounding. *Unfamiliar.*

"Oh, I am so sorry, hon-ey." She stepped out of the way.

I looked up at Daddy and noticed that he was smiling, grinning even. Warning hairs stood up on the back of my neck. This was no ordinary auntie. We followed her into the house.

The house smelled like food and a pine cleaner, the kind Gramma used, making my nose sting. My eyes darted around the room and landed on pillows, fancy pillows everywhere. Some with words. Perfectly placed. Lots of lace, too.

There was a little table in the hallway. It looked like something was missing. There was no dust anywhere in the house, like Granny Hambay-el's bedroom.

Auntie Frances never stopped talking. "Yawl ready to eat?" She talked without pausing, like she was nervous, not bothering to give us a chance to answer. "I hope so, I cooked collard greens and potato salad and chicken with dressing and Marie come on down here, girl!" She flitted about and through the house, straightening this thing and that and opening and closing pots. Watching her was making me tired.

We followed her into her house with little figurines all over it. Little Man looked about ready to reach out and grab one of those little dog statues. I would have told him not to but I didn't care what he did.

"These kids look hungry, hon-ey. Go wash your hands."

She flicked her wrists in our general direction and I

realized she meant us. I looked at Daddy and wondered if he was suddenly speechless because he had nothing else to say or because she was talking so fast that he just couldn't get a word in. He nodded at us. She kept talking and calling him honey.

"Over there. The water closet is over there." She flicked her wrist again in the general direction of the "water closet."

The house was narrow and I only had to take one step to be able to open a little door I thought was a coat closet. The water closet was a bathroom, with no tub. It just had a toilet with blue water and one little sink. The wallpaper was pale yellow with purple flowers and was almost as busy as that at Granny Hambay-el's house. It took a moment for my eyes to focus.

Everything was frilly in there too and it was so small that only one of us could fit at a time. I went first. Even the extra toilet paper roll was covered in frills. Outside the door, I could hear Auntie Frances still talking.

"Marie! Don't make me come up there and get you!"

This was the second time she had yelled for this Marie person. This time I heard a heavy clunking coming down the stairs. I was finished washing my hands, so I opened the door and stepped back out in the dining room. The clunking continued.

"I am coming, Mother, geez!" Marie bounced down the stairs and burst into the room, another shorter girl in tow. She stopped short when she saw me.

"Oh-"

Marie was tall and thin and her hair was frilly too; she had lots of curls with bows all over the place that matched her clothes just so. Her friend was dressed so much like her they blended together like the wallpaper in the water closet. I wanted to sink through the floor because I felt her eyes examining me.

"What do you mean, oh? And didn't I tell you about using the Lord's name in vain?"Auntie Frances had her hands on her hips.

"I mean, I didn't know we had company. And get with it, Mother." She rolled her eyes.

Her friend sniggered.

I looked down and my eyes landed on my shoes, scuffed on the toes. I would have never talked to my momma that way. I blinked back nonexistent tears. Marie looked to be a big girl, about twelve or thirteen. I felt her and her friend staring at me, their eyes roving over my clothes and I recognized the feeling. They were checking me out from head to toe.

"Sweetie, honey, this is my daughter Marie and her friend Vinca. Help me finish setting the table, Marie."

Marie moved to help her mother and Little Man came out of the bathroom. They didn't bother to introduce him; they probably thought he was too little. Vinca continued to look at me, standing next to me outside the bathroom door. She mouthed my name at Marie, as if they didn't believe that I let myself be called that.

Marie made a face.

They giggled.

Daddy was standing on the other side of the table with his hands on the back of a chair, still smiling. Marie started to chatter on and I immediately saw the resemblance.

"Mother, you didn't tell me that Mr. Junius had a daughter. All the times he has been here!" She plunked plates down on the table as if they were plastic, but I could tell from the sound they made that this was china like the kind Momma would have used for special occasions. Her mother cringed at each plunk.

"Be careful with those, Marie darling. I did tell you, you weren't listening. Maybe you could help her with her hair and things. Fix her up." She waved her free hand in my direction.

Vinca looked over at me closer and my face burned.

"Hmm. She needs a lot of work."

I knew I was red and nothing was going to hide it. How did they know I wanted to be *fixed up*?

Alice in Wonderland was happening again and I was again aware of my throat knot. I looked over at Daddy, hoping he would save me. He kept smiling his frozen smile.

I hated it when people talked over me like I was not in the room and they were doing it now. I held my breath and noticed the clock ticking in the room. It was barely past noon and we were about to eat what Gramma would say was dinner.

Time moved its slowest yet, slower than I thought possible. This was the longest table-setting process I had ever seen. And there was chatter the whole way through. We finally sat down at the table and I wondered just how many times Daddy had been here since Momma died.

I scanned the room and looked around some more. Once you got past all the lace and little dog statues, it was a nice, clean place. It even smelled good, like our house used to. Auntie Frances did talk a lot and her daughter chattered nonstop about nothing, but that could be gotten used to.

Daddy sat at the head of the table and said grace, just like he used to with Momma.

"Thank you, Lord, for this food we are about to receive…"

His words ran together for me. I wanted to say "any minute" when he was done, but I didn't think he would like it.

Little Man and I sat at one side, across from Marie and Vinca. Plates were passed around and they put some of everything on our plates, like we were little kids, without even asking us what we wanted. We sat, watching the two girls whisper and titter across from us like they had some major secret that they were not willing to let us in on. I didn't feel as left out as they wanted me to. They were just not as important as they wanted to be. Besides, I was used to feeling like I was on the outside of things.

The silverware clinked against the plates. Frances continued to chatter. I imagined her voice sounding like the grown-ups on Charlie Brown. She was no longer an aunt. Not the way Daddy kept grinning at her from the other end of the table. I concentrated on my food, moving it from one area of the plate to the other.

Eating at Granny Hambay-el's had made me a master in the art of food rearrangement, and I rearranged mine skillfully so that it appeared that I had eaten a decent amount of it.

Little Man cleaned his plate, eating his food so fast that it seemed like he hadn't eaten anything in a long time. I hoped he did not end up sick. Again.

Auntie Frances mentioned June-Bug. Her words drew me back to the table, breaking into my thoughts. I looked up from my plate, suddenly interested.

"You shouldn't have to put up with mess, Junius, not even from your *own* children. Have you talked to him? I would, you know, he would be right out of my house. Faster than you can say, dog, kiss my foot."

I snapped to attention, looking up at Daddy. He had not said anything at all yet, instead sat there grinning at Frances while she talked. I wanted to hear what he had to say now. What could she possibly have known about it all? I didn't believe she had even ever met June-Bug.

"We discussed it." Daddy chewed methodically, his mouth seemed to open and close in time with the ticking of the grandfather clock in the corner.

"That was a hard thing that Elva was asking you to do anyway." The chattered continued. "You know a lot of them boys came back messed up in the head. I *de*-clare it is a wonder he can even carry on a conversation, you know."

Daddy cleared his throat. "I don't want to talk about it. Not now."

"Well, I do. I mean, we should." She paused. "Don't you think?" Frances put her fork down and wiped her mouth with her linen napkin which she then carefully placed back in her lap, smoothing it.

I looked back at Daddy.

His face was tense, but she didn't notice. She kept right on talking.

It was Daddy's turn to speak, and Frances didn't give him much time to respond. If he was going to respond, he was going to have to hurry up to be able to say anything at all.

"Junius, I –"

"I said, enough!" Daddy interrupted her. He waved his fork in the air for emphasis, then dropped his fist, heavy, onto the table. Our plates jumped in the air in response.

The table was silent. Everyone stopped eating, our motions frozen.

"If *we* are going to be together," she said, "I think *he* should go." She looked down at her plate, not at Daddy and scooped up a forkful of food.

I felt slapped.

What did she mean, if they were going to be together? The table was so tense that the air was too thick to breathe, like midsummer with no wind.

How could they talk about being together when *we* weren't even really *together*?

"Do you think *we* should go too?"

Everyone at the table turned to look at me, including Little Man. Disbelief filled their eyes.

They looked at me like I had committed a sin by speaking up.

Vinca smirked, then moved her hand to cover her mouth.

I was not sorry for what I have said. Why wouldn't she want us gone too? It made sense to me.

"I didn't mean—" Her hands trembled as they flitted around her perfectly made-up face.

I didn't wait for her to finish. I pushed myself back and got up from the table all in one movement, not bothering to push my chair in the way Momma taught me to.

Marie covered her mouth now too; I knew she was laughing underneath her hand. Her surprise passed and she looked over at her friend, who was paused with eyes so wide she looked like she was in shock.

I started toward the door, and without even turning around, I waved at Little Man to follow. He too got up from his end of the table and ran behind me, taking my hand.

Daddy followed. "Sweetie," he said, "wait, where are you going?"

"I didn't mean to upset her, Junius. I am not used to children just saying what they want. I told you they need a mother. She is losing her home training—"

He didn't stop or turn around. Instead he talked at her over his shoulder. "I didn't ask you. Just be quiet. Wait, Sweetie."

I heard Frances' mouth close with a pop. It was too late, her plan had already spilled out of her mouth.

She wanted to get rid of us.

I stopped near the front door and crossed my arms. My face was hot with anger and I stood with my back to Daddy. Little Man stood next to me, silent.

"I want to go."

"But we are eating." Daddy's voice pleaded with me.

I began to enjoy my newly discovered power, my way to make grownups listen.

"I am done. I want to go." I sniffed extra loud, on purpose, suggesting to Daddy that I might cry.

Frances and her family were still sitting at the table in the other room. The house was silent. No one moved. They were waiting to see who would win this battle. I just wanted to leave and get away from this lady who used to be my mother's friend. I understood now that she wanted to try and take her place and send June-Bug away and perhaps both Little Man and me too.

Daddy moved behind me.

I refused to look. I knew he was looking back and forth from me to Frances, trying to decide what to do. Finally, he reached around me and put his hand on the doorknob. I looked up at him and stared into his eyes, trying to identify what I saw there.

"You would let her send us away, Daddy?"

He sent us away, to the sitter's house every night. Would he send us away for good to someplace worse? Would he make us leave with June-Bug?

He didn't answer. Instead he opened the door, turning to Frances, still sitting at the table. "I'll call you later tonight." He didn't wait for an answer.

We paused outside on the steps. Little Man was crying now, all the tears that I couldn't. Daddy had a stern look on his face.

"I didn't mean to ruin dinner for everyone," I said.

Daddy nodded. "You didn't."

No one spoke as we walked down the steps. Daddy let us into the car. We slid across the leather seat. I held Little

Man's hand and we waited for Daddy to get in. He moved behind the wheel of the car, pausing for a minute before he started it.

"I am not letting anyone send you anywhere or take you away," he said. He was looking at me in the rear view mirror.

I lifted my head, poking my chin out just a little. "I know."

He nodded, still looking at me.

"We had a mother." My nose flared and my lips were pressed together tight. I stared back at Daddy.

He cocked his head to the side just a little and his face got even more serious. "I know," he answered. "I am just trying to do the right thing. For all of us."

I nodded again, as if we had reached some new, higher understanding.

Daddy started the car, and we headed home. No one sang this time either.

TWENTY-ONE

June-Bug left last night. He didn't even say good-bye. When we got home, there was a note for me.

"Sweetie," it said. "Take care of Little Man. I will see you when you come South for the summer. –J"

That was all.

I gasped as I read it, holding it in both hands so tight I almost put holes in the paper. I stuffed it in my pocket when I was done, feeling my throat lump get just a tiny bit bigger. I knew he was leaving, I felt it before it happened, but I wished he could have said good-bye. I was used to that now, I guess, people leaving without good-bye or doing things without bothering to explain to me. I was a kid, after all, only nine years old.

I dreamed about being left all night long. I kept seeing myself standing in the dark, in the light of a streetlight on a corner. People I knew kept passing by, but they would always leave me there, my face half lit by the dim light like I was half hiding in it, not daring to look in my direction. No one else was around or came by to see why I was there by myself.

The funny thing was that I was not scared in the dream, instead, it was okay. I wasn't bothered and felt normal about being alone. That part scared me when I woke up, the idea of alone being normal.

I took extra time folding up the bedding from my cot today. The morning sounds were the same outside the bedroom door. Little Man (who wasn't so little anymore) being yelled at, AM music that used to annoy me, I didn't even hear. Granny Hambay-el seemed to have given up on the strap for now. It was about time, beatings obviously hadn't stopped Little Man from wetting the bed. I heard her consulting with her daughter, behind the dining room partition about what they could do to make him stop, what herbs they could give him. I didn't think anything would work unless they had an herbal remedy for sadness. If they did, I didn't care what it tasted like, I wanted some, too.

Breakfast moved in slow motion. The numbness that crept inside my stomach deadened the taste of the food. I didn't want to talk or go to school. I just wanted to sleep the day away. But that had no chance of happening here. We had to all stick to the plan, someone else's plan.

Granny Hambay-el spooned out her farina as usual. It was flavorless and too thin. She sprinkled it with a brown powder that I hoped was nutmeg and not something she ground herself last night, some miracle cure she thought up or someone told her about. Her mouth was formed into a scowl, but I couldn't tell if that was because she did it so often that her lips had hardened that way, or if they looked drawn because she wasn't wearing her teeth. Whatever the case, I wondered if she smiled at her real grandchildren or laughed out loud, even while we were gone at school or at home with Daddy for our few hours a day. I guess that was like the question we were discussing in school, something I would never know, the question that asked that if a tree falls in the forest when there is no one around, does it make a crashing sound?

Little Man and I walked to the bus stop in silence. We just walked, both hoping for the end of school soon. I didn't even notice when we got to our corner. The other kids were already waiting there.

I stopped walking because Little Man did and I looked up, realizing where I was, dropping my backpack onto the sidewalk with a thud. No one said hello, they just all stood and stared at us, whispering to each other. I drifted back into my thoughts while we waited for the school bus to appear, wondering what June-Bug was doing down South.

"I got Vaseline in my book bag if you want to grease up, Sweetie. And you betta take off them earrings too." Manuela Jackson squeaked and I realized that she was talking to me. She was the shortest girl on the school bus. She barely talked to us but she didn't tease us either. When she first came the kids used to tease her because she is half black and half Puerto Rican.

I put my hand on the part of my body where my hip should have been. "I didn't need no Vaseline. Why do you care?"

I sucked my teeth and my head rolled with my words. Momma never put anything like Vaseline or oil on me and Little Man's faces like some of the other kids' mothers did. I remembered her saying it would clog up our pores. Manuela even used Vaseline to make her baby hair stick down on her forehead.

"'Cause. They is out to get you, girl. I know you know how to get ready for a fight. Nobody wants any scratches on their face like you left on what's-his-name. Whatever." She waited for me to respond. When I didn't, she waved her hand in the air, dismissing me. "I was just trying to help. It's up to you."

Little Man and I looked at each other as Manuela turned, stepping back into the crowd of waiting kids. The last thing on either one of our minds was a fight. Usually people waited till the afternoon to fight anyway, but things were different lately on the school bus. A new girl named Suenice transferred into our school and took over as the new ruler. We all took one look at her the first day and knew she would be the new queen, she was as big as a junior high school kid. And she made friends with the boy whose face I scratched before.

I tried to think fast as my chest rose and fell a little faster. "We got a couple of minutes till the bus comes, you want to go to the store?"

"What do you want from the store? We don't have any money, anyway." Little Man looked at me with wide trusting eyes. He was sometimes a little slow, or at least in his own world, but I knew he would go along with whatever I said. If I said the right things, there would be no way he would go to school without me.

I felt my pocket. Today was lunch money day. I was supposed to pay for both of our lunches for the week.

"I have money." I held up a small white envelope that held our lunch money. It all made sense, there were more fights on lunch money day than any other day; some kids didn't have to pay for lunch and of those, some would want to take advantage of the ones who did, hitting them up for their two dollars. Suenice must have picked us this time.

"We can't spend that!" He moved back and forth from foot to foot.

"Why can't we? You don't think they will take it at the store? I know you want some Now-N-Laters…" He needed enticing. I waved the envelope in front of his face.

Little Man paused for a minute. I had him. Now-N-Laters were his favorite. "But—"

"C'mon." I picked up my book bag. He didn't need too much time to think, and just as I thought, he grabbed his small red bag and followed me. The other kids didn't even notice as we walked away from the bus stop.

The small candy store was a block and a half away, and although the school bus was expected any minute, I didn't see any reason to rush. We bought Now-N-Laters in grape for Little Man, and red shoestring licorice for me. When we were done we had a whole dollar left.

"Here." I handed it to Little Man.

"What I am supposed to do with this?" he asked.

"Put it in your pocket. You deserve it." I almost believed it myself.

"But what about lunch?"

"Don't worry about it. I will take care of it." I searched his face for some reaction. I did not have the slightest idea of *how* I would take care of it, but it looked like he still believed just as he did when he was two and three.

We started back to the bus stop, Little Man eating his Now-N-Laters like he had no intention of saving any for later. The grape flavor smelled artificial and strong as it caught my nose and by the way he sucked on the candy he seemed to be happy with it. I was glad that someone was happy about something; it wasn't him that was going to get jumped by the mob of school bus bullies, maybe scarred for life.

He was totally unaware of how I looked out for him now, since Momma died. And now that June-Bug was gone, I was the only one that really could. June-Bug told me to, so now it really was my job.

The bus stop looked very empty. From across the street, I could see that all the kids were gone. My heart did a flip. Relief flooded over me. A warm feeling flowed down through my body to my toes. What I hoped would happen did. We had missed the bus. There was no chance of getting to school at all now.

Little Man noticed it an instant after I did.

"Sweeeetie! Look!" he shouted. "What are we going to do?" He reverted to his babyish whine, a whine that I gave up eons ago.

"Well, we are going to hang out all day until it's time to go back home to Granny Hambay-el's house." I caught myself, not believing that I almost called that place home. "It's not like we can go there now, you know. She would beat us for sure." I thought about the thin brown belt she used on Little Man every morning and the welts it created when it made contact with his skin and I winced. No siree, not for me.

"H-h-hang out?" He sniffed.

I sighed. I really had to break things down for him sometimes. "Yes, like a holiday. Like Huckleberry Finn or something." If they could cut school in books and on television, then we could do it too. We were far smarter than any of those kids.

Little Man seemed to relax a little, his shoulders dropped from their tense position. I held his hand.

"We can just hang out in the neighborhood, okay?" I tried to use my best Momma-like voice, at least the best one I could remember.

He nodded.

We could do this.

I picked a spot, not far from the bus stop and we sat on the sidewalk, under a shade tree. I tried to get Little Man interested in playing tic-tac-toe in the dirt. I made up games. I knew this couldn't last; I was bored too and I had no idea how much time passed. We walked around the block. I tried to get Little Man to play tag. He was no more interested in the game than I was.

We counted red cars.

Then blue ones.

We ran out of colors.

Finally we got up from the sidewalk and brushed ourselves off. We walked back toward home, neither one of us knowing if we dared go there. The neighborhood streets screamed with emptiness. I always imagined cutting school would be fun, but this seemed more lonely than fun. No one else was around, they were in school where they belonged. All of the parents were at work.

We walked on the side of the street that we never did, I was making sure that we were varying our normal routine, doing some of the exploring we were never allowed to do. I felt like I was stretching my wings the way birds did first thing in the morning. We passed in front of the school where I went to kindergarten. I stared at the big gray building, surrounded by a black wrought iron fence with massive gray steel doors. I remembered avoiding the cracks on these sidewalks while Momma was in the hospital. Today I played the opposite game, stepping on each and every one, with Little Man following behind me, trying to do exactly as I did.

Our game was interrupted as we passed the second door. It opened suddenly and I stopped short, causing Little Man to run into me from behind. I turned my attention from the cracks in the sidewalk to the school steps. A small man in a pseudo-cop outfit stood there, watching us. A security guard. I reached beside me and took Little Man's hand.

"Ur-uh, what are you kids doing outside the building?" He took a few steps in our direction. I tried to pull Little Man away, so we could leave, but the man spoke again. "Hello," he sing-songed. "I'm talking to you! Come over here." He pointed down to a spot right in front of him with a brown finger that was the longest I had ever seen.

I held onto Little Man as tight as I could. Daddy had told me over and over again not to talk to strangers. I knew that, Little Man even knew that, but there was a sense of authority about this man, something I could not resist, that told me I needed to do what he said. Finally, I spoke instead of moving.

"We don't go to your school. We missed our school bus." My voice was too loud. I released some of the tightness of my hold on my brother.

"You don't? You think I believe that?" he said, his voice stern. "Just come here." He paused. "Now."

I dropped my head. We were in trouble at a school that wasn't even ours. Reluctantly, I stepped forward, Little Man in tow. The security guard opened the door and held it for us. He motioned for us to step forward.

"Inside." He pointed toward the building with his head.

The building seemed extra dark from where we were standing. I held my breath, trying to avoid taking too much of it in. It smelled of darkness and paper mixed with industrial cleaner, a smell that only schools could have. I paused for a minute to think about my options, realizing that we couldn't run. The man stepped around behind us. One, if not both of us, would surely be caught. We stepped into the building.

It was now as unfamiliar to me as a place I had never been. Paper attached to the walls fluttered in a slow, artificial wind. No one was in the hallways, but I didn't recognize the bulletin boards or the doors, even the blue tile on the floor looked different to me than it had before.

"The principal's office."

His voice boomed through the still hallway. I jumped, startled, I had almost forgotten that he was there. He stepped in front of us and we followed him to our doom. I imagined that we were part of a spy movie, that the enemy had captured us. I silently vowed to give him no more information than necessary, no matter what torture they used.

The office was lit more brightly than the hallways, and he motioned toward a long wooden bench.

Little Man was two minutes from crying. We both took a seat without further prodding. My stomach fluttered from the familiar feeling of nervousness. I put my hand on Little Man's to offer him some comfort.

The man walked toward a door to the left and back of the room. I watched him go, noticing that his pants had the creases sewn into them and he had hips, like a woman. He looked more like a janitor than a security guard.

"We in trouble?" Little Man poked me in the side and I jumped. His eyes were filled with tears. I shrugged, but patted his leg at the same time. Butterflies flitted inside my stomach, and I realized that what I was feeling was not fear but a slight sense of enjoyment. This felt good to me. At least I was feeling something.

The hippy man returned, asking us for our names.

"Do you know your phone number?" he asked.

I looked at him, not believing he even asked me that. Did he think I was a baby or something? Did I look as if I was not in control? I gave him Daddy's number, at work. I dared not give him Granny Hambay-el's number. Daddy might as well hear the truth from the source instead of some version that got more inflated as it was retold.

He left us, walking over to a phone on a small desk sitting in the corner. The top of the desk was clear, except for a blotter and one single pen. It didn't look as if anyone used it regularly at all. Instead, it appeared to be reserved for prisoners like us, to make one last phone call.

We watched, and the man dialed the phone. "Lieutenant Wooten, please." I felt my stomach tighten as he asked for

Daddy. I had not counted on this. I really had not counted on anything.

"Sir, I am calling from Richmond Elementary School. We have your children here."

Little Man and I teetered on the edge of the bench. We wanted to hear what he would say, hear how he would tell on us. At that moment he noticed us listening and lowered his voice, turning his back to us. The tears in Little Man's eyes began to flow down his face. He was a softie.

After a few seconds, the man turned back around to face us, the phone still to his ear. "Your father would like to talk to you, young lady," he said. He extended his arm, holding out the phone in my direction.

I stood up from the bench slowly, a feeling of dread creeping over me. I didn't want to get in trouble with Daddy, and couldn't remember the last time I had been. I just wanted to avoid a fight at school. I crossed the short distance and raised the phone to my ear. At first I couldn't speak but the man, now standing behind me, shoved me, very lightly on my shoulder.

"Dadd-ee." I puffed my cheeks full of air.

"I am disappointed in you, Sweetie. I will deal with you later. You stay there, okay?" His voice was too calm.

I suddenly hated what I had done. I hated that I was supposed to be the big girl, and instead I let him down.

"But can I tell--" I wanted to explain about the bullies.

"I have nothing to say to you now. They will take care of you and we will talk later." He used his "boy, are you gonna get it" voice. He hung up.

I let my hand drop and looked over to meet Little Man's gaze. Daddy said he would talk to me later. I knew that I was in for at least a long lecture. But at least we would talk. I knew I should have been feeling more remorse, but I couldn't find it inside me. It seemed to be missing. Instead I felt a little happy in the place that feelings of remorse and regret should be occupying. We would talk, and that was making me happy. We had not really talked in a long time. Momma was the one who had done the talking, and then June-Bug. Now Daddy would, too.

⁂

The school bell rang, and I was relieved. We stayed at that school the rest of the day, being put into the classes we should have been in. The faces were different, but otherwise it was the same as our own school.

I reassured Little Man that it would be all right; I lied, telling him that Daddy wasn't mad, that he wouldn't be in trouble. That was almost the truth. He wasn't in trouble, but I knew I was, and in a way, I wanted to relish this trouble, keeping it all for myself.

Little Man met me at the front of the school. He stood waiting, with the security guard-janitor. We didn't speak, instead we filed out in silence. The other kids seemed to be leaving faster than we were and we let the crowd move us down the steps. We were the different ones again, the news of how we, two school bus kids, came to be at that school spread like wildfire all day long. We were, another time, a curiosity.

The unfamiliar crowd made me uncomfortable, the sweat from my palms made it hard to hold onto my school bag. I was more alert now, watching every person who looked our way like a hawk. I caught the eye of a short round boy. He was staring at me and Little Man and was not afraid to hide it, all the while talking loudly to his friends. A small crowd stood near him. A popular one. His big, round glasses took up his whole face.

He slapped his friends five and headed straight for us. I put my hand out and stopped Little Man in his path, just as he reached us.

"You two live on my block. I see you coming and going." He didn't ask, he stated. I didn't recall seeing him on our block, so I knew that he meant the block that the sitter lived on. We didn't know any of the kids there. We were still never allowed to play with them.

"And?" I stared him in the eye, challenging him.

"And nothing, I just saw you." He rolled his eyes. "I heard what happened. You gotta know how to cut school. Can I walk with you?"

Already annoyed, I started to say no. Was he implying that I did not know how to cut school while he did? I wanted to prepare myself to deal with Daddy and Granny Hambay-el.

I didn't want a walking companion.

I said nothing. He was not deterred by my silence, he chattered on about his school and his friends. He fell into step and walked with us, his words occasionally pulling me back from my thinking place. Why had he bothered to even ask permission? He was obviously another one of those who did not care what *we* thought.

"So, how long have you lived there?"

I couldn't stand it any longer. "We don't live there." I spoke through clenched teeth. "Our sit—"I stopped myself. "Our granny lives there."

I didn't want to seem like a baby. At our regular school, kids teased us because of what they knew about our life. I saw no reason to add to that.

"Why don't you ever play outside? We play lots of fun games and stuff. We even have block parties. I never see you there, just going in and out of that house, like clockwork."

"We play, we just play on our own block, or in the backyard." Little Man smiled at the boy. I frowned, stopping his smile in mid-curve. The last thing we needed was a nosy neighbor kid. One who knew it all at that.

"If it was so much fun, you would have something better to do than watch us, right?" I twisted my face into a sarcastic grimace, lifting my eyebrows in "I told you so" fashion at the same time. "It's not your business anyway."

"Well, excuse me for trying to be friendly." He was pushed into silence. We walked the last block listening to our footsteps on the pavement, but he did not go away.

My mind kept wandering back to what Daddy was going to say to us, what he was going to do. As we neared the house, we slowed down. Our new friend with the big glasses walked along with us. Little Man sniffled and I held my breath, hoping he would hold his tears at least until the boy left us.

"So, what are your names?"

We paused in front of Granny Hambay-el's house, an awkward pause. The boy waited, his words triggering a full-fledged crying attack from Little Man. Tears rolled down his face, leaving salty trails on his cheeks. The roly-poly boy watched us, his lower lip hanging open. We did not tell him our names.

We stood close to the hedge, and Little Man reached into his pocket and removed the money left from our candy store adventure. He quickly tore the dollar bill into little pieces, again and again, as if tearing at the dollar bill was the same as tearing away at us missing school in the first place. He stuck his fist through the hedge. The branches tore at his skin, but the pieces of the money dropped into the center of the bushes. He was destroying the evidence.

"Come on!" I grabbed him on his shoulder nervously and turned him around, goading him toward the house. He cried harder. The boy with the glasses stood there with his mouth open again.

We reached the top step and the boy bent and reached into the hedges. He retrieved the torn dollar bill pieces.

"Hey," he said. "Wait!"

He rushed toward us, reaching the top step just as Granny Hambay-el opened the door. I looked up into her face, and saw in the darkness of her eyes and tight mouth that she already knew what we had done. Her gaze locked me in my place. Little Man's cries grew louder, reaching sob status.

The boy reached around us and showed her his open hand and the mutilated dollar bill. I looked down and could hear her head move as she looked from us to the money and back to us.

"What's this, eh?" She shifted her weight over one of her bow legs.

"They tore this up and dropped it in the bushes." His voice quavered, his boldness dissipated by Granny Hambay-el's fierce appearance. He had sealed our fate.

Granny paused, then finally took the money from the boy's outstretched palm.

"Thank you. Go home, now. You two--" She pointed a long, crooked finger at us, seemingly at a spot right between my eyes.

A pain seared through my head as if a bullet found its bull's-eye. She meant business. "You get in here, *now*."

I stumbled through the door just as she reached past me, grabbing Little Man by his collar. He was snatched through the door, his feet dragging the ground. She slammed it behind us before the boy even had a chance to turn around.

He had no idea what he had just done.

Granny Hambay-El continued into the house, her heavy walk causing the floorboards to creak and protest.

Everett appeared from nowhere and stood on the landing from upstairs. He was half in the shadows, but I could tell he was laughing at us.

Her voice trembled with rage. "You dyamn children. Ungrateful things." She talked at us and pushed us down into our chairs, open and waiting. "You gwine make you father think that I am not in control. You upstarts! You gwine see me on you now, you hear."

I expected her to hit us. My shoulder tensed in anticipation. I closed my eyes, and suddenly she thundered away from us toward the kitchen.

My eyes flew open.

Was that it?

We looked at each other, confused. My anticipation changed to surprise and then to dread.

Everett finally came down off the steps. He paused in front of us, his mouth drawn into a half smile.

"So," he said. "You cut school, huh? I didn't think you had it in you. When I was a kid, I would cut all the time but I was smarter than you two." He paused. "I didn't get caught."

If I were standing, I would have stepped back from him. The hairs on the back of my neck stood at attention. I couldn't move. I was frozen in my chair as I gripped the sides.

"But you know, when I did get caught, I sure got it good. Trust me. Yours is coming. Granny doesn't let folk get off that easy. You just wait." He laughed, then, like a TV villain, then left us there to think about what he'd said.

I held my breath the whole time. I realized it was true, what he said. And I knew there was nothing worse than waiting.

TWENTY-TWO

Our punishment would be simple enough. I should have known what it would be, and was not surprised as I stood in the kitchen, listening to Daddy talk to Granny Hambay-el. She marched us straight back through the house and into the kitchen. There would be no plastic chairs today, not yet.

My father sat at the table where we usually sat for dinner. It was covered with a real cloth tablecloth today, a pretty one actually, embroidered, instead of the heavy plastic one we usually got to eat on.

I was not used to being in this type of trouble; Daddy had come home from work early to get here to punish us. My stomach felt heavy and my feelings of defiance washed away.

I was truly afraid.

Granny Hambay-el motioned us into a corner, against the wall. We stood with our backs to the flowery kitchen wallpaper, silent, afraid to speak. I had to go to the bathroom, but I even was afraid to shift, even to do my bathroom dance. There was going to be a storm. I could feel it.

Daddy did not look at us. He sat at the table, with his head heavy in his hands, his elbows pressing down hard. I looked, wide-eyed, knowing that Granny Hambay-el boxed

Little Man's ears for putting his elbows on the dinner table just yesterday, wondering whether she would do the same to Daddy. We all were under her control, even Daddy, and he didn't even know it.

She took a seat at the table across from Daddy, and surprisingly, the stern look that met us at the front door disappeared, and she smiled. She even put her teeth in for Daddy's visit. This was serious.

"Don't you fret, mon," she said. "I take care of these young 'uns. The devil him play his tricks today, but I know what to do." She glared in our direction, her lilting voice sounding sweet and proper, almost musical.

"I can't imagine why they did this. They are normally so obedient." Daddy's voice was low. He didn't look at us, and they both talked like we weren't in the room, like they would talk about a dead person.

Like they talked about Momma.

"If I can't control them, they will take them away, and I don't know if I can bear for that to happen. They are all I have, you know. And Sweetie looks so much like Elva. There is already talk in her family about trying to fight for custody." He rubbed his hand through his hair. "I don't know. Sometimes I think I should let them get what they want. Maybe they can do better than I can. I'm a single man, all by myself now." He paused. "But I would miss them so much. It's like a father's love doesn't count for anything."

Granny Hambay-el reached over and stroked Daddy's arm. I did not know she knew how to comfort anyone. Little

Man and I looked at each other and I sighed. We had not heard one word about people trying to take us away from Daddy since the funeral. I couldn't imagine who would want us. The people who had us didn't seem to want us.

I leaned back onto the wall.

"You leave dem to me, I will straighten them out." The table shook as she pounded her fist on it.

My skin prickled.

"Let them stay here with me for two weeks, Mr. Wooten. I can put them back on the straight and narrow."

"Two weeks? You think that will work?" Daddy lifted his head for the first time since we came in.

"Yeah mon, I can get some sense back into dem. Nowadays, people are too permissive with their chil'ren. Let me. Back home, we have a saying. Spare the rod, spoil the chile. Are you familiar with dat? I can clean whatever demons them got inside them out. I promise." She thumped her chest.

Daddy looked over at us. What were they saying? We would not go home for two weeks? He didn't seem to understand that she really meant she would *clean* the demons out of us! There was no telling what she would do.

The kitchen clock ticked louder than ever as Little Man and I both held our breath. We didn't dare speak a word. Daddy finally answered.

"I don't know about demons, but I do know that two weeks sounds like a good punishment to me. It will be like they are grounded. My mother used to do that to me, right after she whipped my behind." He sat up, seeming more in control. "Will you make sure they have no television during that time?"

"If that is what you want, sir. You de boss. My daughter will teach them some useful things. I will see to it." She pushed herself up from the table, resting most of her weight on her arms first. The table creaked in response. Daddy stood up too, walking around the table.

"It's settled, then. I need to talk with them alone a minute." He paused, waiting for Granny Hambay-el to leave the kitchen.

He looked over at us, speaking to us for the first time. "I hope you two learn something from this. Sweetie, I can't tell you how disappointed I am in you. You are supposed to be my big girl, and you might not believe it, but I do understand where all this is coming from. It's obvious how you feel. The way you acted at Frances' house. Your grades. I talked to your teacher. I know what is going on." He didn't wait for an answer. "I'm doing the best I know how to do."

I thought I spied a tiny bit of softness in his eyes. He looked away quickly.

"I trust this won't happen again."

They left us there, our jailer walking our father out of our cell. He didn't want relatives to take us, yet he was practically giving us away to a stranger. Little Man's tears began to stream down his face again, this time, his nose ran too. From the front of the house, I heard the door close just as surely as a key turning in a prison door. I leaned farther into the wall, closing my eyes, my body crumpling into a sitting position. I was trying to avoid one beating by an opponent I could have probably handled, and instead led myself into one I had not bargained for.

⌒⌘

Granny Hambay-el came back into the kitchen and stood in the doorway, hands on her hips, triumphant.

"What are you doing down dere, chile? Get up! Both of you, have a seat at the table!" She flung her arm in the direction of the table. The sagging skin on its underside waved at us and her wrinkled hand flapped on the end of it.

We didn't answer, instead the fear inside us moved us both. We scurried over to the table as we had been commanded. We sat in our dinner seats, wondering what was next. I could not believe that Daddy left us as he did. The numbness I was feeling grew stronger, creeping from the pit of my stomach and spread throughout my body.

We watched as she took out a pot and filled it with water from the sink. She placed it on the stove with a thud and then lumbered over to the pantry.

The pantry door wasn't actually a door but a flowered curtain, sewn by the daughter. I knew all kinds of mysteries were in that closet, including the Christmas cakes that soaked for months in the over proof liquor she poured on them. If I stood close to the door, I could smell all kinds of smells coming from in there, only imagining what they were. We waited, knowing she would not be coming back out with any cake this time. Minutes passed, me imagining that she actually stepped out the other side of the pantry and into some parallel mysterious place like in a book I read, to bring back some strange instrument of torture.

Finally, she emerged from the closet. She did not say a word. She looked over at us as she passed the table and sucked her teeth, in that long, special way she had. If she were so disgusted by our presence, why did she keep us here?

She held a clear plastic bag in one hand and a small bottle, unmarked, in the other. She placed the bottle on the counter and began to open the bag, placing the contents of the bag into the pot. She had to draw it out; the stuff in the bag was wispy, like hair. She stirred the pot with a big wooden spoon.

"It has taken me a long time to convince your father that I know better than any doctor. We are going to fix a lot of things these next two weeks." The wrinkled flesh on her upper arm sagged as she stirred her pot, jiggling back and forth as she moved her arm.

A picture of Hansel and Gretel flashed in my head. A witch. A cauldron.

"This is for you, Little Man." She nodded her head toward her pot. "We are gwine stop this bed wetting nonsense. You hear?" She banged the spoon on the rim of the pot with each word. "They told me that if I boiled the silk from corn and you drank up the liquor, it would stop the bed wetting. We have nothing to lose, so I try it, right?"

Little Man kicked me under the table, but he didn't look up from the spot he was staring at on the table cloth. I knew he thought this whole thing was my fault. No, she didn't have anything to lose. He would have to drink it, not her.

I held my breath. I was next. I didn't wet the bed, but I knew that I was going to get some remedy or the other if Granny could help it, just because. I could see it in the way she looked at me when we came through the door.

She turned around from the stove to face us, the wooden spoon still in her hand. She pointed it at me.

"And you. I know you did dis. You de evil one, you devil-chile, you. Too many folk telling you that you pretty. That what cause dis. But you ugly, real ugly inside. I know it." She turned and picked up the bottle she set on the counter. "Pretty hair. Pretty eyes. Rotten inside."

"Dis be for you!" She reached into the drawer, pulling out a tablespoon. "You will have a tablespoon of this every night. Do you know what this is, gal, eh?"

I shook my head, shrinking back in my seat as she came forward.

"This is cod liver oil, gal. It will clean everything out o' you. The old food, even de worms that making you act out so." She wrinkled her nose, waving a single, knobbed finger in the air as she spoke.

She poured the oil into the spoon. It was thick and heavy and it moved slow, like molasses that I saw my Gramma use in baking her cookies.

"C'mere. You don't think I am going to give this to you over me good linens, now do you? You chil'ren mess up anything. Slovenly, you are. C'mere. Hurry." She motioned with her head.

Reluctantly, I pushed my chair back. It wasn't like I could run. Or fight. I knew I had to take it. I sighed and got up from the table.

"Does it taste bad?" I took half a step in her direction. She pursed her lips, making them thin out against each other, and raised one eyebrow. She obviously did not care what it tasted like and was not about to share that information with me. She pushed the spoon in my direction, and as she did, the smell of the cod liver oil reached my nose. It even smelled thick. And oily. My stomach flipped.

"Don' make me hold your nose. Just take a deep breath and swallow it. Don't taste it. Hurry up. I got to take care of yu brotha."

She grabbed me by the arm with her free hand, squeezing me. I took a deep breath, closed my eyes, and opened my mouth. She shoved the spoon in and I closed and swallowed. My stomach turned as the thick, oily substance made its way down my throat.

She let me go. I opened my eyes and she gestured for me to go back to the table. She wasn't through with me. Or at least she wanted me to see Little Man get his potion too.

"Hey, Mommy." Her daughter walked into the kitchen, her arms full of grocery bags. Her son, Everett, was right behind her, his arms as full of bags as his mother's.

For a minute her caramel brown arms blended with the paper bags so well, it looked like they were floating in front of her. She dropped the brown paper bags on the table in front of us and smoothed her clothes.

"Watch me linens, gal. Did you get everything?" Granny stepped back over to the stove, removing the now boiling pot from the flame. She reached for a strainer. At that moment I felt my stomach begin to heave. I opened my mouth and began to throw up. It spread over the table, around the bottom of the grocery bags.

"Mommy, what is she doing?" her daughter screamed. Little Man pushed his chair back from the table to avoid the mess. "The linens! The bags!"

"I gave her some cod liver oil! She is doing dat on purpose! She is a devil. You are going to clean them linens, gal! You see me on you!"

I sat with my head down, my hand covering my mouth, trembling. Her voice was making me sicker. The taste of bile fouled my mouth and I retched some more. I didn't care. I hoped I ruined her precious linens.

"I hope she didn't mess up your tea! I had to go all the way across town for that tea you wanted." The daughter began to move the bags from the table, setting them on the sink. "Why don't you put that stuff in some orange juice and have her drink it? I will get it. Are you making the corn silk drink for the boy? You know you are supposed to put a dab of cayenne in it, right?" She finished moving her grocery bags to a safer location, and opened the refrigerator.

"Gal, who you think you talking to? I been doing this since before you were even thought of. Them American friend of yours rubbin' off on you then? You sure soundin' like dem more and more." She finished straining the water in the pot into a glass. "Boy, you come drink this, and you better not throw it up like your sister, or I got something for you."

Everett stood off to the side, all the while sneering at us.

Little Man moved over to the sink. He smelled the cup, and Everett slapped the back of his neck. Little Man jumped, almost spilling it.

Granny pursed her lips and then he took a sip.

"Drink it all." She leaned on the sink in front of him, almost cornering him. She would make sure he got every drop. He sipped, his eyes wide. He sniffled as he sipped.

Satisfied, she turned to me.

"Well, get up from there, you. Why you wan sit in you own vomit? Nasty." She moved a chair near her into the center of the floor. "Sit here. Move like you mean it. Now."

I sat on the edge of the chair and slid back, reaching down to hold onto the sides. My hands were sticky and smelled like garbage now. My fingers were beginning to stick together. She stood on the side and poured more cod liver oil into the spoon. The yellow goo seemed to move into the spoon faster this time. Her daughter moved to the other side of the chair, standing poised with a cup in her hand. Everett jerked my chin farther up into the air. It hurt where he held it.

I thought they would give me time to breathe, but instead Granny Hambay–el straddled me with her incredibly bow legs. She pinched my nose so hard I began to see spots. I couldn't breathe. I tried to will my mouth to stay shut but it dropped open in response, and she shoved the spoon so far back into my throat that I gagged. Everett forced my mouth closed.

I swallowed automatically.

Granny grabbed my nose again and I opened my mouth. I tried to fight, move my hands from where they gripped the chair, but she used her knees to squeeze them down. Suddenly I was drowning in orange juice.

"Swallow!" she yelled. "Now!"

I obeyed. I just wanted them off me. My hands ached from the pressure. They let me go. I raised them and stared at the chair imprints now in the palm of my hand.

"You betta keep it down this time. Humph!" She turned away from me, limping to the pantry. The smell of the orange juice and vomit covering me reached my nose. I wanted to be clean. My stomach did not protest. The cod liver oil would stay down.

Little Man was glued to his seat. He sat with his hands in his lap, under the table, crying my tears. His body was shaking from his almost silent sobs. The daughter hummed and finished unpacking her bags. She didn't say anything else to me. This was not out of the ordinary to her. I wondered if she had to take cod liver oil as a child.

Granny Hambay-el finally noticed that I was still sitting where she left me.

"You plan on sitting here all night? You are in my way. Take my linen off the table and go wash it." She sucked her teeth again, motioning toward the open basement door.

I lifted my head. The tables had now turned. Instead of Little Man being sent to the basement laundry room, this time it was me that had to go.

"Can I ch-change my clothes?" My shirt had soaked through to my skin. The clamminess of it was making me itch.

"No. Linen first. I want you to think about what you have done."

I pressed my lips together hard, rolling my eyes. She noticed.

"Don't you sass me, gal. You wash that tablecloth like I tole you. Take it downstairs. The detergent you should use is on the basin. Wash it by hand. And you better make sure it is clean, too. I will check it when you are done."

⌾

And check she did. No sooner than I reached the sink, I heard her plodding down the steps. I dumped the tablecloth I was holding into the washbasin just as she entered the small washroom at the back of the basement. She stood with her hands on her hips, legs spread wide, daring me to do anything even mildly approaching defiant.

I braced myself on the porcelain sink, with no clue of how to begin. Even my Gramma had a washing machine. It was an old one, still with a round tub and two rollers on the top that wrung the water out of the clothes. Even she didn't wash clothes by hand anymore. I didn't know what to do. I could feel waves of panic rising inside me.

"The soap powder is on your left." She didn't move, motioning with her head.

I plugged up the sink and turned on the water, reaching for the soap powder at the same time.

"You betta hope the sun holds up. You gotta hang that thing on the line outside too. You American children don't know nothing about how to take care of a house. You don't do anything yourself, huh?" Her eyes glared at me so hard I imagined I could see them glowing like someone possessed on television. I knew nothing I did was going to be good enough, but I didn't care. At least I would get to go outside, even for a minute.

She stood over me, watching carefully the whole time I washed the tablecloth. I knew that she liked to sit down all the time so I moved as slow as possible. Inside my head, I counted each move I made by the numbers. She didn't leave. I wasn't going to win. Not today. She stood watch over me like the warden she had become, even in the yard, daring me to let the tablecloth touch the ground. I knew if I did that she would make me trek back downstairs to the wash basin to start over. I braced myself for a long two weeks.

Twenty-Three

I didn't want to go.

Miss Faust stared at me hard. She had called my name and I could tell by the serious look on her face that I was going to have to stand up in front of the class and read my essay. It didn't matter how bad I felt. I tried to ignore her at first, acting like I didn't hear her. There were only five minutes left to her class and then I could go back to my regular classroom.

She called my name again. I sighed, then stood up as slowly as I could. I hoped that the bell would ring and that I wouldn't have to do this. I knew it wouldn't, I just did not have that kind of luck.

I felt hot and just a little weak and sitting down made me feel better. I touched each desk I passed as I made my way to the front of the classroom. My stomach was still a little queasy. After the cod liver oil, I had not been able to eat anything this morning, not even a piece of cheese.

"The Red Fish," I said. "By Monica Denise Wooten." My voice sounded far away, like it belonged to someone else.

My essay was good. I knew it was just as soon as the words flowed out of my pen and onto the paper. I felt bad and there was no way I could make that goodness come out in my voice. I was boring and tired and was making my story sound that way too. And if I wasn't excited about it, I knew that no one else would be either.

Half the kids in the class never paid attention anyway. That was the reason they were here in the first place. But Miss Faust did. Since she made me start coming to this remedial class instead of recess, it was obvious that she paid attention all the time. I kept my eyes on her face. Her nose twitched. She didn't like what she was hearing.

"With some feeling please, Monica. You wrote that so you must have some emotion about it."

I did have emotion, just not about what she thought I should have. I had emotion about feeling sick, about taking cod liver oil, but the work just didn't seem to be as important right now. How was it going to help me?

I looked back down at my paper. She didn't need to know what I felt. She would probably not believe me or only listen half way like the other grownups did when I talked. She would probably just say, "That's nice dear," or something like it.

My nose stung and my face felt hot. I hated to be standing there like that, with her looking at me and whatever other student was paying attention thinking I was crazy or something. Not to mention if someone walked by the classroom and saw me in here with this bunch. I would be teased until I graduated.

The bell rang. Finally. I could feel Miss Faust looking at me, but I forced myself not to return her gaze. Instead, I headed back to my desk to grab my things. The sooner I could get back to my normal classroom, the better.

"Monica."

I thought I was going to get out of the room without having to talk with her. Two more steps was all I needed.

I stopped but didn't turn around. My arms and back were stiff with tension as I gripped my books.

Miss Faust was behind me. "You doing okay?"

Why did she ask me that when she knew that I wasn't doing okay? I nodded anyway.

She stepped around in front of me, blocking my way. Miss Faust put her hand on my shoulder. "Then why do you look so pale? Are you sick? The school nurse is in today."

I shook my head. "I'm not sick. I'm just tired, that's all." I looked away.

Miss Faust didn't move. I must not have been too convincing. The silence between us seemed long and thick, so long that I could hear her thinking about what she was going to do next. The noise in the hallway thundered in comparison to the silence in the room. Finally she cleared her throat. "I see," she said.

But she really didn't.

"I heard that you and your brother missed the school bus the other day." She paused. "You must have gotten into trouble for that."

I could not tell if she really wanted me to tell her what was going on or if she was just trying to be nice.

She studied me and had that thinking line between her eyes.

I just wanted to get on with my day. I shrugged.

"Uh-huh. Okay. What happened to your journal? The one I gave you when you were in my class?" Her voice was lighter now. "Wait right here."

I kept staring at the floor and listened to the click her shoes made on the wooden floor. She stepped over to her desk and then right back to me before I could even think of leaving.

"Let's move on from the old journal, okay? I want you to start a new one." Miss Faust held out a book that looked just like the journal she had given me before.

I didn't take it.

"C'mon. I know you don't like being in this room." She paused, still holding the journal in front of me. "Your writing has gotten so much better since you started coming here. That's good, but I know you have so much more inside you, and nowhere to put it. I can see it. You can use this book to help you. Think of it as writing practice."

I was going to have to think about it. I didn't want to talk and I certainly didn't want to write. I wanted to make up stories, not write down things that happened in my life. I didn't understand the value in that. And besides, she might want to give me a grade on it or something.

"Can I go? I don't want to be late."

Miss Faust's eyes filled with disappointment.

I looked away.

"Think about it." She finally stepped out of my way.

I didn't take her book and I didn't look back. She would never understand that there were some things I would never be able to find words for.

TWENTY-FOUR

The boiled corn silk didn't work. I awoke to the usual sounds of the strap licking Little Man's backside in the next room. I thought it was going to be like any other day, but I was wrong.

I dragged out of bed, peeking out of my doorway, my nose running from the cold that I was now used to. Little Man passed, naked as always. For the first time I noticed red welts in his previously unbroken coppery skin. The strap had not just licked *at* him, it had found its mark. The tears that flowed down his cheeks formed tiny prisms like the kind we played with at school. We made eye contact, and he wiped his tears with the back of his hand.

"She let Everett spank me," he said. His words came out haltingly and his voice was hushed.

I looked away, folding my sheets.

Granny Hambay-el combed my hair just like she had that first morning. I expected silence, as, usual, but instead her voice surprised me. She usually spoke to me only to give commands.

"This afternoon you are going to learn something useful. Both of you."

I didn't answer. I was not surprised. Nothing surprised me anymore. I just wondered how much her version of "useful" differed from mine. What would Faust want me to write down about this? I put my head in my hands and she jerked it up. My eyes smarted from the pain. I knew, in my heart, that Daddy really was under her spell. He had to be.

For those two weeks I came home from school and then worked outside in the garden with Elizabeth, the daughter. At first I was happy because I thought she was taking an interest in me, but then I realized that she was part of the sentence. The gardening was supposed to help with my rehabilitation. I enjoyed it, but tried not to show it too much. I did not want to be stopped from going out into the backyard. I enjoyed moving among the things that were just starting to grow, smelling the outside air. I marveled at no matter how much she tried, the weeds still found a way to grow between the cracks in the cement. The weeds were survivors.

Granny Hambay-el's house was a row house, like our house, so the backyard was small. It was nothing like ours at home though. We used to play in our backyard all the time before Momma died, but we hardly went back there anymore and it was so overgrown it looked like a jungle. Granny Hambay-el's yard was the opposite; they had concreted everything, except for small patches around the edges. That was where Elizabeth planted. It was almost as if life was allowed only where and how they let it. The first day working in the yard I noticed a few weeds poking through anyway, and this made me happy, a little anyway. Some things couldn't be controlled, no matter how hard you tried.

Elizabeth grew lots of things in the backyard that they used in cooking or teas. I thought that most of the things that Granny made into tea came from the supermarket, but I knew now that was not the case. They grew as much of it as they could. She told me that they even sold it to other people sometimes.

The stuff they grew wasn't like Gramma down South. There was no corn or cucumbers or tomatoes, no obviously practical stuff. Most of it didn't look like food, but flowers and weeds. She said that was the way they did it back home, where they were from. Doctors were hard to get to there, so they did what they could with what they had, she explained.

She taught me all of the plant names. There were lots of different things, some common, some not, some I even had to wear gloves to work with, things like rhododendron and azalea and savin. Common things that I thought were just decoration could be used to cure this thing or that thing. No wonder Granny didn't believe a doctor could fix what was wrong with Little Man.

Baneberry grew at the back of the yard, its tall bushy look scared me, the only plant I didn't want to work with at all. The furry underside gave me the creeps and I kept as far away from it as possible.

The plant work did have a saving grace. I finally got to see the inside of the mysterious pantry. It smelled sort of like a hospital mixed with cigar smoke; it almost grabbed your nose as soon as you stepped through the curtain. Every day Elizabeth selected different plants and clipped them. She took a wooden clothespin and pinned them together, and then placed them in a basket she carried. The basket looked like an old-fashioned picnic basket, like the one Dorothy carried in *The Wizard of Oz*.

After about the second day in the yard, she made me clip the plants together for her and carry the basket, and then she took me in the house. I followed her to the pantry, where she showed me how to bag, label and date each plant we took inside. I could hardly concentrate for all of the smells and sights that were assaulting my nose. I forced back a sneeze as I wondered what they all were for.

There was an elaborate filing system, with everything in its place, like in the rest of the house. One full side of the pantry had herbs and plants and things, and the other extra food. I tried to memorize where everything was in the few minutes we were in there; I even saw cookies. This was important stuff to know. I could open the pantry curtain much quieter than I could the refrigerator door to sneak a piece of cheese. After that, I volunteered to do all the filing of plants the rest of the week, just so I could see what was in the pantry better. I had to tell Little Man!

That was easier said than done. We were kept pretty much separated, except for meals. I was working in the garden and he was inside most of the time, sitting under the steps. He was learning to weave or something. I heard Granny say that it was important for a young man to know a trade. It taught them discipline, she said. Every night a new remedy for his bed wetting was tried, and every morning he was still wet. We watched Granny Hambay-el try all kinds of mysterious remedies from her closet, from leaves to powders to ground-up apple seeds dissolved in hot liquid. She would usually brew the tea or fix the remedy as she drank her daily cup of tea. I wondered what she was giving herself or what she was trying to cure; none of her teas smelled good and none of them looked like they came in a Lipton-type tea bag. As I learned about the plants in the yard, I was also learning to be even more wary of the mysterious teas than I had been. Some of the plants could make you very sick if they were used incorrectly or even if they were brewed to the wrong strength.

Little Man drank the teas that Granny gave him and only once did he screw up his face or complain.

"Blah!" he said as he drank the apple seed juice, trying to use his napkin to wipe his tongue clean. He never complained before, and hardly ever spoke to me anymore, but this time he whispered to me that this new remedy tasted like burnt almonds. He sucked the sides of his mouth and puckered his lips. Little Man hated nuts of all kinds. Nothing worked, at least not to stop the bed wetting.

I had to take castor oil along with my cod liver oil almost every night. My mouth had a permanent oily taste to it and a slight burn. I threw up a few times. We were both getting skinny and feeling sick. I could only use my knowledge of the pantry's wealth one time, when I managed to snatch a few cookies. They were dry and crumbly sugar-free cookies, but they were the best-tasting thing we got our hands on since the punishment started.

Our punishment was cut short the morning after Little Man was given the ground-up seeds for a second time. I think they were apple seeds again, but they could have been apricot or something else. Little Man was still wet when he woke up, but I did not get to hear him scurrying past my door with his wet linen like normal. Instead, after I heard Granny yelling at him to get up, I heard a thud, and I knew that he had fallen on the floor instead of standing up when he got out of bed.

I dropped my sheets back on the bed and stepped outside my doorway. Little Man's room was at the end of the hall and I looked directly into it. He was stretched out on the floor, with Granny standing next to him, feet spread, hands on her hips. Everett was next to her, the now famous belt in one hand. It was wrapped around his fist with its end trailing down by his side.

I was frozen.

She yelled at him. "Stop it now. You get up from there, boy! You gwine see me on you now!" Every time she said that I imagined her all over us, like a germ. The thought made me itch and my stomach jump. For a minute it looked like she would nudge him with her foot. I was glad for her bow legs; one of them would not be able to hold her up should she attempt to kick him.

Little Man did not move. He clutched his stomach instead, drawing his legs up closer to his body. He moaned. His moans reached my ears, feeling like a slap to my face. They released me and I did something I knew to be forbidden; I went to his room and kneeled by his side. Granny Hambay-el sucked her teeth. She did not have to speak, we had been told time and time again that girls and boys would not be allowed in the same bedroom together. She never even allowed us to look into the other's room. She said that it was asking for trouble.

"Sweetie," he said, "I am so dizzy!" Little Man closed his eyes. "My head hurts too. Can you call Daddy?"

"Shhh." I touched my hand to his head and drew it back quickly, rubbing my fingertips together. Little Man felt hot and cold all at the same time. The feel of his forehead reminded me of the cool clamminess of a snake's skin. I didn't think I had ever been scared before at Granny Hambay-el's house, but this was scaring me. I knew that calling Daddy first was not the answer. He was working. Maybe he would not believe us.

"What are you doing, gal? You should be going down to the yard!"

"He needs a doctor! He's sick!" I looked down at Little Man. He looked too weak to even cry.

"How could you know what he needs? This is all your fault anyway, you upstart! You Amer—"

Her words blurred, and I silently finished her sentence for her. She talked about American children like they were roaches or like being American was something else she could cure us of.

I got up and walked around her to the phone. My legs felt hot and my hands were sweaty and clammy as I dialed 911. I could sense her following me, but I was not afraid, although I expected her to make my legs fall out from under me at any minute. I had promised that I would take care of Little Man. I had to try.

"You put that phone down now!" Although my back was turned, I could feel the air move as Everett raised the arm that held the belt. I braced myself to be hit as the phone rang for what seemed like an eternity. The blow didn't come. I turned slightly to look at her as the operator answered and I gasped. Granny Hambay-el had come up behind him and grabbed the end of the belt in mid-swing.

TWENTY-FIVE

*D*addy met us at the hospital. Although I was angry with him, I was happy to see him. I fought hard to look sad, but I felt a smile spread across my face anyway. If he was not there, I would know that he truly did not want us anymore. All of this was his fault, not mine, but I was the only one to see this. Granny Hambay-el told me over and over again that it was all my fault, and that I was the troublemaker.

Daddy hugged me right off and some of my anger slid away.

"What happened?"

I shook my head. My sadness was confusing me. I wasn't sure. "I think Little Man got sick because of her food." I stumbled on my words.

Daddy smiled at me softer than I ever remember him doing. He rubbed my head. "Aw, Sweetie," he said. "You are being a little over dramatic I think. I'm sure that's not it." He paused. "I know you don't like this any more than I do, but let's not make things up, okay. Why don't we wait for the doctor to tell us more?"

Little Man was going to be all right. They said he had a stomach virus, but I didn't believe that for one minute. I knew that he really suffered from heartache mixed with bad herbs. The doctors poked and prodded me too and asked me a few questions about what we had eaten, but in the end, I think Granny Hambay-el "sweeted" them and wrapped them around her little finger too. She was good at it. They sent us home with some Pepto-Bismol-like medicine for Little Man and a prescription for a bland diet with dry toast and cottage cheese. Even that would be an improvement.

Granny Hambay-el spoke in her extra-sweet voice, the one she reserved for Daddy and visitors. "I'll take dem home now. He gwine be fine."

I stood stiff as she put her hand on my shoulder.

Daddy stood up, clearing his throat. He glanced at his watch. "You know what," he said. "There is no need for that. I think they can just come on home for the rest of today." His eyes were hard and dark. "I'll send them back later."

I couldn't help but look over my shoulder and smirk at her. Once he saw us, the punishment was over. I didn't even have to cry. I wasn't sure, but I felt as if Daddy was apologizing to us in his own way, even if he couldn't bring himself to actually say it.

The house looked the same as it did when we left. Daddy arranged Little Man on the couch and I looked around, checking it out as I searched for evidence of some kind of change, a return to a normalcy that I did not even remember or know how to define. I smiled at my brother as he lay on the couch; if I were him I would milk this situation for all it was worth, for both of us.

I inspected the carpet as I walked through the house. It had been a big deal when it was installed, after the fire in the kitchen. Momma cried when she saw it; it was a surprise, from Daddy to her. The floors were soaked with water from the firemen's hoses, and although the new carpet covered the floors up, I still smelled the fire, even today, years later. The smell of burned people things burned my nose, bringing tears to my eyes. I stopped talking about it, no one else seemed to smell it. Now the carpet was beyond dirty and so matted that the once beautiful multicolors blended together, hair and dust from the years ground down into it. I didn't think that Daddy ever vacuumed. Or even knew how to. I could tell from the way he moved around the house that he was afraid to remove anything, even the dirt from the carpet. It was almost as if he felt that if he did, he would remove her memory too.

The shades in the house were all drawn, making the house seem as dark as a cave. My eyes narrowed as they tried to focus in the semidarkness that lurked inside the house. The front door knocker pounded, causing the dust-covered glasses on the front table to vibrate, clinking together. I jumped. Our doorbell had long since stopped working but it didn't matter. Visitors, at least while we were home, were rare.

Daddy made it to the door first. Whoever it was, I hoped he wouldn't let them in to walk on our crunchy carpet or breathe our dusty air. I could not tell if it was the dust or the sadness hiding in our house that made that air seem so heavy.

Daddy reached for the door, but it flung open. Light streamed into the room. I squinted and raised my hand to shield my eyes as I watched the dust particles dance in the new light. Auntie Jay stood in the door, illuminated by the daylight. It almost looked as if she were glowing.

"Well, Mr. Wooten. From the looks of things, you ain't holding it together too well, is ya?" Her arm was bent with her handbag slung over her elbow. She held a lit cigarette in one hand and was more dressed up than I remember her ever being. "Where they at?"

She walked into the house like she owned it, and for the first time, my daddy did not seem so strong. She got closer to me and I felt her eyes burning into me, almost like she was surveying me, checking me out, down to my bones. She circled me like a vulture, poking me in the ribs.

"She is too skinny, Wooten. How are you, Sweetie? It's been a long while. That woman treating you right? Why don't you buy her some clothes?" She asked several questions, not expecting an answer to any of them.

I had forgotten how much she looked like Momma. Except she was not pretty like Momma was, not because her features were made all that different, but because Auntie Jay possessed a bone-deep ugliness, the kind that makeup and fancy clothes couldn't hide. I rolled my eyes as she fingered my clothes. I didn't have much clothing and what I did have never really was stylish or fashionable, so I had long since stopped paying attention to it. Her touch reminded me that it was.

"Please don't smoke in the house, Jay. And her clothes are just fine. There ain't no holes in 'em or nothing. They got more than I did growing up. More than you did too." Daddy closed the door, finally speaking up. His voice was low, not mad this time, but more defeated.

"Whatever. You and my sister was always picky. Where's the boy?" She moved her purse off the bend of her elbow and held it in her hand, searching for a place to put it down. I glanced over at Little Man. He was still lying in one place with his eyes closed a little too tightly.

"He's on the couch. He's fine, you know, you didn't have to come. I just needed to tell somebody. You know how I feel about hospitals." Daddy ran his hand over the top of his hair. He told us before how he hated hospitals since Momma died. That was the only hint he gave of emotion when he cried back then. Sometimes I thought he didn't feel anything or didn't care. But deep down, I knew that wasn't true. I could see in his eyes that he did. I wasn't always sure he cared about us, but he must have in some way or he would have sent us away already.

"I know I didn't have to come, I wanted to. I haven't seen my sister's children in a long while anyway. Besides, I wanted to try and talk some sense into you. And I knew you were desperate if you even called me to say anything about it. It ain't like I hear from you every day." She brushed off her sleeve and opened her purse, moving closer to Little Man. She dug down into it on the couch as she spoke.

"You really ought to consider sending them South to live, you know, or letting someone else raise them. Humph! You ain't doing it, not really, are you?" Auntie Jay removed a cigarette holder from her purse. It was metal, and she used it to snuff the fire from the end of the still lit cigarette.

"I didn't ask you." Daddy leaned on the door, making me feel like he was ready to open it at any minute. "What do you mean? I am doing what I am supposed to do. They have clean clothes, a roof over their heads and they have food and someone to look after them, don't they? Isn't that a father's job?"

I moved to the staircase and found my favorite spot on the bottom step, peering through the railing. I felt like I should be on guard, like I should step back and watch like I watched the rest of my life.

Auntie Jay ignored him as she put her half-smoked cigarette in the case.

"I didn't say you wasn't doing your best, what you know how to do. But you know I gotta tell you how I feel. But what if your best ain't *the* best? Did you ever think of that? These kids don't need a whole lot, but they need your love. Are you giving them that?" She raised her drawn-on eyebrows. "Frankly, I would prefer you send them somewhere else and not to my mother. She don't need to be reminded about Elva, anyway, God rest her soul." Auntie Jay crossed herself. "And that girl looks just like her momma to me. But be reasonable, you a young man, give yourself a break. You don't need to be reminded either, none of us do. How you supposed to go on with your life, to date? How is the hole in your heart supposed to heal? Ain't nothing gonna change, for them or for you, if you don't get yourself right. You know that, don't you?" She let out a half-laugh and waved her hand in a small semi-circle. "At least that would be better than letting that stranger around the corner raise them, don't you think? That is one *strange* woman."

I sucked in my breath. After all the years we'd been going to Granny Hambay-el's house, I would hardly call her a stranger. Is that what Daddy thought? Were we a burden to him? My stomach felt sick. I was hearing too much, finding out information that I thought about but did not really want to know.

Daddy opened the door.

"Jay, you can leave. These are my children. Elva is gone now, so I got to give what I got. What I can give. I can only be a father, not both. I can't do more than that." Daddy's voice was louder than I had ever heard it, I expected him to start swearing at any moment. "And I am not sending them anywhere, you hear? You are an evil, meddling woman, and it is really not your business. They are all I have too. They need to be near me. No wonder they run you out of Muscoda!"

"Didn't nobody run me nowhere! You need to get smart and do the right thing. That boy killed my sister!" She pointed her long thin finger in Little Man's direction. "If it weren't for him, she would still be here. You know it, and I do too. She chose him over that stuff that could have saved her life, and you let her do it. He should be grateful he even walks the earth, 'cause if it had been my choice he wouldn't be here." Jay reopened her cigarette holder and removed a cigarette defiantly.

"But it wasn't your choice, now was it? You didn't know nothing 'bout Elva. She was more loving than you ever could be."

"How you gone tell me I don't know my own sister? How does that sound?" She sucked her teeth. "They keep getting in trouble anyway." She paused. Daddy's mouth dropped open as his eyebrows raised. A deep vertical furrow returned to his forehead, making it look like his head might divide in two.

"You think I don't know? I talk to that woman, she tells me!" She snapped the cigarette holder shut and moved to the door, switching almost wildly with every step.

"It's time for you to go, Jay. Now. Before I forget that I am a gentleman. Get the hell outta my house and go back to where you came from!" Daddy was straining to keep his cool. I jumped at his harsh-sounding words.

Jay stood at the door and took a last look around. "And you need to get somebody to clean up or I'll call child welfare on you, I swear it."

I was afraid to move from where I sat. I couldn't see her leave, but I heard Daddy slam the door so hard that the house shook, echoing his anger. I peeped through the banister, glancing over at Little Man. He sat up on his elbows. He was not asleep as I thought him to be. He was just pretending when Auntie Jay looked down at him. I would have pretended too.

Daddy headed back for the living room and Little Man plopped back onto the couch, acting like he was asleep again. Daddy paused in the doorway. His chest was heaving. I didn't remember him ever being that angry. He never lost his cool.

"Sweetie, come here." Daddy moved over to the overstuffed chair that sat beside the sofa. It had been around a long time, longer than any other piece of furniture. This was the same chair that Daddy used to sit in when I was very little, reading the paper. I would crawl up in his lap and lie on his belly, sucking my thumb, waiting for him to get done.

I moved to the side of it. I wanted him to talk with me, explain what Auntie Jay had said about Little Man and Momma. I wanted him to give me a nicer explanation than what I already understood, or at least tell me that it wasn't true. He reached out and put his hand on the back of my neck.

"I have a surprise for you guys," he said. "Little Man, you can open your eyes now. I know you ain't sleep."

Little Man opened his eyes and sat up. He grinned. I held my breath, waiting. I wanted him to tell us that we didn't have to go back to see Granny Hambay-el anymore. I wanted him to tell us our punishment was over.

"I am sending you down South. To see your grandmother." His eyes searched my face.

I gulped. He was sending us away, just like he did to June-Bug, even though he told Auntie Jay he wouldn't. He really didn't want us and this was the proof. It was Little Man who spoke first.

"For how long? You sending us away?" I expected him to cry but he didn't. He asked what I was thinking.

"No, I ain't sending you away. Didn't you hear me tell Jay you were mine? You two don't need to listen to the foolishness that woman says. I am sending you to visit, for the summer."

"To spend time?" I smiled too and a wave of relief swept over me. I could get to see June-Bug. I could get to see Gramma.

"To spend time. You haven't been since your Momma passed. It's time you go. You need to know who your people are."

"When?"

"As soon as school ends."

For the first time that I could remember, Daddy hugged me. I drank in his smell, burying my face in his soft tummy. My body sank into his like he was a glass of water and it was very, very thirsty. I knew then that he didn't hate us or not love us anymore. He was just as stranded as we were.

TWENTY-SIX

I sat straight up in bed. The absence of the usual morning noise was so loud that it woke me up. There was no talk radio blaring, no yelling voices. Granny Hambay-el didn't say anything at all to us or even yell at Little Man for wetting the bed. She didn't even suck her teeth, not one time. I took her silence to mean that she disapproved of us leaving, our sentence ending so soon. If it were up to her, she would keep us locked up from the world forever, in our own special type of purgatory.

After breakfast, we sat and waited by the door, our bags packed. Daddy was coming to get us to take us to the airport. The front room was as silent as the rest of the morning, the only sound was the plastic slipcovers protesting when Granny shifted her weight. The only one that dared to speak to us was Elizabeth, on her way out the door.

"Sweetie, you look for anything new for me. Any different plants." She waved her hand in the air nervously. She looked a little sad, but I couldn't imagine that she actually would miss me. We would be gone the whole summer, for two months. I nodded and looked down at my shoes.

"You remember how to put them in baggies, right? So they won't break up, right?" She straightened her perfectly fitting jacket, fingering the edges that she was so proud to have sewn herself.

I nodded again. I could see Granny Hambay-el roll her eyes. I didn't know what she wanted me to say. Elizabeth shifted from foot to foot awkwardly, then walked out the door.

We were going to fly to Gramma's house. There would be no bus this time. And by ourselves. Daddy finally arrived and we sat in the car with Daddy lecturing us, giving us a whole list of dos and don'ts for the airplane. Little Man grinned so hard that his face looked like it was going to hurt any minute. Daddy talked to us like we were real little kids, telling us that we should be polite on the airplane and remember to say please and thank you. We shouldn't talk to strangers. He was more nervous than we were. I stared out the window, but this time it was a happy stare, interrupted only by the occasional jittery flip that my stomach seemed to take. I was going to get away from Granny.

At the airport, we got big old name tags that we were supposed to wear around our necks the whole way. I started to grumble about not being a kid but changed my mind. I was going to be eleven in the fall.

We were going to have all summer at Gramma's. It was all going to be okay. We would be almost like normal kids for a change. All of the normal things I would do kept running through my head, things that I didn't get to do at Granny Hambay-el's house.

We finally arrived, and I looked for June-Bug at the airport. He wasn't there. People rushed past us and I felt my heart sinking to my feet, and then I saw my Gramma. I peeked around the stewardess and she was standing right outside the door. Her brown skin, still wrinkle free, glistened from the remains of morning oil. I smiled, remembering the way she slathered it on daily. It wasn't "store-bought" stuff, as she called it, but homemade gold that Gramma fashioned from natural things that grew on her property.

I wrestled free of the stewardess's hand and ran to greet her, Little Man right behind me. We ran into her open arms.

"You gon' knock your old Gramma over. Let me look at you," she said, stumbling backward from the weight of us hitting her. We released her and stood back so she could get a good look. I twirled around so she could see all of me. I had grown up a lot since that last time she saw me, in a lot of ways.

"My, my," was all she could say. I could see her eyes begin to look watery as we made our way out of the airport. I looked at her tears and wondered if she were crying because she was glad to see us, or if she was crying for us.

◦◦◦

Things were different the very first morning we woke up in Muscoda, I noticed it right away. Smells from Gramma's kitchen massaged my nose, bringing me close to waking up, but not quite. I thought it was a dream and I wanted to hold onto the aroma of fried steak and eggs with buttery rice as long as I could. It was like I was really little again, when I would close my eyes and try to imagine the doll I saw on television into existence.

Gramma sat right on the edge of the bed, and although my eyes were still shut, I could feel all of her there. For a minute her smell reminded me of Momma's smell all mixed up with the smell of camphor and cooking.

She put her face close to mine and whispered in my ear.

"Wakey, wakey," she said, just like Momma used to. Her silver hair was braided and pinned back tightly. I inhaled and took in the smell of Dixie Peach. I almost forgot what it smelled like; Afro Sheen had replaced Dixie Peach back home.

I smiled.

"You better get on up from there, gal, before you sleep the day away. It is almost seven o'clock."

I opened my eyes, glad to be up. I inhaled, taking in the breakfast smells. I didn't smell farina, like back home, and I didn't hear no talk radio.

I bounced out of bed, making a beeline for the kitchen. Little Man had beat me awake. He was sitting right at the table, already eating his breakfast of scrambled eggs, grits and bacon. My mouth watered, the grits still had a puddle of melted butter right in the middle.

There was an empty plate waiting right beside where he was sitting.

"That for me, Gramma?" My eyes widened at the thought.

"Sure is. You just got to tell me what you want in it." She was already moving over to the stove, smiling all the way.

For a minute I flashed back to Granny Hambay-el's house. I actually had a choice for breakfast. I wanted everything, except the bacon. I knew that that was bacon from Gramma's own hogs and I couldn't imagine eating anything that I might have known before.

"No bacon?" she asked.

"No, ma'am. I can't eat anything I might have looked in the eye."

Gramma held her sides, laughing. "I don't know what they teach you folks up North." She reached over to the stove and dipped a ladle into the can of grease on the stove, putting it into her waiting cast iron skillet. The sound of the grease hissing as it heated was music to my ears, unlike any I had heard in a while. I felt a little sad, realizing that I used to hear music all the time, even when there was none. That rarely happened anymore.

Gramma fried my eggs and then filled up my plate with everything except bacon, just like I asked.

"Sweetie, you eat up, now. Then go get dressed. Folks be coming by here directly." She wiped her wet hands on her clean apron and reached into the pocket for her handkerchief. No tissues for my Gramma, she still used old-fashioned handkerchiefs, sewn by her own sister, that she washed and starched every week.

We ate ourselves into a new sleepiness. Gramma stood around and watched us, smiling.

"You kids act like you ain't never seen no food before," she said. She picked up her cast iron skillet to move it to the sink.

Little Man and I looked at each other, then back down at our food. I couldn't remember the last time I had an egg fried just right. We had not been here twenty-four hours, and I wanted summer to last forever.

There was still no sight of June-Bug. I couldn't help it anymore, I finally asked Gramma where he was.

"Well," she spit her snuff in the old coffee can she carried with her. The brownish-blackish wad that came out of her mouth hit the bottom of the can with a thud. My stomach felt queasy. "He done got himself in a little trouble." She paused.

Little Man and I looked at each other and he raised his eyebrows. For a minute I could see Daddy in his face.

"He and his girlfriend had a little disagreement, and your brother got to spend a few weekends in the county. I don't know why he picked this weekend, but it was already done before we knew you were coming. He will be out Monday though." Gramma grabbed her metal cane and walked toward the front door. "I told him I would take you to see him. Maybe it will make him feel better, act right. He just ain't been right since the good Lord called your momma home. That boy been mad at the world. Can't blame him though. I been a little mad myself."

I looked at the floor. I generally did not speak of Momma out loud and I felt like Gramma had disturbed something by talking about it. I felt as if I could no longer imagine that she had just taken a long trip and would be back any day now. And I couldn't believe that June-Bug had gotten into any kind of trouble. He must have hit her. On TV, that was usually why men got in jail when it came to their girlfriends. My mind raced, I couldn't believe that either. He never would hurt even a fly. When he lived with us, he would take the cheese off the traps that Daddy set for the field mice so they wouldn't get hurt.

Gramma stopped and turned back toward me. She reached down and took my chin between her fingers. "It ain't your fault, baby. Sometimes people make choices that make no sense to anyone but them. And he won't be there long. I promised him I would bring you to see him, first thing as soon as you got here. Would you like that?"

"Yes, ma'am." I nodded. Gramma released my face and we followed her.

"I figured you would." She removed her apron, folding it on the way to the door the same way it had been folded for years. I touched it as I passed where she placed it on the edge of the sofa.

Gramma smiled. "Your Great Auntie Ella Mae made that apron for me. From old linen sacks she got from the white folks she used to work for. Years ago."

I didn't answer. I knew the apron was special. Gramma's sister made her sheets that way too.

"We know how to recycle everything down here in Muscoda. Not like them northern folks. We even recycled this here land. Used to be sharecropper land. And before that, part of a plantation."

I felt as if she were letting me in on some kind of secret, but I knew that there were lots of things Gramma could tell me, and we had to go. There would be time enough for that later.

The county jail was but a minute away. The southern dust swirled around my legs even downtown where things were paved. The hot Alabama sun brought beads of sweat to Gramma's nose and forehead more than once, but that did not deter her as we walked the few blocks to the jail. Every time the beads of sweat appeared in her forehead, she would stop a minute, reach down in to her bosom and produce a white linen handkerchief. She patted, not rubbed, the sweat away and then stuck the hankie back down where it came from, leaving the smell of moth balls lingering in the air. I watched her and wondered if we had other lives the way my Great Auntie's linen did.

Her metal cane made a steady thump-click sound with every step. She still walked faster than we did and we had to almost run to keep up.

Gramma had a cane for as long as I remember. Last time we came to Muscoda I ran my fingers down the whole length of the very one she was using now, memorizing the dents and the scrapes in the metal. She needed a cane because of her stroke. She had her stroke a long time ago, before I could remember.

Daddy said that every dent in that cane had a story behind it. Her stroke didn't stop Gramma from being a hell raiser. Daddy loved to tell us how she chased some man and beat him with her cane when he messed with her daughters. And from what I could tell, seemed like Auntie Jay was the one always in trouble. Someone was always trying to beat her for messing in other people's business. But I guess that didn't stop her from doing it.

The jail was no more than a room inside a square gray building that seemed to rise up out of the dust. It was right in the center of town. We didn't walk up to the front or in any doors, instead we walked past it, right behind Gramma around to the back. She stopped opposite the only window on that side, a window with bars in it.

"Now, you go on up and call him and he will look out," she said. "And here, give him this." She handed Little Man a brown paper bag. She wiped her forehead with her handkerchief again, and then she stuffed it down inside her bra.

It took June-Bug no time to come to the window. He peered through the bars. All I could see was his face from the middle of his nose to the top of his head.

His was still wearing his afro but it was almost flat, it laid down, almost like it was parted on the side.

"Hey, Sweetie. Little Man. Your old daddy let you guys come South, I see. He must be getting mellow in his old age."

I couldn't answer him. I could feel myself getting angry. My face got hot.

"You are getting so big. I guess I am missing it, huh?"

Little Man fidgeted. He played with the bag that surrounded the bottle that he held in his hands, making a scratching sound.

"Oh," June-Bug said. "You got something for me, huh? Gramma give you that?"

I didn't answer. I folded my arms in front of me. Little Man nodded.

"Just hand it up and I will be able to get it." He stuck his fingertips through the bars.

Little Man handed the bottle up. It was thin, and it fit right through the bars. I expected someone to come running and yell at us to get away from the window any minute.

June-Bug unwrapped it. The bottle was an old alcohol bottle, refilled with Gramma's brew.

"Grandma's finest," he said. "This will get me through the weekend." He kissed the bottle.

My stomach churned. I thought I'd be glad to see him, but I wasn't. Instead, I remembered that he left us.

"Sweetie, you haven't said a word. How you been?" June-Bug smiled, showing me his teeth. The two in the front were discolored, like he hadn't brushed his teeth in a while.

I sniffed. I wanted to punish him. I felt like he should wonder like I wondered about him every day. *If you really wanted to know you would write or call.*

"Everything, okay?"

We eat and have somewhere to sleep. I guess you could call that okay.

"You know you look just like Momma. More and more every day." He smiled at me. He was missing two teeth on the top. My eyes stung.

"Don't be mad at me, girl. I couldn't stay there with you. I wasn't wanted. Muscoda is my home. People love me here."

We loved you.

"I will be out before you know it and we can hang out, like old times. Don't worry about me. This here will get me through." He raised the bottle we had stuck through the window.

I shrugged and turned away from the window. Gramma was standing on the other side of the road, wiping her forehead. I walked toward her, leaving Little Man by the side of the jailhouse. I swallowed. My throat felt dry and I was reminded once again of the lump that grew in my throat after Momma died, my lump of tears that got stuck there. I had lived with it for so long that I almost didn't feel it now, only if I thought of it. It seemed to grow bigger and I was suddenly thirsty.

I reached Gramma and stood as close to her as I could, willing her skirt to wrap itself around me and hide me.

She rubbed my shoulder. "Ain't no use fretting about things you can't change, baby. He chose his life, like most of us do. He loves you like crazy, he is just hurting inside."

I moved my face from Gramma's skirt. My nose was drinking in her smell. The mixture of camphor and black ointment and steak and eggs was comforting to me.

"Daddy says that everybody hurts about something."

"That is true, but that boy has more than his share. First, Uncle Sam made him a hero without a job. And then your momma and that girl he hangs out with. That is just too much. He don't need no bars to be in prison. He is in prison all the time. He carries it with him."

I blinked. Little Man was done. June-Bug waved through the bars. I waved back. I wondered if his prison felt like mine.

TWENTY-SEVEN

I didn't count on making any friends. I didn't know how it happened. I let down my guard for one minute, and it happened to be the minute that September came to Gramma's house with her dad to buy some brew.

Gramma sold her brew by the glass, and it was famous for miles around. When I asked her what was in it, she just smiled at me and shrugged her shoulders.

"You know, my momma told me, and I am sure that her momma told her. It ain't time for you to know yet, Sweetie. It's a family secret." She stopped in the middle of her sentence and reached for her spit can. She swished her snuff around in her mouth and then spit a big, thick wad of it into the can with Robin Hood-like accuracy. Then she changed the subject. "Think it looks like rain, Sweetie?" She went right back to stirring.

I knew my Gramma well enough to know when to pry and when not to. She started humming and that was that.

Gramma didn't seem to tell anybody when a new batch was made, but folks would just know somehow and come. They would line up outside the door and stand around and stay till real late in the morning. Gramma set up hours for them to come by or I believe they would've come all hours of the day and night, even on Sunday. Ten in the morning until two in the afternoon, and then six until eight. The hours were posted nowhere but everybody knew them. No exceptions. Little Man and I made up a song, "Ten to two, come get brew."

Most of them that came were men, and most came alone, looking all sad and stuff when they arrived, Mason jar in hand. Everyone brought their own glasses, and the Mason jar seemed to be the glass of choice. Gramma charged them by the size of their glass, either one or two dollars. That seemed to be a lot of money for something they drank so fast. Many of them would get three or four refills by the time they left. Their bellies would be full of Gramma's brew, and they would be as happy as they could be until the next batch, laughing and joking with one another like they were the best of friends. The room would be full of smoke from all sorts of tobacco, cigarettes they rolled themselves and musty-smelling cigars. When they had enough brew, they bought other things, tomatoes from the garden, cucumbers, corn, and on slaughter days, they bought every part of the pig that Gramma would sell.

Gramma would usually send me somewhere on brew days.

"A young girl as pretty as you are shouldn't be hanging around no men. You git now." She would swat at me with a dishtowel or whatever she had in her hand.

I asked her why the first time. "What's wrong with men folk?" I smiled, hands on my hips. Gramma always laughed when I mimicked her.

"Don't you stand there sassing me, girl. You just git to going. The North is supposed to be better but they ain't teaching young girls the basic knowledge. The basic stuff. The things that get you through."

My smile disappeared. She was not amused by my antics.

"Men folk can't help themselves. Most of 'em can't keep their hands off of girls. It's like bees and honey." Gramma grabbed a broom and started sweeping dust that wasn't there. She looked down at the floor, almost like she was avoiding my eyes. "You just remember that, Sweetie. Times are different now, not like when I was young. A young girl has a say about her body nowadays. Don't let none of them touch you. And if any of 'em do try, you just holler as loud as you can. You understand me? You are yours and nobody else's, you hear?"

She raised her eyes, her gaze meeting mine. I looked away this time. I nodded, not wanting to ask any more questions. Gramma was more serious than I had seen her since we arrived.

I started to leave before she told me to, but I had a slow start this one day. A new batch of brew was waiting. Gramma let in the usual four people at a time, and on this day, four was five because September walked right in with her daddy.

She was the skinniest girl I ever saw, so skinny that her daddy's leg almost hid her entirely. Her knees were knobby, sticking out in front of her leg more like a sore or something than a joint. I thought I had become skinny while Granny Hambay-el was busy "cleaning" me out, but September made me look like I needed to go on a diet.

She also had the biggest eyes I ever saw. She peeked around her daddy's leg, and it was like the sun suddenly came up in the dimly lit room. At first I didn't even know she was talking to me, I had become so used to being ignored by other kids my age, or at least ignoring them.

"Hey!" She drew out the word with a sing-songy voice until it was three syllables, in the way they do in Muscoda. I always thought extra long when I heard it, whenever I said hey, Daddy always said, "Hay is for horses." I looked around, just to make sure. She said it again.

"Hey!"

I realized that she meant me, and I felt suddenly defensive, like I ought to get ready for some smart remark like I did at school.

"Excuse me?" I said.

September stepped around from behind her father. He was busy having a conversation with one of the other men.

"Hey, like hello. Don't y'all speak where you come from?" She put one hand where her hip might have been if she had any.

"My name Septemba," she said. "But everybody call me 'Tem-bo. You can too. You Miss Nell's granddaughter, right?"

I nodded. I was so used to being avoided or teased that I did not know how to react. I also knew she knew who I was, everyone did. Everywhere I went someone was identifying me as "Nell's grandbaby" Or "Elva's girl." Usually they would say how much I looked like Momma, too, and then click their teeth or something afterward. Tembo did neither.

"You don't talk much, huh? I got a sister that looks like you. She got them funny eyes you got too. You wanna go outside?" Tembo ran everything all together, like she forgot that sentences ended in punctuation, or like she was just opening her mouth and the words were running out by themselves. I didn't even mind that she called my eyes "funny." I never thought that much about them before, maybe because back home there were lots of people whose eyes were gray or hazel or green. Daddy said that something funny must happen when Indians mixed with Black people and sometimes the eyes just come out that way.

I looked around the room. Little Man was nowhere to be seen and Gramma was busy conducting her brew business. I nodded again.

Tembo took my hand, and I almost drew it back surprised. She tugged harder and we headed for the door. The whole time, she never stopped talking. I listened to her as best I could, trying to catch all the words that flowed from her mouth. Her accent made them seem full of rhythm and it took a minute after she said stuff for me to get it all.

The old wooden door slammed shut behind us and we sat on the back steps. Tembo talked nonstop for about fifteen minutes, telling me about her school, her sisters, her mother, just about everything. I acted like I was looking down, but I was studying her clothes, her hair, even the way she spoke. Granny Hambay-el often talked about "American children" like they had some kind of plague. I knew this was silly, but I found myself avoiding other kids, whether they made fun of me or not. Tembo looked pretty normal to me, right down to her dusty and knobby knees that were sticking out below the well-washed shorts that she wore. She was different.

I learned all about her and her family, her five sisters, and her mother that was a nurse, just like Momma had been. The sister she said looked like me, looked different than her other sisters. Tembo described her as having red hair that even Dixie Peach couldn't press and funny, funny eyes. She stopped talking so abruptly that I almost missed it.

"So, who takes care of you?" The pause in her non-stop speech was almost loud. "My daddy told me about your Momma, so who takes care you and your brother? Who mends your clothes and stuff like that? Your Gramma lives here with us and daddies got to go to work, right?"

I hesitated. People back home asked me this same question over and over again. Most times I would just tell them that Granny did, to avoid problems later, to avoid the teasing or the comments.

"We have a granny." I almost whispered, shifting my seat on the steps.

"You mean like your daddy's mother?" she asked. Her eyes seemed to stretch open wider.

"No, she isn't really related at all. I guess she is just a babysitter. My Momma picked her before she died."

Tembo paused and squished an ant that happened along in front of us. "That's amazing. Like someone giving all their stuff away before they die because they don't want to do it after. I saw that on TV once. Well, you don't look like no baby to me. My daddy told me that your momma had cancer. That is some serious stuff," she said. And her talking started up again just as suddenly as it had paused, and she was telling me about her school, just like that. Tembo didn't cringe or run away, or make fun. She didn't even ask me a whole lot of questions or cluck her teeth or say so much as one "I'm so sorry."

Tembo and me were friends after that, all summer, stuck together like glue. We understood each other. Sometimes we let Little Man hang around with us, and sometimes we didn't. Sometimes we did nothing, but sometimes we climbed trees or teased the chickens. She helped me pick my tomatoes and okra sometimes, and sometimes I would go to her house. Tembo liked to make believe she was a witch a lot, and we would make our own brew, except ours put spells on people instead of making them drunk.

Tembo and her mother lived behind Gramma, through the field and across the alley, but her mother worked all the time so she didn't grow anything on their property. I really didn't remember ever playing outside before I came to Muscoda, but I did with Tembo, every day all day, until Gramma made me come inside. I never missed the games of tag and hide-and-go-seek that the kids at school would not include me in, Tembo and I played much better games. Sometimes in our tag and hide-and-go-seek we included blocks and blocks and even the supermarket down the road. And her house was the most fun; they had music there all of the time, just like we used to before. Sometimes we would act like the singers in the music and make believe we were singing the songs. We would dress up and sing *"Then Came You"* like Dionne Warwick or *"When will I see you again"* like The Three Degrees. My favorite was when we would be the Supremes because her sister would play with us, even though she was too old to play dress up. We would let her be Diana Ross, except she wouldn't pretend she was singing but would sing for real over the top of the music. Her voice was so pretty I would get goose bumps every time she sang. You couldn't help but hold your breath when she opened her mouth. That girl could make plain old "Happy Birthday" a musical event.

I knew that back at home we would never be allowed to wander all over like Tembo and I did, but in Muscoda it didn't seem to matter. Tembo knew who everyone was, and the folks that she didn't know sure seemed to know us. Instead of nosy neighbors it felt like we had a thousand Grammas all looking out for everybody. We couldn't get in no kinda trouble without anyone knowing about it. It wasn't like back home, where people would just walk by and try to act like they didn't see you, even if you were standing on the corner crying. Everyone spoke to everyone else, even if they were just passing across the street.

Gramma never had to send me anywhere else during the brew days, I went before she asked.

We played our made up games every day. This day was beautiful. My back was prickly from the heat well before lunchtime and sweat ran down it and made me feel like little bugs were in my shirt, but I didn't stop playing. There was not a cloud in the sky, but I knew that could change faster than you could say "cornbread and buttermilk." I had learned that the sky in Muscoda was unpredictable, not to be trusted, and it could erupt into an Alabama shower at any minute, maybe even raining on one side of the street but not the other. Tembo told me that happened because the devil was beating his wife, and her face was so straight when she told me that I didn't even question her. I made Little Man "it."

He had not played with us in a long time. He'd just spent a few days being really sick; he'd snuck into the refrigerator like we did at Granny Hambay-el's house and ate Ex-Lax, which he thought was chocolate. I know he was a little mad at me for laughing, but I couldn't help it. The way he keep running out to the outhouse tickled me, and we never did tell anyone about the food at the sitter's. Old habits were hard to break, but he didn't have to sneak food at Gramma's, she let us eat anything we wanted and nothing we didn't. Gramma stroked his head and told him that if he was hungry, all he had to do was ask, but he couldn't seem to do it.

We made up a special combination of hide-and-go-seek and cops and robbers just for him. We had our own rules and they changed whenever we felt like it, usually when we were about to lose. Little Man started counting and I started to do my bathroom dance back and forth. We took off running before he got to two.

"I gotta go pee, Tembo." I whispered so Little Man couldn't tell which direction we were going to go.

"If you go to the outhouse now, he will find us right away. I know where you can go that will give us a minute." Tembo's little legs carried her faster than anyone I knew. She motioned to me to keep following her. I was struggling to keep up, and having to go to the bathroom didn't help, but I was not too eager to go into the outhouse anyway. It smelled in there, and it was a good distance from the house, back through the corn. It seemed like every time I had to go, there would be a snake in my way, blocking my path. Gramma was on the waiting list for a septic tank, but from what I heard folks saying, it would be a good two years before they got out to her place.

Tembo headed toward the supermarket, and I followed, not wanting to be "it" early. I was glad to follow her, they even had air conditioning in their bathroom. The supermarket was about a quarter mile away, and I looked out over the almost open field. Sweat from the Alabama heat was making my shirt stick to my back. I licked my lips as I looked at the suddenly overcast sky, hoping for rain to cool me down. We were used to the rain, it seemed like it rained every day of August at the same time. The sky would just open up and buckets of water would fall out, then stop.

The field had one lopsided shack in the middle that was all that was left of what used to be a house. The house burned to the ground mysteriously, leaving only the outhouse standing. Thick bushes grew up around it here and there, and we cut around it on the road to get to the supermarket.

The icy cool greeted me and I felt my body relax, glad. This was the only store in town with air conditioning. Gramma certainly did not have any at her house. The only ones on the block who did were the neighbors three houses down.

Their house had a big old unit that sat on top of their roof, but they never invited anyone in. It was said they were rich, but folks never spoke of where their money came from. Everyone gossiped about them though, especially when they bought their sixteen-year-old daughter a car. She was the only teenager this side of the railroad tracks that owned a car. Many of the adults didn't even have one.

We slowed down our run inside the store, we didn't want anyone to stop us from running or send us home. Someone always seemed to be lurking around, eager to give us some kind of direction or stop us from doing something that seemed like fun.

"You can go to the bathroom in here," Tembo said. She panted, trying to bring her breathing back to normal. "Little Man ain't gonna look for us in the store." Sweat was rolling down Tembo's face and she used the back of her hand to wipe it away.

"How do you know that they will let me go?" I resumed my bathroom dance. I shifted my weight back and forth from foot to foot.

"They will. And if they don't you ain't lost nothing. My momma used to clean for Mr. Frank, before she was a nurse aide. He knows me. When he started out, he had just a small store, now he has three." Mr. Frank's store was just a small store last time I was in Muscoda, so small I couldn't even remember it. Gramma said that he waited around for folks to die so he could buy their land and pave over where they had farmed for generations before. He was building lots of stores, all over Muscoda. She didn't like them, they were big and fancy and no one in them knew your name, not like it used to be. Gramma didn't want Muscoda to change at all. If she wanted change, she would say, she would move to Birmingham.

Tembo always seemed to know what she was doing, and when she didn't, she made believe. She did not believe in hesitating in asking for anything, and most of the time she got what she wanted. I followed her to the back of the store, where she knocked on a gray door that had a small window in it. A wiry white man appeared, bald on top of his head, with thin tufts of hair on the side. He was wearing a red apron that was spotted with dirt that I suspected was blood from meat he had cut up. He smiled at Tembo.

"Well, September Jackson," he said, "you are growing up to be one fine young lady. How's your momma doing?" He rubbed his hands on his apron and grinned at Tembo like she was a steak, showing every yellow tooth in his head, from ear to ear. The two in front stuck out farther than the rest, making them seem larger than usual. He had a clipboard under his arm.

"She fine, Mr. Frank. Can we use your bathroom? We gotta go real bad." Tembo grinned back at him just as big. She showed all of the gap between her two front teeth.

"You know you can, little miss. Let your mama know that if she ever gets tired of that nursing she got a job with me, okay? I was just on my way out too, but you two can go on back."

"Yessir." Tembo grabbed my hand again and we made our way past Mr. Frank. I wondered what kind of job he could possibly have that would make Tembo's momma go from nursing back to cleaning, but I didn't ask. I had to go so bad, I couldn't stop to care.

We hurried up back out of the store. Little Man was sure to be heading down toward the grocery store by now. I tried to look for him, but I couldn't see a thing. When we went inside the store, the parking lot was empty, now there seemed to be a crowd of people milling around. We made our way through the crowd and decided to double back and go back the way we came. He would not think to look where we began.

Tembo reached out and grabbed my arm, hard, stopping me from going forward into the parking lot. I was surprised, and I looked over to find the closest thing to fear that Tembo was capable of reflected in her face. Her brown skin looked blanched.

"We need to go the other way," she said. "Run."

Her lips trembled as she spoke and I did not stop to ask why. I followed her, and we headed across the field that we had skirted earlier. Tembo went behind the outhouse, and crawled into a bush. I hesitated at first, but the way Tembo made her way into the bush told me that she was not just afraid of being caught by Little Man. This was not part of the game.

I stooped down, and my heel caught me right between the legs. I felt a sharp, shooting pain radiate throughout my groin area. Cockle burrs scratched my legs, my arms, even my face.

My eyes stung from the pain that was confusing me. Tembo kept whispering, "Oh, my God, my sweet Jesus," over and over. I was suddenly afraid as I listened to her. For Tembo, saying, "Oh my God" was the same as cussing; she even went to church on Wednesday nights in addition to Sundays.

We sat in the bushes for about ten minutes. The only sound I could hear was breathing mixed in with the din of the locusts. Sweat poured down my back and dripped between my legs; I fidgeted, feeling as if a thousand sticker bushes were prickling me. I would find my socks full of those sticker things tonight.

The bushes rustled and Tembo grabbed my arm, harder this time. The bush we were hiding under moved aside, and more heat and light streamed in. We jumped, and Tembo let out a low scream. We looked up into the eyes of Mr. Frank.

"I'm so glad I found you gals," he whispered. "I saw you leave but didn't know where you went." He looked over his shoulder nervously. "Them rider folk been hanging round here every day like that. It ain't safe here."

"Riders?" My face stung from where the bushes scratched it and sweat was dripping down into the wounds.

Tembo looked at me like I had been living under a rock. "Klan, guhl," she said. "KKK."

The only time I ever saw the members of the KKK was on television, and then they always had on white sheets. I wondered if he meant those folks gathered outside the store, they didn't have any sheets on them. And weren't they supposed to be on horses or something? Standing around in a field at night? I looked at them in disbelief, I don't think I really ever thought that the Klan was real at all, they lived inside the television like Scooby Doo and the monsters on the 4:30 movies.

"C'mon, let me take you two home." Mr. Frank motioned to us and we stood up to follow him. Mr. Frank and Tembo stood looking at me with their mouths open. I looked down to where their eyes were pointing. My sky-blue shorts were soaked in blood. Mr. Frank looked away, his face flushed with embarrassment.

My stomach caved in. Is this what it felt like? I suddenly remembered stopping down into the bushes, the pain shooting through my groin area. Was this what happened when you "become a woman" like Gramma said? Or had I hurt something? I wasn't sure, the only thing I knew about a girl getting her period was from the *True Love* magazines I read while hiding in the back of Gramma's closet and from "*Are you there God, It's me, Margaret.*"

Tembo's touch snapped me back. "C'mon, girl, we can go to my house." She was relaxed and seemed to be back to her normal self. "I can get you fixed up."

I nodded. Mr. Frank took off his apron and handed it to me. I took it gratefully and wrapped it around my waist.

Mr. Frank led us through the field past the leaning shack while Tembo and I held hands. I remembered her telling me that it was haunted and I felt my stomach rumble as we walked too close to it for comfort. We drew in our breath. In the short time since we passed the shack earlier, it had changed. The boards still looked like someone had nailed each and every one up by hand and it still leaned to the side at a peculiar angle, like it shouldn't even be standing at all. But it was different. White letters now ran around and around the shack. It was as if someone had gotten detention and used the shack as their chalkboard to write out their punishment one hundred times. I gasped as I read it; instead of saying, "I will be good in class," the shack carried a much more somber message. In red spray paint, someone wrote, "KKK still lives," over and over again.

The sight stopped us in our tracks. I could feel the sweat on Tembo's palm as she held my hand. My ears felt hot as they filled with every sound in the field. Every cricket, every locust, every rustle sounded like an irritating commotion as we stood stock still. Mr. Frank finally cleared his throat and shooed us on. My stomach ached and I was acutely aware of the hot wetness in my pants, but now I couldn't tell if the feeling was from the blood or if I had peed in my pants too. I pulled the apron tighter around my waist and my face flushed from the shame. I couldn't tell what I was more ashamed of, the mess below my waist or us walking through this field with this white man that reminded me of the scarecrow more than a little bit. I could not help but wonder if he wore a sheet at night like on TV, too.

We went to Tembo's house. She didn't live far from Gramma, just across the field in Possum Quarters. Muscoda was not a wealthy town. Some of the houses sat up on stilts and you could look right under them. Dust swirled around most of the houses when the wind blew; there were no fancy lawns to hold it down. It was a good thing it rained every day; rain was the only thing that gave a temporary reprieve from the dust. But once you crossed the alley into Possum Quarters, the houses were poorer and the dust seemed thicker.

Gramma called Possum Quarters the bottom of the bottom. It was small, no more than a dozen houses, but there was only one way in and one way out. I wasn't even sure that the road was paved or just packed down really hard.

Most of the folks that lived there did not have land to grow anything on or raise any animals like Gramma did. They made a living any way they could. At any time of day you could find adults milling around, waiting for work, waiting for a truck to pick them up to take them to work, or just waiting. The houses were more broken down-looking, but I knew a lot of those people. They all came to Gramma's for brew, sometimes spending their last dollar to get a drink of her magic potion.

Mr. Frank said his good-byes at the corner of the dead-end block. I wondered if he were afraid to go any farther. Possum Quarters had an unspoken rule that was almost never broken except by the tax man and the sheriff: No Whites Allowed. I could feel his eyes in my back watching us all the way to Tembo's front door. People milled around, a few called out to us as we walked by. "Haaaay, Tembo, girl," they said, voices sang out in the way they could only here. She nodded back in brief acknowledgment as we passed while I looked at my feet, counting the steps until we were inside. The shirt around my waist covered up the spot but nothing could hide my embarrassment. My yellow skin flushed red as I smelled the heat from my body.

The wooden front door to Tembo's house slammed behind us with a bang and I jumped, startled as a small splinter that broke free whizzed past my head.

It took my eyes a moment to adjust to the light. The inside of the house was much darker than the bright outdoors, and it smelled like no fresh air had been let into the house for days. Scratchy music played somewhere inside the house. I followed Tembo, squinting. It seemed as if one hundred people were in the room, but I knew it was only her brothers and sisters. She had six sisters, and four brothers. No one looked like anyone else and I never could tell who came first and who came second. I wasn't even sure if they were all really related or not or if they were folks that her momma took in because they had nowhere else to go.

The house only had a few rooms, just like my Gramma's house. Someone called to us, and Tembo answered in her usual Muscoda "Hey," but we didn't stop. We headed straight for the room that Tembo shared with four of her sisters.

The small room had two sets of bunk beds, one on each side, with a small brownish dresser in the middle. I could barely tell that the beds were made, each of the lower beds had piles of what I took to be laundry on top of them. The room smelled like Tembo, a smell that reminded me of Pumpkin Pie spice.

She opened a drawer while I looked around.

"Here," she said. Tembo threw a white pad in my direction. It looked like a narrow diaper. I bit my upper lip.

"You know what to do, right?"

My face burned hot again, and I knew she could see it. I nodded and tears stung my eyes. I swallowed them. How was I supposed to know? This seemed like something that mothers told daughters. No one had told me anything. Not really.

Tembo pulled new underwear from another drawer and some shorts that I knew were not hers. She was too skinny for me to fit her clothes. Gramma said she looked like a skeleton with skin stretched over it.

I examined the underwear as I took them gladly. She had given me the Sunday pair even though it wasn't. I never had underwear that was anything but white and on sale and I ran my hand over the frilly words.

"Go to the bathroom and fix yourself up." She pointed with the underwear and sat on the bed. I looked down at the floor.

Tembo jumped up and took the panties back from me. "You peel these things here," she pointed toward the pad, and then you stick it here, like this." She demonstrated.

I nodded and let out the breath I was holding. She handed me a plastic bag from Frank's store. "Put your shorts in there and you can take them home, okay?"

She was waiting on that same spot on the bed when I got back. Tembo immediately started to talk in her all-in-one-breath way. I anticipated her talking about what happened, but she didn't. She held a small purple book in her hand. She held it up.

"Do you have a diary? I do. I write letters to myself in it." Tembo opened her book and started to flip through it.

I almost gasped. I didn't know that anyone really kept a journal like Miss Faust suggested I do. Tembo's journal was smaller, and the cover wasn't as pretty as the ones Miss Faust had given me. I wondered if she wrote secrets in there, too, things she didn't want to tell anyone.

"I will probably write about those Klan people we saw today in here."

"How do you know they were Klan? They didn't have sheets on them or anything." I sat next to her on the bed.

"They don't always wear sheets around here, but they were Klan." She nodded her head up and down and twisted her mouth to the side. Tembo's legs didn't quite reach the floor. She clicked her heels together, bouncing them off each other. "It ain't the first time, you know. I got lotsa stories about them and their kind in here." She tapped on the cardboard cover of her diary.

I blinked. I didn't know.

"I know you a city girl, and you think it is so much better where you live, but my daddy says it's all the same, even up North. Y'all folks done ran up there, thinking things would be different, but the only thing that's different is we just know who they are down here, that's all. He said he told your Momma that when she left here, but she went anyway."

"Ain't you afraid? How often do you see them?"

Tembo opened the book and flipped a few pages. "A lot. Usually after something political happens. And no, I ain't afraid. They thought that we all would be afraid, after all that mess up in Birmingham with the riots and the marches and the bombs. I'm too young to 'member it all, but my daddy does. He says you can't let things make you afraid, you just gotta keep on going for what you know. Do you have a diary?" She grabbed a pen and made a short note.

I didn't tell her about the book that my teacher gave me. I hadn't written in it in a long time, especially not any secrets.

"You could write about your granny in it. I write down everything. It helps me sort things out sometimes. I make a note to myself whenever something klanny happens." She scribbled some more in purple ink, not even blinking at her "Tembo-ism." She didn't say but I knew exactly what she meant by the word klanny. "Klanny" things were hateful things. Granny Hambay-el was hateful to me and Little Man sometimes, but I didn't really think she meant it. It was the only way she knew how to be.

She closed her book. The purple fabric cover was worn and thin in places. I wanted to touch it. I envied her and that book. Tembo had someone to tell things to, even if it was only a book.

"You never ever talk about your granny. Why not? You live with her, right?" She turned to look at me. Her big eyes seemed wider than normal. She was full of questions that she could not wait to ask. I could not believe that my boring life was more interesting to her than our chance encounter with the Klan. I knew I must've been strange to her. I bet we were the only kids she knew that lived the way we did. She was certainly the only person I knew that was like her.

"Well, sort of. We stay there but I never thought of it as living. She's just different." The smell from the room tickled my nose and I rubbed it.

"Different than what?" All summer we let her talk about her life and her parents and her school, but I never told her much about me. I was so busy trying to live in the here and now, I didn't want to think about going back home. In Muscoda I could be like everybody else. I even wanted to run outside barefoot because the other kids did. It didn't matter to me that they did it because they didn't have any shoes. They had *lives* that they let me and Little Man fit into.

I sighed. "Well, she is old, and has really bow legs. She grows things in her yard like people do here, except not vegetables. Mostly plants and things like that. She makes tea out of a lot of it and she saves a lot of it. She even sells some to people. I think she would make tea out of anything if she could." I remembered her making tea from corn silk and things I couldn't name. I gulped. I also remembered the taste as I drank it.

Tembo stared at me like I was telling her a fairy tale. "For real? I don't know many people that drink tea. Everybody drinks coffee here. Or brew." She looked at the floor. I knew she meant her daddy. "Anything like what?"

I paused. I was not sure how much I wanted to tell Tembo. Up until now she treated me pretty much as just like her.

"Like anything. All kinds of things that grow in the ground. We were stuck there on punishment once and I helped to gather everything. She labels it all in plastic bags and then drinks what she needs depending on what she feels like that day."

Tembo threw back her head and laughed. Her braids danced around her face, the beads at the end clanked together and made little clicking sounds. "You lie, city girl. I imagine that some things wouldn't even taste good as teas. And she probably can't even tell the difference, not like you say. You make her sound like a witch or something, a root worker like that old crazy lady that lives up the way. How does she know which leaves are poisonous and which aren't? My momma says that a lot of things that grow around here every day will make you really sick if you ain't careful. People make themselves sick all the time by accident. Momma told me a story once about some girls that got real sick on account of them trying to roast marshmallows using sticks from an oleander bush. Another time they was playing tea party with shrub leaves and had to go to the hospital 'cause they couldn't stop vomiting." Tembo bounced her legs on the sideboard some more. "Can you imagine that? Just plain old shrub leaves."

I smiled, I couldn't help it, even though she called me a liar. Tembo was that kind of person, she would insult you and make you laugh in the same sentence.

"I think she knows which is which. They know a lot of things about plants and have books and more books about what cures what." I never thought of Granny Hambay-el as a witch before, but I knew that was what they would call her if she lived in Muscoda, probably a few other things too the way she talked about American children and things. The witch woman up the way probably wasn't no witch either, but folks did go to her for help when the doctor couldn't figure out what was wrong. She had funny ways, that one. I heard a few stories of people going to see her when their husband ran away too. Maybe Tembo was right. Perhaps Granny Hambay-el couldn't tell the difference. They all tasted terrible to me. I shrugged.

At that moment, Little Man came down the hallway and me and Tembo looked at each other like we had been caught red-handed doing something that we shouldn't. We had forgotten about our game.

"You cheat!" he said. He pointed in our direction. "You can't go in the house!" He stepped toward us.

Tembo smiled at him.

"Stop whining like a baby," she said, standing up. She put one hand on her hip and sort of jutted it out to the side. "Now I know why they call you Little Man."

"Did you see the Klan people?" I asked.

Little Man twisted his face as if he did not understand me, then he shook his head. It was probably best that he didn't. He probably wouldn't know what they were anyway.

"Tembo doesn't believe that Granny drinks teas made from everything." I rubbed my nose.

"She makes me drink them too. It's true. Most of them are real nasty and they have funny names like Billy web bark and horehound tea." Little Man stuck out his tongue and scraped it with his teeth like he was trying to remove the memory of a taste.

I remembered the home remedies all too well. A chill ran through me and I was suddenly cold in the August heat.

Up until the day we left, Granny Hambay-el was still trying to cure Little Man of his "problem." She had not made him sick again, though. Funny thing is, he had not wet the bed at all at Gramma's house. If he did, it was their secret and kept from me. I squinted at him just a little bit. I didn't recall him ever really having an emotion or showing that any of the things that went on at Granny's house affected him before. I tried to be silent through it all. I put myself outside my body and watched. Little Man just seemed to cry and take it, but I knew that our very life was eating away at his insides.

"I still don't believe you, but if I was you, I would be real careful about what I drank," Tembo said. She looked at me and Little Man sideways, from the corner of her eye. A strange little smile sat on her face. "I think you should give her some of her own medicine. Test her. See if she really *will* drink anything."

I gasped. Little Man moved closer to me. "I can't do that."

I never thought of disobeying Granny Hambay-el, and that was what we would be doing if I did what Tembo suggested. I never really thought of acting out at all. When we got in trouble before, it wasn't really because of what we had done, but because of what we had not done. The idea of switching tea was interesting for some reason. What would happen? I wondered. Would she be able to tell the difference? Would she say she felt better or would her legs suddenly be straight? Why was she drinking all that stuff anyway? But what would happen if we were caught made me afraid. The thought of it made my stomach jump.

"Yes you can, girl. My Daddy says you can do anything you want to. Just change a few leaves around." She waved her hand in the air. "And then write to me and tell me about it. I dare you." Tembo picked up her diary and put it in a drawer. When she opened it, I could see her pretty underwear peeking out. She told me it was all purple and I could see that it was true. My own plain white underwear was still hidden in the little bag she gave me. Remembering it made me flush and I squeezed my legs together. My private areas throbbed and I felt the pad between my legs. It felt more like a diaper than a barrier between me and further embarrassment.

Little Man hit me in the arm, grunting as his fist hit my shoulder. This was the hardest punch he had to offer but it barely stung me. He was letting me know how upset he was that we went inside without him. And I still hadn't told him about the Klan and the shack. The other stuff he didn't need to know.

"Let's go back out. It's safe now," Tembo said.

I rubbed my arm and we followed. I put the idea of the tea leaf switch to the back of my mind although I was curious. Safe was relative, I realized. We were supposed to be safe at Hambay-el's house but she was always giving us some thing or the other that might make us sick.

Little Man and I followed, looking around at her many family members as we passed through the dark house. I thought hard about what she said and was beginning to wonder if Granny really would drink anything. If she would, it would prove that she was really crazy. At least to Little Man and me. But we would not dare bother her tea, right? I didn't have time to wonder long, though. We were barely out in the sunshine again when a group of kids approached us. The muscles in my neck tightened. I felt a familiar rumbling in my stomach. I had trouble-sense and I could smell trouble coming, right from the middle of those kids. We hadn't even started home yet and Muscoda was starting to feel like we were home, back in Granny Hambay-el's house. First Tembo asked questions almost like the kids at school would, and now the kids approaching us reminded me of the mob scene that had become so familiar at school.

I had not noticed the kids at all when we came onto Tembo's street. My face felt warm. One girl seemed to be leading the group of kids, and she stopped in front of us. Little Man and I stood one step behind Tembo, on either side.

They stood in front of each other like a mirror, each with their hand on one hip. I recognized the girl as Angie, her father was the Muscoda sheriff. She didn't even live in Possum Quarters. They barely lived in Muscoda. Gramma said her house was as close to the other side of the tracks as they would ever be allowed to be.

Angie stared at me, challenge plastered across her face. I blinked but dared not look away. I knew that to seem weak was sudden death. I tried to hold my body as still as possible, to stop the shake I felt building inside.

Angie's hair was long and almost flat, but I knew that she did not spend Sunday afternoons under the straightening comb like the rest of us did. She tossed her head. It was well known that her mother was Indian, they told everyone about it, like Indian heritage was supposed to make her better than the rest of the kids in Muscoda. My daddy told me that we all had Indian in us somewhere and a lot of other things too. Her hair flowed over her shoulders and rearranged itself as she moved her head.

In the few seconds that we stood there, everything seemed to stand still, even the air.

"Hey, Tembo." Angie removed one hand from her hip and used it to smooth her hair. "We don't see you round much anymore. Where ya been?"

Tembo shrugged her shoulders. She shifted her weight to her other hip. "I been around," she said.

The group of kids chuckled.

"You been hanging out with your new friends, huh? We ain't good enough anymore?"

"I ain't never said that, Angie."

"How are things at home? Did your daddy get a job or is he drunk this month?" She rolled her eyes and looked back over her shoulder, and the kids behind her laughed again.

I looked into the face of one boy standing behind her on the right. He looked away.

"My momma says he spends most of the day drunk as a skunk. I know you been hanging out at that bootleg lady's house. You gonna be a drunk too?" Angie moved her head back and forth, her piercing voice turning into a battle cry.

Tembo was silent. I looked at her well-scrubbed face for a reaction. Her eyes were narrowing. I looked down and she was clenching her fists, opening and closing them again and again. She did that when she was angry, and I knew that any talk about her daddy was asking for trouble. An explosion was coming.

Little Man stood behind Tembo with his arms crossed in front of him. I looked around for a way out, but Angie and her friends blocked the exit from the dead-end street.

Angie caught the reaction on my face. "Oh, you got something to say, city girl? You think you bad just 'cause you from the city and you talk all proper? You ain't about nothing." She moved over and stood in front of me, re-assuming her hands on the hip pose. She let her eyes travel freely up and down my body, examining my clothes, my hair, my face. I felt naked. That was the second time today that I had been called "city-girl," but coming from Angie there was nothing amusing about it. The hostility poured through her gaze.

"You ain't gonna be nothing but an alkie anyway. That's what my momma says. Punishment for your grandma for doing what she does."

The sun hid behind a cloud and rain drizzled on the other side of the street. I had only seen that happen in Muscoda, I knew that it was doing the devil-rain this time not because the devil was beating his wife like Tembo said, but because Angie was being hateful for no reason. Anger welled up in my throat now too.

Little Man came around to the side of me. Angie saw him move over.

"And where you going, Little Man? Ain't that what they call you?" She put her other hand on her hip. "No wonder you ain't got no mama."

The group of kids gasped and grew silent. All whispering stopped and I drew in my breath. I knew I was outnumbered, but I raised my hand anyway. That was the last straw. If we were back home we would have been fighting already. I closed my eyes and threw a punch right at Angie's mouth.

I hit nothing. Before I could land on my target, Tembo pushed through Little Man and me, jumping through us like a lioness pouncing on her kill. She wrapped her slender arms and legs around Angie, pushing her backward. Angie fell onto her back with Tembo on top of her, a small cloud of dust rising from where they landed. The other kids started to yell and moved into a circle, closing around the two girls, now on the ground.

I looked over at Little Man. He was as surprised as I was. My face felt hot. The other kids were occupied, yelling and screaming around Tembo and Angie. They chanted, "Fight, fight fight," as Tembo and Angie grabbed and pulled each other. The clouds on the other side of the street grew closer. Tembo held her own, although Angie must have outweighed her by at least twenty pounds.

She had hold of Angie's hair in one hand, holding onto it so the girl could not move her head too far. She punched her anywhere she could reach with the other. Angie was using her hands to cover most of her face. She let out a howl and Tembo let her go. Both girls staggered to their feet.

Angie covered her mouth with her hand. Blood trickled through her fingers. Her hair, no longer smooth and shiny, was all curled up into a ball on one side. It looked like she had a fight with a hairbrush. Her shirt, once perfectly pressed, now had black smudges on the back and front. The front pocket was torn off and hung on by a few threads. Her shoes, white when we started out, were covered with red dust. Tembo had a small scratch on her face. Both girls labored as they struggled to catch their breath. Tembo's eyes shone with hatred and she suddenly smelled of sweat and dirt all mixed together. Her fists were still clenched, one with a few strands of Angie's precious Indian hair peeking out from between her knuckles.

Angie sobbed. She removed her hand, staring at the blood on it. She held one of her teeth in her hand.

The mob behind her was no longer a mob, just a bunch of kids with surprised looks on their faces. A few of them moved their mouths as if to say, "Ooo," but no sound came out.

"You are going to get it, September Jackson!" Angie spat her words at Tembo, and then a big wad of blood on the ground, right in front of me. She backed away from us, her crowd backing away behind her. "You think you are so bad. They ain't no better than us." She pointed at me and Little Man. They got to go back home sometimes! They didn't even help you, dummy!"

"I ain't need no help! You better get on home now before I give you some more!" Tembo raised her fist as if she might throw another punch. Angie jumped back.

I couldn't help it. A little smile escaped my lips.

"Let's go." Tembo was our leader now. She stood up for us when she didn't have to. She was no bigger than a kid two years younger than herself, and she stood up to the biggest bully in the neighborhood. We walked toward the field, back toward Gramma's house. She didn't even brush herself off.

"What made you-?" I had to ask her. I knew I would have avoided the situation if possible.

"Sometimes you can't get out of a situation, but you can try to control it," Tembo said. She brushed off her clothes. "You better learn that."

Little Man and I exchanged glances but didn't say anything. Both of Tembo's knees were skinned, and a little blood was rising to the surface. She didn't even flinch as she stopped to pick a few tiny pebbles out of the scrapes. I knew they hurt; the scrapes were centered right on the spot where the knee bends. It was going to be my turn to fix her up.

We headed for the alley. Tembo didn't even go back in the house to change her clothes. She looked scuffed up, not neat and pressed like she normally did. She was going to wear her battle scars like they were medals. I knew she would probably get in trouble for fighting and would have to sneak back into her house. She would probably have to write Bible verses over and over or something. Her mama didn't take no mess. Tembo didn't look like much, but she had some smarts that you couldn't learn in school.

There was no talking as we headed back across the field to Gramma's house. Tembo was the one to break the silence.

"Did you know that your momma used to be my daddy's girlfriend? That makes us almost sisters." She held her head up proudly and didn't look at me when she talked. "He told me he didn't want her to go to New York. He didn't want to be left here."

I shook my head. I didn't know. Tembo seemed to know more about my family than I did. Little Man walked a few steps ahead of us and we locked arms. I had a friend. I was sad about leaving when I got up this morning, but this new knowledge was like cement between us.

Twenty-Eight

We had two days left at Gramma's. The knowledge that we would be leaving soon weighed me down. The familiar dread of Granny Hambay-el's house seemed to be waiting for me in the shadows. My shoulders felt like someone was sitting on them and everything moved in slow motion again.

Today was a brew day. On these days Gramma usually sent us somewhere away from the house so we stayed away all day. She let us sleep late this morning, I was surprised not to be awakened for breakfast like she had every day since we had come to visit. I sniffed extra hard before I opened my eyes but I couldn't smell anything cooking. Mothballs and percolated coffee, hours old, were the only smells that greeted my nose when I opened my eyes. Even the crickets seemed more quiet than usual; their din was more noise than song again, like it had been when we first came to Muscoda this year.

I glanced over at the other bed in the small room. Little Man was still fast asleep. We both slept so soundly here. Our room was at the back of the small wooden house. We had to walk through Gramma's room to get out. The feather mattress cushioned us from any possible noise or disturbance, and the sounds of the Alabama cicada bugs served as our lullaby.

I shook him awake. He jumped first, like he was afraid, then rubbed his eyes, realizing where he was. I felt a pang of sadness, knowing that he still dreamt about being greeted by an angry belt first thing in the morning. I felt bad for waking him up so suddenly.

I went to the small dressing room to check my panties. The blood stopped in only one day. I put another sanitary napkin on just in case. Everything I remembered from the book I read said it was supposed to last longer than that. Maybe I was special and would be spared. Gramma told me it was the curse of all women. She would be surprised that it happened to me so early. She told me that I would be at least twelve. I was. I didn't even have any hair on my legs nor was I anywhere near needing a bra. All the girls I knew that got their period at least had a little hair on their legs. I sighed, realizing that all I got was embarrassed in a field.

Little Man was already dressed when I came out. It was his turn to empty the pee-pot. I knew he hated doing it, but he also knew that Gramma would get him if he didn't do it first thing. I laughed at him as he struggled with the pot with one hand and held his nose with the other. The liquid inside sloshed back and forth and made a tinny sound as he moved. It would be a long struggle; he had to carry it all the way out to the outhouse and dump it down the hole.

Grandma left a note. She had business to take care of in town and would see us later. I was curious. I wondered what the "business" was. Was she taking June-Bug another bottle of brew? I expected to see him soon, but we still hadn't. Gramma said he was still spending his weekends in jail.

This was the first time she left us alone in the house since we came. The kitchen didn't smell like anything had been cooked. That was fine with me, it meant I could have my favorite breakfast with no one to complain. I grabbed the day old corn bread from the stove and sat it on the table. I put some in a bowl for both me and Little Man, and poured buttermilk over it. It cascaded over the top like I imagined rain would run over rolling hills in the mountains, filling in the crevices between the bread. The smell of the cornbread and buttermilk pinched my nose. My love of fried eggs had become a distant memory, especially since Gramma made me go and get the eggs from the chicken coop every day. The chickens always squawked at me, making me feel like a thief that would eat their chicken babies.

Gramma came in before we were done. The front door banged open and she thump-clicked through. She didn't smile or look at us as she placed her cane in the corner. I caught a glimpse of her face and her mouth was drawn into a tight line almost like she had no lips. There was no smile for us this morning. She put her cane in its usual corner and reached for her spit can. She wound up her mouth in the way she did before she spit, and I closed my eyes. Gramma had been spitting in that can as long as I could remember but it still made my stomach feel queasy to watch it. The front door banged open just as Gramma's spit hit the can, drowning out the sound.

"Big Ma! How you doing, today?" My eyes flew open as Angie's father walked into the room. He was a big man, tall and wide, and he filled up the door as he passed through. His uniform was crisp, like it had just been pressed, and the smell of new starch tickled my nose. He took off his hat as soon as he entered and held it to his massive chest. I immediately looked at his hip; the largest ring of keys I had ever seen flanked his left side, and he had a gun as big as daddy's on the right. I wondered if one of those keys could open the door and let June-Bug out.

Everybody called Gramma "Big Ma" or Miss Nell, and she wasn't even that big, not really. She took care of everyone in the neighborhood once or twice, although not everyone liked her. Tembo told me it was usually the women whose husbands spent their pay checks on the brew that had a problem. If they just learned to make their own, it would keep the men at home and the women wouldn't have to worry. Everybody was safe at Gramma's.

"Fine, fine. What brings you my way? I don't usually see you until after dark." Gramma tied her apron around her generous waist. "You know I ain't open yet." She grinned and reached up to pat him on the back like he was still the sneaky little boy that lived around the corner.

"My visit ain't all pleasure, although I don't mind if I do." He rubbed his nose with a long boney finger.

Gramma produced a mason jar, filled to the brim with her brew. The murky brown liquid colored the glass and I imagined the vapor that rose from it was like witches brew on television. She set it on the coffee table, like I saw her do a thousand times before. I realized that I had never seen her hand someone a mason jar directly. She always put it down first. I wondered if that made it better for her.

The sheriff did not wait for Gramma to invite him, he sat right down on her small brown sofa. It seemed to have grooves worn into it where people who had come to have brew sat over the years. Angie's father placed himself into the dent in the middle of the couch and he slid right into it as if it were the perfect size.

Little Man and I retreated farther toward the back door, out of sight but not out of earshot. I wanted to hear every word he had to say. I couldn't help but wonder if he had arrested Tembo or if he knew about the last time we went can hunting with her. I told her that we shouldn't steal those folks' cans off the back porch. One man had even shot at us. We collected a whole four dollars and had lots of candy for days after that. We would be in trouble now for sure. I wondered if the jailhouse was big enough for us all in there at the same time.

"It's about your grans, Elva's kids."

He made a slurping sound and I knew that he had sipped the brew and wrinkled up his face a little. Just about everyone that drank the murky brown concoction did that. I couldn't help but wonder why people kept drinking it if it made them do that.

I held my breath. Gramma's shuffling stopped.

"They got into a fight with my girl, Angie. Now, you know I had to come talk to you. Anybody else I woulda had to pick them up, but I respect you, Big Ma. She said it was right in the middle of the street too."

Gramma cleared her throat. "My babies didn't tell me 'bout no fight."

"No, of course they didn't. Angie said it was both of them. She lost a tooth. They ought to be 'shamed ganging up on her like that." The Mason jar clinked down on Gramma's table and his wad of keys jingled. Gramma polished that table every day and I knew she was frowning. The clink meant he didn't think to use a coaster.

"They's just kids, Walter. Kids will be kids, you know that. I remember when you was a snot-nosed kid yourself. You remember that time you got caught stealing candy? You was about eight years old then, weren't you? I helped. I was in the store and I helped you out. I paid for the candy so you wouldn't have to tell your momma about it. You remember that?"

There was a pause in the conversation for a minute and I could hear glasses clinking again and keys rattle. I knew that Gramma wasn't drinking brew with him, she never drank it herself, not even to taste it. I imagined her taking one of her glass coasters with her initials etched in it and placing it under the sheriff's glass for him.

"Maybe so. But do you think you are going to be able to control them?"

My face burned with shame at the thought of any kind of "control" coming from Gramma.

A knock on the back door startled me, and I jumped. I looked up to see Tembo peering through. I tried to be as quiet as possible as I tiptoed through the door, holding it carefully so it wouldn't slam shut behind me. I was glad to see her, but I knew we were going home early now for sure.

"I saw the sheriff is here." Tembo held her finger to her lips and talked in a hushed voice. "Angie musta told that we had a fight."

The three of us moved away from the house together.

"She sure did." My eyes were wide and I instantly felt myself begin to sweat. "She said that it was us fighting her. Me and Little Man."

"Sometimes folks get jealous for no reason!" Tembo tapped her foot on the ground. She seemed to do that whenever she was upset. She crossed her arms in front of her and that was when I noticed that she had a package in her hand. It was square and wrapped in brown paper, but the brown paper was tied with a wide piece of yellow and gold cloth that crisscrossed the paper like a ribbon. I couldn't take my eyes off it. It was as if someone had real gold right down into the fibers.

"Well, it won't matter soon anyway. We go home real soon." Saying it out loud made me suddenly feel sad. A sinking feeling tickled my stomach. I let out a slow breath and Little man started picking up rocks and trying to skip them across the dirt but only managed to kick up a few dust clouds. We were all real quiet and a small lizard scurried away from Little Man's rocks and back into the corn.

"I know. I'm a miss you both. I brought you a gift." Tembo extended her cloth-wrapped package and I took it. I felt sad, and the lump that lived in my throat back home reminded me that it was there. I swallowed, then sniffed. I had no gift for her. I couldn't even say thank you.

"I know you can't call me or anything, but I want you to try and write to me, every day. Tell me what happens, so it will be easier to catch up next time you come. Write everything down and then bring this back to me. I will do the same for you."

I nodded. Tembo had obviously seen the way I looked at her diary when she wrote in it the other day. Mine would be like a secret friend, almost like I was talking to Tembo every day like we had all summer.

Gramma's voice interrupted us.

"I gotta go," I said. "I think we are in a lot or trouble." I sniffed and ran my foot along the sandy red dirt. Tembo didn't answer but she first hugged me and then Little Man. We watched her as she walked back toward her house. She was taking the long route by choice.

⊙∞⊙

The sheriff didn't stay long. Gramma didn't even call me back in when he left. After Tembo snuck away, he was just gone.

She didn't say nothing to me at first. I watched her sweep the room and the rug under the coffee table even though there was no dirt there that I could see. It was like she was trying to sweep the memory of the sheriff out the door. She spoke to me after about ten minutes.

"You fight that girl?" she asked.

"No, ma'am. I wanted to though. She was picking on Little Man. Tembo jumped in the way and knocked her over."

"I didn't think you did. Some things around here just don't change."

I didn't know what she meant by that, but I was too afraid to ask her. Gramma busied herself dusting the room, moving imaginary dust.

"Muscoda was too small for your momma. She left everything behind because of it. She was something else."

This was the first time I ever heard her talk about Momma.

"I didn't want her to go, but she was determined. She wasn't up in New York three weeks before she met your daddy."

I wanted to ask her about what Tembo said about Momma, but I didn't. If I didn't say anything, I felt like Gramma would tell me what I wanted to know.

"He was so smooth. Her car broke down, and he was the officer that went to help her. I bet he took one look at my baby and his good sense just left him. Your momma had that effect on people," she said. Gramma sniffled, then took her handkerchief out of its keeping spot down in the front of her dress. She used it to wipe the sweat that had accumulated on her face. "She was so happy when she told me about it. Meeting a colored police officer and all." She paused. "I didn't want her to go."

Gramma stopped then. Her face looked tired.

"Go on out on the porch. June-Bug coming home. He might even be out there now."

She shooed me away.

At first I didn't think June-Bug was outside. I sat on the metal porch swing and waited. I wanted to see him, although I was disappointed when I saw him in jail. I could only see his head, but I knew that he was somehow smaller than I remembered him being. But if Gramma said he was coming, he would be there.

It was the end of summer, but the heat still made the air so heavy I was searching for a breeze. Instead voices came to me through the azalea bushes. It took me a minute to realize that June-Bug was there, down by the side of the house with Little Man.

"They shouldn't be calling you Little Man anymore. You ain't so little."

I imagined Little Man shrugging his shoulders the way he did.

"Yeah, man, you don't want to end up in jail. But you know, I did the crime. It ain't like it is in New York. They don't take no jive down here. You better believe that," he said. "The man will lock up a brother up in a minute."

Part of me wanted to run down the front steps and around the porch. I sat where I was, but stopped swinging so I could hear them better. Little Man was telling June-Bug about Granny Hambay-el.

A thud hit the wood siding and I jumped in surprise. June-Bug must have punched the house.

"I can't believe that. You too big to be getting beat. She ain't even no kin. That is madness. I tried to tell your daddy."

I could hear the anger in his voice.

"Listen up. You ain't no baby. You almost grown. You need to make your own choices now. No one will ever treat you like a man if you don't act like one, you understand me?"

It was strange hearing June-Bug and Little Man talk. When he was in New York, he barely paid attention to him, then he was gone. We had rarely heard from him since he moved back South. I missed him.

I used to love being his special little sister, but I realized now that Little Man needed him more than I did. Daddy was working all the time, and he had no one else. Hearing June-Bug giving advice to Little Man made me feel proud of him again. He was right. Little Man did need to act more grown up and make his own decisions. So did I. The more I thought about it, I realized that he had been maturing all summer. South had been good for him, too.

TWENTY-NINE

Gramma sent us home early. It was only by a day but it was still early to me. She called the airport and changed our flight, and before I knew what happened, we were back up North, just like that. I thought I saw tears in her eyes when she dropped us off. She hugged us at the door while the stewardess put those big tags on us again. All she said to me was, "Be strong," and then she thump-clicked away.

Summer changed us both. I realized that on the flight home. I sat, watching Little Man and the way he asked for a drink. He almost seemed to be taking care of me for a change; he checked three times to make sure I was not cold or didn't need a pillow. I was going to have to start calling him by his name soon, but "Kenny" sounded just as strange to me as "Monica."

Daddy was not going to meet us at the airport. We knew that before we left Muscoda. The whole city back home was in some kind of emergency. Gramma told us that there was no electricity anywhere and that Daddy had to work extra-long because people had gone crazy. There were stealing and burning things down around them.

I was not expecting to see Auntie Jay, but she was waiting when we walked through the door into the airline terminal.

She stood right in front of the door looking as if she were admiring a nearby poster. Her hip was slung to one side and she wore a pin-striped man-styled pant suit with a contrasting scarf tied around her head. Her hair was now somewhere between wavy and bushy, and it stuck out from underneath the scarf. A cigarette dangled in her fingers and I could not help but wonder if it was the same one she lit last time I saw her. She held it exactly the same way she did back then, and as we got closer the smell from the cigarette tickled my nose and made my eyes water a little.

She didn't smile when she saw us; instead she scowled, her mouth twisted to one side. I would have been surprised if she did, as I realized that I didn't remember her ever smiling at me. I sighed, hoping to shrink back inside my baby blue pant suit. I knew she did not approve. I hated it too. Granny Hambay-el's daughter made it from leftover material. It itched and always felt like there was too much material between my legs. It wasn't stylish, it was basic. It didn't even have bell-bottoms like the clothes I saw Tembo's mother buy her for back-to-school. I knew now that most kids, even down South, got new clothes for school. And Gramma told me that Momma moved to the North because things were better there. Maybe they were at one point, but the look on Auntie Jay's face made me wonder if they were ever going to be "better" for me and Little Man.

"Well," she said, "at least you two got a little sun back home. Let's go. Your daddy didn't send any clothes with you?"

I shrugged my shoulders and followed her. I didn't realize how much Gramma's house now felt like a home until she said it. It was the only place I felt happy in a long time. My suitcase was full, but I knew what she meant. Her eyes attacked my hair and my clothes before she even greeted me.

The familiar feeling of emptiness was already taking over me. We just stepped off the plane and I was already feeling like I was on the other side of the street, the side where it rained all the time. Other people, the people around us, were walking around in the sun.

Little Man said nothing. He automatically walked behind me, his face permanently fixed with an expression that did not say he was happy or sad, it just said he felt nothing. He looked like I felt all of the time. I never noticed that before. I knew he wanted to put as much distance between himself and Auntie Jay as possible. This made me worried. More people than I had ever seen in one place in my life were in the airport today. I didn't want him to get lost in the crowd, at least not without me. Up to now I never thought that he cared, but for the first time I felt like I could lose him.

On the way from the airport, we passed many streetlights that were still blinking red or yellow. Auntie Jay didn't say much to us, she just kept her radio tuned to a radio station that played church music, the kind that they played back in Muscoda in Gramma's church. I guess she had somehow found religion recently.

The few stores that we passed had broken windows, and I could see smoke in several places, off in the distance. I still smelled it like it was right next to me, but I was used to that. I had smelled it for years. I learned not to talk about it and had stopped believing my nose. People looked at me funny when I did.

All the stories I read in books about homecomings said that I was supposed feel relieved coming home from a vacation. I felt none of this relief and could tell by the look on Little Man's face that he didn't feel any either. Instead I felt like I was waiting for something. A not good something.

Auntie Jay took us straight to Granny Hambay-el's house. For a minute I was relieved, then surprised. Anything was better than staying with her. I could not tell if she really did not approve of the way Daddy was "raising us" or if she just did not approve of us. She turned around a little as she parked the car. She scowled openly, not trying to hide her disapproval.

"You know your Gramma would have loved to keep you down in Muscoda. I woulda took you, too." She pulled the car into its space along the curb. "Anything is better than this. At least we're family. Your daddy can be so selfish sometimes. He would rather have you here than with me when he is working or out with his woman friends."

I didn't talk to her at all, just listened to what she said. She turned around and looked at us in the back seat.

"You know you can call me when you need me, right, Sweetie?"

I nodded. I thought I saw a trace of softness in her face.

The front yard looked the same as I remembered, except the azaleas were blooming and so full of funnel-shaped flowers that they looked overloaded. These were Granny

Hambay-el's favorite, I heard her tell her daughter that these reminded her of "back home." They planted them so that they alternated. A pink one followed by a white one, looking almost as if a candy cane surrounded the house. I smiled at the thought. Wasn't the witches house surrounded by candy canes in Hansel and Gretel too?

This yard was smaller than Gramma's front yard in Muscoda, and not as welcoming, even though the azaleas made me almost want to go in. Their hedges formed a sort of fence that kept you from seeing fully into the yard from outside, or outside into the street if you were sitting on the grass. Gramma's yard was full of color too, but it made you want to come in and visit, even if poisonous oleander was growing there. You could be in the front of the house and wave at neighbors, and they could wave back at you. All summer long, I watched Gramma nod her "How dos?" to people passing by. The warmth from the yard was enough to make even the oleanders seem harmless.

Granny Hambay-el's house was sort of a fortress. We were locked in once we entered, away from everyone and everything outside, like Rapunzel locked in a secret tower. But I didn't think that any prince was coming to rescue us. I knew now that that only happened in fairy tales.

Missing Tembo already, I grabbed a few of the azalea leaves as I passed by. "Plain old shrubs" flashed through my head. Maybe she was right, maybe Granny Hambay-el would not drink tea made from anything. What was the worst that could happen? I stuffed them into my pocket feeling like a thief. I wanted to dry them out and save them for later. I did not know what I could find in the pantry that looked like them, but I knew I could find something. I remembered Tembo standing up to Angie. If she could fight back even though she knew she would surely take some licks, I could stand up for myself, too. I just wasn't sure how I was going to do it yet.

When we finally arrived at the door, Auntie Jay surprised me by walking up the steps with us and waiting for someone to open the door. For a minute I felt like she would act like a taxi driver and slow down just enough for us to get out. The grandson opened the door and the feeling of constant dread that we lived with here flooded over me. Little Man grabbed my hand and I stepped as far around Everett as possible. Just seeing him was making me sick.

Auntie Jay surprised me as she smiled and chatted like I had not seen her do in a long time, she was a different person. She batted her eyes at him like the ladies on TV and she even laughed a little with him. I was even more surprised that he was up and about. If he wasn't lurking in a dark corner or behind his grandmother, I didn't recall him ever being anywhere but out in a disco or asleep in bed recovering from his night with "loose women." And except for his help giving Little Man his morning whippings, he always managed to sleep through all the morning noise.

Auntie Jay did not come in. Instead, she herded us inside the door and set our small bags in behind us, hugging each of us at the door. I didn't ever remember her doing anything like that to us, especially to Little Man. She did not smile or anything; instead her mouth was drawn into a tight line, her thin lips pressed together.

Everett closed the door and stood, eyeing us with his hands on his hips, a slight smile curving his mouth.

My stomach felt queasy.

It was much darker in the room than outside and for a minute I could not see. The runner was still on top of the red rug, and I noticed specks of dust swirling around me in the air as the smell of furniture polish mixed with broiled fish met my nose.

I instantly felt despair. Granny Hambay-el's broiled fish was one of my least favorite dishes, right next to liver. She never took the bones out and it still looked scaly, even after it was finished cooking. She cooked the fish with the head on and I always felt like the fish was looking at us as we ate.

Everett smiled a big grin at us like we looked as good as fried chicken, showing us the huge gap between his two front teeth. Gramma told me that there were some tribes in Africa where a gap in one's teeth were so prized, fathers would force little girls to have them by placing a wedge in their teeth for months. Everett's gap provided no such attractiveness, instead it just added to his clown-like look.

He looked at us for what seemed like too long and licked his lips. He motioned toward the inside of the house.

"Well, Monica and Kenneth," he said, "we sure have missed you this summer." He bent down just a little at the knees as if he were talking to very little children. I jumped, startled by the sounds of our given names. Even in school, almost no one called us that. Couldn't he see that Little Man and I both had grown almost two inches this summer?

"How was your summer? Did you have a good time visiting your grandmother?"

His voice sounded strange and proper, like he had been practicing his English. There was almost no hint of the singsong accent that Granny Hambay-el had. He picked up our bags and walked into the house. We followed in our old familiar careful way. He couldn't see, but I smiled. When Everett was around, I was uneasy, usually, but I appreciated that he took the time to actually use our names. Hearing them out loud, the names somehow fit now.

"Granny wants your bags in the washroom. Monica, you sure have grown into a pretty young lady."

My stomach flip-flopped. I was instantly embarrassed as we walked straight through to the kitchen. I felt my face turn hot. Everett placed the bags on the kitchen floor, in front of the door that led to the basement and stood there, hands on his hips again, staring at me. Could he see that my period started this summer? I wondered. Did I really look different, perhaps somehow more adult by my shame in the field? I knew that I felt like I grew a whole year over the summer.

"You should say thank you when someone gives you a compliment, young lady. I guess these young boys your age don't give too many, huh? Granny will be right back. She and my mother went to the grocery store." He winked at me, but only managed to look strange without an eyebrow framing his eye.

I nodded, feeling suddenly awkward. It was true. I had not received a compliment from anyone in so long that I did not know how to act. I could not bring myself to say thank you or anything else. He finally walked away and left us standing there, shifting our weight from foot to foot.

Little Man moved first, heading for the chairs. They were just where we left them before we went to visit Gramma. They had not been touched by anyone; the metal along the back of the chair was coated with a thin layer of dust. It was a miracle that any dust survived in this house at all, Granny always seemed to be cleaning something, reminding all around her that "cleanliness was next to godliness."

"When do you think we will see Daddy?"

Little Man was almost as tall as I was. I couldn't answer him. Where had his "littleness" gone? Instead I shrugged.

We took the chairs to our usual places in the living room. Everything about the room looked the same to me, like we had been there just yesterday, not two months ago. I held my journal in my hand. I wanted to write all of this down, so I could share it with Tembo next time I saw her. She seemed to drink up life and I knew she would want every detail. I wanted to write down the things that happened before too, so she could understand how we got here. I opened the book to the middle to begin writing. Little Man interrupted me again.

"Do you think you could stop calling me Little Man?" He looked at me with wide eyes, like he was asking something very hard.

"But I have always called you Little Man."

"But I am not *little* anymore. Everett even said so. I want you to call me by my name." He rubbed his nose with his finger, just like I remembered my daddy doing, and I felt, just for a minute, that I was looking at a miniature version of Daddy.

It was going to be strange, but I was sure he was right. I was so busy "taking care of him" that I didn't even see him growing up and never allowed him to have an opinion. I realized that up to then I made all the decisions for him, for both of us.

"Okay, Kenneth. Or can you just be Ken?" I smiled at him and took the top off my pen. It felt weird calling him by his name. I felt like I was talking to a stranger.

"Ken is good." He puffed out his chest a little bit.

I nodded and began to write in my journal, inhaling deeply. The air in the house smelled different. I could smell the change.

How would I start? *Dear Diary*, I thought, *Auntie Jay met us at the airport in a suit Gramma would surely say was mannish.*

That was as good a start as any. But what would Tembo really want to know? She had a hard time believing me when I told her how my life back North was. She didn't believe me about the folding chairs or anything else, not really.

I took the pen off my cap and wrote my beginning. I shielded my paper, even though no one was really around. This was going to be my book of secrets, meant for only one other person to read. The words flowed more easily than I imagined they would.

We went straight to Granny Hambay-el's house, and Everett was there, almost like he was waiting for us to come back to entertain him.

It makes me feel like we are his toys, like the main attraction in the traveling fair like the one we saw when we went to town, to Birmingham. I feel like he looks through me like some kind of alien on Star Trek or something, waiting to eat my insides if I am just a little careless.

–Sweetie

That didn't seem right anymore. I crossed it out and signed my name the right way.

–Monica

THIRTY

I got lost in my words as we waited for Granny Hambay-el to return. They poured onto the page as if opening the journal opened a floodgate inside me. As I wrote I realized that I had stopped feeling a long time ago, and now these feelings were coming through my pen onto the page. Gramma told me before that feeling was hard for men. Somehow I had let it get hard for me, too.

My fingers started to ache from holding the pen so tight. I stopped and saw a dent on my third finger. I rubbed it with my thumb; my fingertips were turning white.

I never noticed how quiet the house was without Granny in it. Every noise seemed larger than it was before, but I could not tell if it was because she were gone or because we had somehow gotten used to the more pleasant sounds of Gramma's house.

Everything seemed to be waiting for something here, just like us. The clock ticked louder than ever, but neither one of us would dare turn on the television or make much noise. I think we were convinced that maybe we *would* break anything we touched, just like Granny Hambay-el said we would. I was even more aware now that this was not home and never could be, although I knew we would still spend most of our waking and sleeping hours in this house, sitting in the same place.

Over the summer, I began to feel like I needed to find a place where I belonged, or make that place exist somewhere. I wanted to go home. I wanted Daddy to be glad to see me. I wanted him to remove the layers of dust that gathered over Momma's things and clean the carpets. I wanted to let sunshine into our dark house and invite friends over. And although I sometimes hid upstairs in the middle of the closet still full of Momma's things, searching for her scent in the middle of the moth balls, I wanted Daddy to throw them all away and make room in the closet for our life.

Sunlight suddenly streamed into the house, lighting up the snowflake-like dust specks in the air again. Elizabeth came through the door first, followed by Granny, and it seemed as if the house was noisy all at once.

Elizabeth pulled a metal shopping cart with her, filled to the brim with brown paper bags. It squeaked and complained as she pulled it behind her. She stopped the cart on the runner in the doorway.

"The kids are back, Momma." She paused and removed her coat, actually smiling at us.

I could hear Granny Hambay-el's famous teeth sucking from the other room. Elizabeth walked over to the small radio behind us and pressed a button. Marvin Gaye filled the room. Down South, they played his songs all over the place. I smiled. The time in Muscoda had been good.

Granny was still in the front room, I could hear her fumbling to close the door. I couldn't see her, but I could smell her smell; she still smelled of Ben-gay mixed with mothballs and Ultra Sheen, just as she did two months ago. The big brown door had four locks inside, and I could hear her closing them systematically, one by one. Finally, she waddled into the room, her legs still bowed and her step heavy.

She did not say hello or remark on how big we had gotten. She did not extend a hand or offer a hug. Touching her was taboo; she was off limits the same as the furniture and the rug.

"Little Man, come on and give us a hand wit' dese bags." She sucked her teeth again.

I expected Little Man to jump up, say "Yes, ma'am," and run to her aide. Instead he stood up slowly and stood his ground. He looked at his feet.

"Please call me Kenny." I almost didn't hear him.

Granny's head snapped up and her hands immediately went to her hips. Her eyes grew wide in disbelief. Elizabeth's mouth dropped open. I could not believe my ears either. I didn't remember him ever speaking up for himself and I could not help but smile a little. He wanted to be free too!

"What did you say?" Granny's eyes got wide and her accent became more pronounced. "You wan' me to box your ears?" She moved closer to Little Man, challenging him.

He stood his ground and I held my breath. Granny Hambay-el said "box" his ears but I knew she really meant punch him in the head. It wouldn't be the first time. Every time she did it, his ear and whole side of his face would turn red, her knuckles outlined on his face for what seemed like hours.

"You upstart! You get ovah here and help like I told you!" Her cocoa-colored skin was suddenly infused by a tinge of red. Anger seeped from her pores. I could smell it.

He didn't move.

The smile left my face. What was he doing? He was taking things too far. Granny Hambay-el moved forward and I cringed, expecting her to hit my brother. Elizabeth caught her breath.

She pushed him aside so hard that he fell to the floor as she lumbered past. He glared at her in an unspoken challenge. She didn't hit him, instead she muttered under her breath and continued on toward the kitchen. Elizabeth scurried behind her. She glanced over at Kenny and narrowed her eyes, drawing her mouth into a tight line. I imagined fire coming from her nose, but he did not drop his gaze. I think he won. I just didn't know what.

The tension that had been building up in the back of my neck loosened a little, and I realized that my diary was still opened. I snapped it shut before Granny or Elizabeth could notice. There was no need to give them an excuse to be angry with me.

THIRTY-ONE

*T*he quiet in the house was so loud that it woke me up. I opened my eyes and stared at the ceiling. There was no fan making me cold or noise from the radio blaring on AM. No voices were coming from the kitchen. Instead there was just silence. I held my breath for a minute, waiting for the familiar sounds of Granny Hambay-el hitting Little Man for wetting the bed and then chasing him down the hall. When it didn't come, I let my breath out heavily, moving the hair that had fallen into my eyes. This could not be a good sign.

I sat on the edge of my bed and slipped my feet into the pink fuzzy slippers that Gramma had given me as a going home present. The fuzz felt good, like a good hug, and I wiggled my toes.

Although the fan wasn't going, the window was open. I could feel my skin prickle from goose bumps. The air from outside smelled wet, like it did before the rain that I hated so much up North because it made my hair get fuzzier and stand up, but loved to run in barefoot back in Muscoda. I pulled my bathrobe around me and stepped out of the open bedroom door, into the hallway. My plan was to look down the hallway and see if Kenny was still sleeping or if the quiet had awakened him too. I knew I would be able to see him, his cot was right across from the doorway. It seemed that the only one who closed the door at Granny Hambay-el's house was Granny. Everyone else just left their doors wide open, as if there was some unspoken pact that she owned everything and everyone in the house. She never knocked on doors if they happened to be closed, instead she just threw open every door and burst into the room. If we left doors open like that in Muscoda, Gramma would say we acted like we lived in a barn. No one here seemed to care. Instead of closing the doors we had learned to just look away, it had almost the same effect as the door.

I walked right into Everett, or at least into his stomach. I had not realized just how big he was. Other than yesterday, I had never been this close to him before. My face flushed red; he placed his hands on my shoulders and he backed me up away from him. I was afraid to look at him. His chest was bare and he was wearing exercise shorts. He smelled like sweat.

"Slow down, Sweetie. Where are you going?"

I shrugged my shoulders like I was caught doing something I shouldn't. I rubbed my hand over my face, hoping to remove any of his sweat or sweat smell that might have ended up on me when I bumped into him. I could taste his salt.

I expected him to suck his teeth like his grandmother would in her particular Central American way. Instead, he was silent. I finally looked up to see that he was smiling at me.

Something about his smile looked more like an evil grin than a friendly gesture of welcome. I had seen the look before, on TV, before the villain committed his crime. The hairs on the back on my neck tickled me and my stomach felt weak. I expected "danger" music to begin playing in the background any minute.

"You should be more careful and look where you are going."

I nodded and tried to look around him for Kenny, but he stepped to the side to block my view.

"Looking for your baby brother?" His voice was teasing me.

"No." I crossed my fingers behind my back.

"He is still a baby-baby. I think this is the first time he didn't wet the bed that I can remember. Not like you." He stopped me from looking at the floor, lifting my chin up with one finger. I tried to pull away from his touch. "You grew up into quite a young lady this summer."

I shrugged my shoulders again and turned my head away from him. Was it possible for me to grow into anything but a young lady? I could smell his breath; it was mixed with the smell of stale coffee, and the hotness of the smell made my eyes water. I didn't know what to say. I had to go to the bathroom now and started to shift my weight back and forth. I wanted to step back into my room, but Everett put one foot behind me, trapping me in the hallway.

My stomach tickled from butterflies and the hallway closed in on me, making me feel smaller than the ant I squashed on the front walkway yesterday.

Everett reached over and brushed my hair back from my face. The bangs that Tembo and I cut into the front of my hair were flat from sleeping. He moved them back from my eyes, but my sandy hair refused to obey and the bangs immediately dropped back down on my forehead, skimming the tops of my eyebrows. He stroked the side of my face with one finger. I pressed myself against the wall as the rough skin raked across my cheek. There was a wart on the side of his forefinger, growing out of the crease on his joint.

"You hair is growing so nice and pretty. You are going to be one beautiful young lady." He licked his lips. "Don't let any of these little boys around here mess you up. I can take care of you. Tell you what to expect."

He pressed himself against me so hard I felt like my bones would be crushed any minute. His body lifted mine off the floor so that only the very tips of my toes skimmed the floor. His sweaty smell invaded my nose and I turned my head away from him; hard parts of his body pressed into mine.

My head felt tight. I hated that he invaded my space without asking. I wanted to kick him but he was too close. I was trapped. My ears were hot and I burned with anger. I felt as if his hand had burned my face. Where was Little Man? Where was Granny chasing him with her strap this morning? Gramma had told me about people like him, he was of the lowest kind. She tried to tell me in her old-fashioned way about the way some men would take advantage of little girls. This was the reason she wanted us out of the house on brew days and the reason she would not allow me to sit in anyone's lap, related or not. "Little girls just don't," she had told me.

Everett stepped back away from me as suddenly as he had blocked my way. He backed down the hallway toward his room.

"Sweetie!" Granny was calling me from downstairs. "You get down here now, gal!"

"Don't tell anyone, okay?" he whispered, almost running back to his room on his tiptoes to keep the floor from announcing him with its tell-tale creaking.

After his warm reception yesterday, I felt it was possible that he might become our friend here, but now I knew different. Friendship was not what motivated his warmth. Hate welled up in a fierce wave. I did not even hate Granny for her indifference toward us, but I knew I hated Everett for even suggesting that he might touch me in the way he did.

Hate changed to embarrassment and my face flushed red. I felt marked as if he had left an imprint in my body, dirty, as if I had somehow invited him.

"Sweetie!" Granny's voice was louder, more insistent this time. I could tell she was standing at the bottom of the steps.

I wiped my robe and my face, trying to remove Everett from me. I felt marked. I did not want to be touched like that again.

"Coming! I will be right there! I am getting dressed now."

"No, come right now! I want to see you right now, in Elizabeth's room." She banged her fist on the post at the bottom of the steps and the entire banister shuddered all the way from the bottom to the top. I closed my eyes and sank into the wall again, the chair molding sticking me in the back this time. I did not have time to feel anything other than dread. I was being summoned to the room behind the partition.

We were never allowed there. The created room had no door, only a dark blue curtain that parted in the middle like the pantry. It served its purpose and separated the room from the rest of the house just a securely as a jail cell door. We didn't even look that way, just listened to the sewing sounds that came from within every night, sometimes way into the night. Elizabeth never invited us in and we never peeked, making the room as mysterious as the pantry had been before.

I was surely in trouble for something, although I did not know how that could be; we had not been in the house for twenty four hours. I started down the stairway and was relieved to see that Granny had moved from the landing. I thought that she might have seen what Everett had done to me. I hoped that she could not smell his smell on my clothes.

I crossed the runner and parted the curtain to Elizabeth's room. The rug was red in there too. She sat on her small bed, a cot similar to mine, and Granny was standing with her back to the door, hands on her hips with her bowed legs spread wide. She turned around as I entered.

"So, Sweetie, how was your summer?"

I sank back. Granny's voice was lacking its usual shrill quality. I was on guard.

"Fine."

"Did you have a good time visiting your grandmother? Is there something you want to tell me?"

I looked at the floor and wondered what this was all about. I searched for the right answer, the one that would let me go back upstairs and get dressed. I didn't have to wonder long.

Her daughter reached down the floor on the other side of her bed and picked up a white plastic bag and handed it to Granny Hambay-el.

My heart sank. I recognized the bag as the one from my luggage where I had hidden my soiled underwear still inside.

"I see you became a woman this summer. Why didn't you tell us?"

I was paralyzed, my feet glued in place. I remember the sticky feeling in my panties like it was yesterday. At the time, it wasn't something I wanted to share with anyone, much less them. I hadn't even told my Gramma. Our almost meeting with the Klan and being sent home early seemed more important.

"Momma, I think she is embarrassed." The softness in Elizabeth's voice startled me. I needed someone to be on my side.

"She should be embarrassed, mon. She hid her nyasty panties in her suitcase. Didn't you know you were supposed to wash dem out with cold water, girl? These are ruined. You might as well just throw dem them away now. I don't see why you even carried 'dese back here."

She flung the plastic bag in my direction. I wished I had thrown them away. And how was I supposed to know to do anything? I never got "the talk" like I heard other girls did. I had to read it myself in a book I found in the back of the school library.

"You have nothing to say for yourself then, gal? Let me tell you something you need to know. I talked wit' you father

and he asked me to talk to you about this. It's time you know."
She didn't wait for an answer from me. She looked over at
Elizabeth, who nodded in agreement and picked up some
stitching she was working, turning it over and over in her
hands.

"You see where that blood come out? Well, a man's
business go in there and a baby come out that little hole!
Don't you forget that! You understand me?" She shook her
finger in my face but I dared not move away. I looked at the
floor some more.

She lifted my chin with her finger, poking me in the soft
spot on the underside of my chin.

"You understand me? Look at me when I talk to you!"

I nodded, my eyes wide. It was not hot in the room, but
small beads of sweat formed on her brow.

"You keep your legs closed, you hear?" She held her finger
under my chin, stopping me from looking away.

"Yes, ma'am," I said. I couldn't manage anything else. Was
this "the talk"? The story of the birds and the bees?

"Here." She handed me a large brown paper bag. "This is
for your private t'ings. Elizabeth made it for you. Open it."

I opened the bag cautiously and removed a white elastic
belt. I frowned.

"Don' be frownin' up you face. Do you know what to do?
What did you use when your menses came?"

"My friend gave me some things. They stuck to my
panties." I could not keep from croaking. My throat was
tight from fear.

"No, you use this." She grabbed the belt from my hands. "You pin the napkins to the belt in the front and in the back. It is the best way. Those new things they make aren't too good. This will keep your clothes clean and fresh. I am not washing any blood out of your clothes. You understand me? You stain, you wash. It is bad luck for someone else to wash your panties."

"But on TV they say—"

Granny dropped the belt into the open bag and then poked me in the shoulder, pushing me back. Instantly, I regretted my mistake. My shoulder throbbed from the pain as I dropped the paper bag and rubbed my shoulder. She sucked her teeth. Elizabeth stood up and stepped around her.

"You can't believe everything they say on TV. When I was a girl, all I had was rags that I washed every day in the river. We couldn't afford all those fancy things that they sold at the market. This is better. There is no way that those new thin things work as good. Trust me. Women have been doing it this way for years."

"Look, gal, let me tell you something." Granny moved her daughter aside. "I birthed ten children without no doctor, and I know what I am talking 'bout. They haven't made up anyt'in new about a woman's body. It has been the same since Adam and Eve. And you watch too much TV, anyway. All them t'ings they show on the TV are for fast women! Fast women! I never heard of any of those thin's in my day. Young girls don' have no business with the likes of no Massengill or Tampax! You can't do that thing until you have babies! And you betta not be having any no time soon. You hear me?"

I heard her. Loud and clear. I was sure that everyone in the house did too; the partition that made Elizabeth's room did not go up to the ceiling. A picture of Little Man and Everett sitting out there listening flashed in my head and my face felt hotter than it did already.

Elizabeth picked up the brown paper bag and handed it to her mother. She shoved it in my direction and I took it again, peeking inside. I closed my eyes and opened them again. The pads were as thick as the boards that me and Tembo used to build our tree house. I hadn't even put one on yet and I felt as if there were bricks between my legs. I was sure I would walk funny. My shoulder ached, daring me to protest again.

I breathed out heavily, and I felt hate simmering inside my chest for the second time in an hour. Over the years, I never really let myself put an emotion around the way I felt about staying in the sitter's house. I didn't let myself really feel anything at all; I watched my life happen to me the same way we watched television in the afternoons. I was never mad at Daddy for working such long hours or going out with his girlfriends, if that was what he was really doing, like Auntie Jay said. I never allowed myself to be anything more than uncomfortable, and I ignored that half of the time, just waiting for it to be over. I realized then, standing there looking at the floor with these two crazy women, that us being at the sitter's house was our purgatory, our place in the middle. It might never end, just continue to be interrupted a few hours a day, a few times a week by a visit to a house that had become a shrine to Momma. I hated being here more than I ever hated anything else, but there was nothing I could do about it. I was still a child. The only thing I could do, like Tembo said, was to try and control it for my benefit. I just had to figure out how.

THIRTY-TWO

I was going to junior high. Most of that first weekend home we sat in the house, anticipating Monday. Before I went down South I was scared about going back to school. I was still afraid, but in a different way now. School would be more of the same, but there would be kids there from the other school now, too. The new school right next door to the old one, but I knew I was going to find new things there.

When we finally got out to go to school, I had to blink when I stepped through the front door. It was bright and the air smelled like autumn already, filled with the smell of leaves about to break away from branches and cover the sidewalk with their blankets of fall colors.

There was a temporary break in the never-ending rain this morning, the first one all weekend. Clouds hovered in the distance, signaling that it would not last long. Granny consulted the Farmer's Almanac, her Bible, and she said that we were in for lots more rain. I believed her and let myself be dressed in the dime store ponchos she purchased from Woolworth's even though they kept all the moisture in and made me feel soggy.

It was early September and some of the leaves were already turning shades of yellow and red. The chrysanthemums were blooming and I was surprised that Elizabeth had not already harvested the large flowers from the front yard. She ground them up and used them all the time to help cure headaches.

It started raining again before we even got on the school bus, pouring really. I felt as if the sky opened up and dumped its load on my head. This northern rain was not like the rain in Muscoda. It was cold and clammy and made me feel heavy and tired. The memory of welcoming the storms and the rainbow that came after was so far from my mind now that I found it hard to even remember, but I was determined to hold onto the bits of anticipation I was feeling about going to the new school. If I let myself feel sad, then things would not be good. Tembo would have been happy about going to this new school with new people, even in this terrible weather, so I was going to be happy too, even if only a little bit.

Between the gray skies and the rain and all the new people around me, I found it hard to concentrate. My stomach trembled with excitement right through lunch every time I spotted a new face. Other returning students were happy to see familiar faces, but I was excited to take in all the new ones. I looked closely at the students I did not know. Were any of them as happy as I was to meet new people? Would any of them want to know what I did for the summer? For the first time in a while, I felt that I might not have to hide things about my life from other people. I had not hidden anything from Tembo and she had become my friend anyway.

I wanted to hold onto the fun times I had with Tembo this summer and keep them from fading as my memories of Momma had. All I could remember of her now was the way her hair smelled when she washed it, perhaps because I had not shared those memories with anyone but myself. Maybe I had somehow used them up that way. I wanted to make new memories, too, with new friends. I half-listened to the teacher and realized that I had never wanted to make new friends before. I didn't know how. I scribbled in the margins of my notebook. My stomach was still in knots.

The first day of school was over. The bottom of my stomach felt like lead. Tembo had made friends with me. She had been the one to get the ball rolling and pushed me when I tried to retreat the way I was used to doing when I was home. I'd thought I could perhaps turn over a whole new leaf today, but I still felt friendless and odd. The feeling was a familiar one, I had not forgotten it, only pushed it to the back of my mind. The familiarity made it okay.

The bell rang and I jumped, but then moved slowly to gather my things. I looked around quickly, hoping to maybe make eye contact with one of the other new kids. It didn't work. I held my books close to me and made my way out of the classroom.

Someone called my name just as I was about to reach the bus area. I let out a deep breath as I turned around slowly, prepared to smile.

"So nice to see you here. You sure have grown." Miss Faust stood smiling at me.

I was confused. What was she doing at this new school?

"I am vice principal here. Tell me, how was your first day?" Her voice was filled with enthusiasm.

Slow to answer, I stumbled over my words. "It was okay," I said. "But I thought you were a teacher."

"I am. But I was in graduate school. This is my new job. Isn't that exciting? You were always one of my favorite students, now I will see you all the time."

I tried to smile.

"How was your summer?"

"I went to visit my grandmother. It was very nice." My journal was on the top of my stack of books.

"Good for you. And have you been writing? Practicing?"

I nodded. I didn't need to tell her that I had just started writing again. It didn't matter. I had written enough in the few days since Tembo had given me my new book that I had almost filled it up. "Sort of. I have been keeping a journal. Writing my stories down so I can share things with a new friend I met down South. I guess we are journal pals." I flipped through the pages of my book, letting her get a glimpse of the ink-filled pages.

A smile spread across Miss Faust's face. "Good. Maybe you can share one with me."

"Well—" I hesitated. I had never intended on sharing anything that I had written with anyone but Tembo. Shame burned my face. What would she think of me if she knew? "I'm not sure. They weren't really for that-"

She held up her hand. "That's okay. I understand how journaling can be. Many times it is very private. But promise me you will find just a piece to share with me. I want to help you develop your talents. You used to love writing so much."

I nodded. "I will. But I have to get my bus." I motioned toward the door.

"You go then. Good to see you."

I could feel her eyes on me and I left her standing there. Sharing my private world with someone other than Tembo would be hard. I would have to think about it. But it was still good to see Ms. Faust. She was the only friendly face I had seen all day.

THIRTY-THREE

We were to meet Daddy's new girlfriend. Right after homework was done, we were going straight home, and for the first time in a long time, we were going to have dinner with Daddy in our own house.

I heard Granny Hambay-el say that we needed a new mother. Every time they mentioned that, I still didn't understand. Daddy might find a new girlfriend, but the mother I had could never be replaced.

It was still raining, so Daddy came to get us from Granny Hambay-el's house. Granny opened the door with her fake smile plastered to her face, as usual. And then, behind Daddy, a woman I had never seen before appeared. She followed him inside and took off her coat without being asked. She laughed nervously through her thin lips. She had only walked from the car to the door but she looked soggy. Her wispy brown hair was wet and hung down past her shoulders. She even smelled wet. She was thin and I had a sense of having met her before somewhere.

Daddy hugged me first and then Little Man. I felt my time move slower for a minute as I stared at her, unable to refocus my eyes on anything else.

"You answer her, Sweetie." Daddy's voice was firm.

She was talking to me. All I could do was nod. Her mouth was moving and she was confirming, not asking, my name.

"I am Janetta," she said, extending her hand. "I have heard so much about you and I am so glad to finally meet you, although I had hoped the weather would be better. I had hoped we would be able to picnic, but we are just going to have to have an inside dinner this time." Her words flew out of her mouth. I could not take my eyes off her teeth.

So this was her. *Was she planning on sending us to boarding school too?*

"Has the cat got your tongue, honey?" She put her hand on my back and I jumped.

"You..." The cat didn't have my tongue. A ghost did. She looked exactly like my memory of Mama. Exactly. Who was this woman and where had she come from?

"I what?" she said. "Look like your mother? Your father said you would say that." She laughed a girlish laugh. "But we can talk about that later. Over dinner."

She turned to Daddy. "We have to get to the house before my food dries out."

As Daddy hurried us out into the car, the reality of the situation set in. This new woman had cooked in our house. And she looked like Mama. What happened this summer that we missed?

❦

My stomach trembled as I walked into the house. I could tell it was different before we got out of the car. The grass was neatly edged and trimmed. From the outside, it looked too orderly to be the place that had fallen into chaos since Mama died.

The house was filled with the smells of Janetta's dinner. My stomach betrayed me and grumbled. I scowled. No one had cooked much of anything in our kitchen for years. Why was she different?

She rushed straight back to the kitchen and started making pot and pan sounds. Little Man and I stood in the front room, watching.

He crossed his arms, scowling, and plopped himself down on the green velvet sofa.

I looked around the room. The rug seemed less dirty, as if someone had actually vacuumed, and the layer of dust that had blanketed the bookshelves was gone. Once again, I felt like I was a stranger. The newness of this was overwhelming. Little Man's unhappiness was obvious. It was going to be a long dinner.

I finally let myself slide onto the couch next to him. We didn't talk, we just sat there with our thighs touching, noticing the differences in the room. There were new statues in a few places, things we didn't recognize. Surely none of them had been put there by Momma.

Her picture was moved to the back of one of the shelves, instead of standing in the front of it where it had always been in front of all the other family pictures. Little Man stood up and moved them around again, back to the familiar order we knew, without speaking. Neither one of us wanted to voice what we thought was going to happen next.

I kept swallowing to try and rid myself of the lump in my throat.

Little Man barely moved.

Daddy chattered away every time he came into the living room. "How was your summer?" he asked, then walked back into the kitchen.

His heavy voice carried and I could hear him about the cooking sounds that were coming from in there, the room that had been silent for so long. "Is it ready yet?" he asked her.

"Soon." She giggled. "You better stop." More giggling. "I'll tell you when."

And then he was back again, with more questions. I got the feeling that Daddy wouldn't really hear us above his nervousness, so I stopped trying to give him any more than a yes or no. He was treating us almost like we were guests in our home.

"Time to eat," Janetta yelled even though she didn't have to. Her voice was cheerful. She came out of the kitchen with a large white dish in her hands, held between big, green oven mitts that I did not recognize. She had put on small checkered apron that matched her outfit and made her look like one of those wives on TV.

"Y'all heard her. C'mon to the table."

Kenny and I made eye contact but said nothing. We moved to the table as Daddy asked.

"Junius, you sit here, Kenny, you here."

"Don't make a fuss, Janetta, it's just dinner," Daddy said.

"No, it's not. They have never had dinner with me before and this is the way I do it. I want it to be nice for them. For all of us."

"Just don't make a fuss." Daddy's eyes darted around the room nervously.

Kenny stood behind his chair but he did not sit down.

"And Sweetie—"

"Monica."

Her mouth dropped open and her lip quivered slightly. She was nervous. I had caught her off guard.

Daddy cut his eyes at me.

"I thought—" Janetta pushed a lock of hair back from her face. She looked flushed.

"Just Monica." I pulled out the chair she had indicated and slid into it.

"Okay." She paused. "We have some good stuff here. I hope you like it. Your father really didn't tell me what you liked so I had to guess.

Daddy and Little Man sat down.

"Can you say grace, Junius?"

Little Man stared at his plate.

I tapped my foot on the floor.

"Stop shaking the table, Sweetie. Monica." Daddy lowered his eyes. "Lord, thank you for this bounty that you have given and this woman has so lovingly prepared."

Lovingly? "Are you going to marry my father?"

Janetta looked from me to Daddy and then back again. She opened and then closed her mouth.

After what seemed like the longest time, Daddy finally tried to answer me.

"Sweetie, you shouldn't ask her that type of thing—"

Janetta found her tongue. "Your father and I haven't discussed marriage yet, but I suppose it is always a possibility." She cleared her throat.

"Oh," I said. "Where did those new statues come from? And the throw pillows?"

Daddy's exhalation seemed very loud in the small room.

He twisted his neck, then rubbed the back of it with his hand as if he was trying to release some of the tension that was spread across his face.

Janetta smiled. "Do you like them? I put them there. I thought the room needed a little updating."

"Not really."

"Monica Denise. I will not allow you to be rude."

"It's okay, Junius. She has a right to an opinion. Is something wrong with them?"

I shrugged. "I just think the way my *mother* had it was fine."

"Monica."

Little Man pushed his chair away from the table, then stood up.

"Where are you going?" Daddy's face darkened.

"I'm not hungry." He didn't ask or wait for permission.

Janetta called after him. "But aren't you—"

Daddy shook his head and she stopped mid-sentence.

"Let him go."

She nodded but didn't answer.

We finished our meal in silence. A lot more than the pillows had changed this summer.

Thirty-Four

I could hardly sleep last night. I didn't ever remember Daddy raising his voice to me the way he did yesterday, and I kept reliving it in my mind. He yelled at me, and I yelled back. I think we had an argument. That had never happened before.

I didn't mean to make him so angry, and I couldn't believe he didn't realize that what I was saying was true. I had heard him say that people should not kiss in public, or act all silly, and he was doing it himself. He kissed Janetta right in front of our house, in the middle of the street. And then when I told him that it was not the right thing to do, he yelled at me, right in front of her.

I wasn't sure if I should've be mad at him, her, or both of them, and having no sleep made the afternoon at school very hard. I couldn't concentrate in my last few classes and had been daydreaming for the last twenty minutes or so, and the ringing of the last bell jolted me back from my daydreaming, to the here and now. I stopped at my locker to get my rain slicker, throwing the books I didn't need inside. They hit the bottom with a loud, dull thud.

"You should treat your books more kindly." Miss Faust had walked up behind me.

"Oh. I'm sorry. I guess I didn't know my own strength." I gave her one of my best smiles.

"Did you have a good day?" she asked.

I inhaled. The spice of her perfume met my nose. Ms. Faust still smelled as she had in second grade. "It was good, I guess."

She looked surprised at my answer. "You guess?"

I nodded. "I couldn't concentrate much. I had fight with my father."

"Really? You want to tell me what it was about?"

I shook my head.

"That's fair, I suppose. How do you like junior high school?"

Now here was something I didn't mind talking about. "Well, I think I like that I have a whole lot of teachers instead of just one. Some of them are nice."

"I'm glad." She paused. "I don't suppose you have some writing for me? You could use that anger and you said you would give me a sample."

I had said that. I thought a minute, then thought about an essay I had written. I opened my journal, lying in the bottom of my locker, and stopped. My face flushed. Almost ashamed of what I was going to share, I took a deep breath. I tore the pages from my journal slowly, almost as if tearing carefully could rip them from my life. The ripping sound made me cringe. Without giving myself a chance to change my mind, I spun around and handed them to Ms. Faust.

"Here's something." I forced a strained smile. "I gotta make my bus."

She didn't speak, but instead looked at me with her mouth half open.

I almost smirked, and hoped she would enjoy my story of getting my period this past summer. I wanted her to know how grown up I had become since last year.

I left her there and made my way to the front of the building with the rest of the kids who rode my bus, to the staging area for both the junior high school and the elementary school. I usually met Little Man there although we still would not sit together on the bus, we had just moved farther back.

My nose ran as I stood in the rain. I felt like a wet banana in my dime store slicker. The rain clouded my mind with a gloom that I just could not shake off. Little Man got out of school ten minutes after I did, and the kids from his school had started to pour out of the door to the staging area. One of the kids bumped into me. I didn't bother to complain.

The monitor blew the whistle, our signal to board our bus. I blinked the raindrops and the haziness from my eyes and looked around. My pulse quickened and my ears felt hot. Where was Little Man? No one else was coming from his school.

"Wait, we can't go. Everyone's not here." Rain was caught in my eyelashes. I tried to blink it away. "My brother isn't here." I noticed that two other boys who rode the bus from his class were there, but he was nowhere to be found. I searched my memory for their names.

I held the sides of my hood back away from my face. I did not like the feeling of the clammy plastic on my skin.

"Have you seen Little Man?"

They looked around, surprised that I was talking to them. The taller one opened his mouth to speak but the other one answered. He had a big knot on his forehead and his eyes were black and blue. "He was here before lunch but I can't remember seeing him after."

"He wasn't sick or anything was he?" I wondered if he would go home without them telling me, knowing he wouldn't.

"No, I don't think so. He took the bathroom pass and I don't think he came back. I thought maybe he went to the office or something."

I squinted and my throat knotted up as I watched the monitor enter the school building to ask about Little Man. My nose started to run again and I wiped my face with the back of my hand. The principal followed the bus monitor back out of the building, holding the megaphone in his hand and an umbrella in the other. It must be serious if he was going to venture into the rain.

"You don't know where your brother is?" His mouth was drawn into a line.

I shook my head, feeling hollow. I remembered how quiet he was on the way to the bus stop this morning. I thought it was because I was quiet, realizing that I was so preoccupied with myself that I had paid no attention to him. He ran away on purpose. Without telling me.

"I'm sure he's fine. Maybe they sent him home without telling you. I will check with his teacher. You go on home and I will call your father to check. He will probably be there waiting for you when you get home."

I let myself be herded onto the bus with the other kids and the principal walked away, whispering to the bus monitor. I knew that Little Man wasn't at home. I could feel it in my bones, along with a dampness that had crept in from the rain. I was happy and sad at the same time. Little Man was out. He had done something. But his action made me painfully aware of where I had failed. I was supposed to be watching out for him. I was the big sister. The responsible one.

He wasn't there when I got there. I knew that he wouldn't be. Granny Hambay-el and her daughter where waiting, Granny sitting on the plastic-covered arm of the sectional. Her hands were on her knees and she rubbed them back and forth like she was rubbing at some unknown pain. She glared at me when I walked in, like it was all my fault.

"Sweetie, do you know here he is?"

"No, ma'am," I said. My stomach quivered.

"You sure? You know you evil chile and you always leading dat boy into trouble. It betta not be one of you tricks, you hear?"

Her words stung as if she had slapped my face. She wasn't concerned for Little Man. She wasn't concerned about us. She was just worried that Daddy would blame her.

I nodded. I knew Little Man was okay.

"Your father be here in a minute. You children think this is funny, but let's see what you say when he gets here."

I went to get my chair from under the steps and just as I reached my usual spot the doorbell rang. Elizabeth hurried to the front room, tripping over the plastic runner. I looked down at the floor, noticing that the runner had yellowed in some places.

It was Daddy. My heart jumped and I wanted him to grab me and hug me. He didn't. Instead he took off his jacket and folded it neatly, laying it across the back of the sofa. He wore a white shirt with his black under-shoulder gun holster. The gun that was concealed by his jacket now glared at me.

He didn't say hello.

"What do you know about this, Sweetie?" Daddy rubbed his hand over his mouth. He used the voice he reserved for work, like he as interrogating a criminal or something, and he looked scrubbly, like he needed a shave.

I sucked my teeth this time. Instead of worrying about Little Man he was already convinced that we had cooked up some kind of conspiracy. There was no telling what Granny Hambay-el made him believe before I got home.

"Excuse me, young lady!"

"Nothing. I know nothing." I sat in my chair, folding my hands across my chest. My breath came hard and my nose was hot. I could not help the pout that found its way to my mouth. He didn't even look at me.

"Watch your tone with me, you hear? And put those lips back in your face."

I didn't want to help them. Little Man was free, and that had to be better than this. I was mad at him for leaving me behind.

Daddy let out a big breath, and then sadness peeked through his stern exterior. He suddenly looked sad. "He could be hurt. There are so many crazy people out there." He talked to no one in particular. He put his hands on his hips and paced the runner two times, then stopped. "Sweetie, we have to find your brother." He was back to his calm voice. "Did you notice if he was upset this morning or anything? I don't understand what could have happened that would make him run away."

My mouth dropped open. How could he not see?

"Monica?"

"Daddy, He's mad at you. Because of Janetta. Everyone else gets included in your life except us. He ran away because of you."

Daddy didn't answer me, he didn't even tell me to lower my voice this time. He and Granny Hambay-el walked into the kitchen, leaving me in the living room and out of their discussion. Once again, they did not think to include me or ask what I was thinking. I got lost in the four-thirty movie. Gidget danced on the beach with her friends. They laughed in the sunshine as it thundered outside. Every now and then I could hear the deepness of my father's words drift to my ears from the kitchen. The phone rang and rang. I wondered where the police were. On TV, when children disappeared the police came. Maybe Daddy was it.

I imagined Little Man off somewhere, sitting directly on someone's furniture and eating food he liked. He was getting children's aspirin for a slight fever he got after being wet in the rain instead of some mysterious herbal remedy. And he would not get cod liver oil on Friday that normally made us gag so much we had to drink orange juice right after. And Gidget danced on the beach.

The rain came down harder, making a drumming sound on the roof. The doorbell rang. Elizabeth opened it.

"I came as soon as I could."

"They are in the kitchen." Elizabeth used the voice she reserved for visitors and my daddy.

Janetta was here. She said hello to me but I ignored her.

She kept talking. "Your father called me. About Kenneth."

She stared into my eyes for a minute and then left me there as Elizabeth herded her into the kitchen.

Elizabeth came back from the kitchen and I was still standing.

"You okay, Sweetie?

"No."

"Are you sick, then? Maybe you need some air. All this rain—"

"Can I go to bed? I want to go to bed." I didn't intend to scream, but Elizabeth looked shocked.

"Don't get hysterical. He will be okay. We have it under control. Let's step out for some air."

I let her push me out the front door, then she stood with me in the rain.

We didn't talk. My breath came easier as I listened to the sounds of the raindrops on the aluminum awning. I ran my hand through the azalea bushes and pulled off some leaves. Elizabeth let me stand there, silent. I pushed them in my pocket.

"I'm okay now."

I stared at Elizabeth. Her face was softer. She left me outside the door and Daddy opened it and came outside to stand with me.

His hands were in his pockets and he stood next to me. He was quiet and he stared out across the street.

We listened to the rain together for a few minutes. Finally, Daddy spoke. His words seemed to come slowly, as if speaking was suddenly hard for him.

"I didn't mean to make either one of you upset. I just wanted you to like her." He put his hand on my shoulder.

I didn't move.

"Maybe I did come on too strong, Sweetie. I didn't know what to do. I certainly didn't mean for this to happen."

I nodded slowly.

"We'll find him." He opened the door for us to go back inside. His voice changed and he went back to using his all business voice. "I have it under control," he said.

I slid through the doorway and took off my wet shoes. They had nothing under control and just didn't know it.

THIRTY-FIVE

*I*t wasn't butterfly season. It was the fall. I couldn't understand how Little Man turned into Kenneth and flew away somewhere. I kept waiting for my own metamorphosis to happen, too like I read about in the nature encyclopedia from my closet. I wanted to become Monica instead of Sweetie so I could fly away to a new home and drink from some sweet flower. I waited three weeks and it didn't happen. And it was surprisingly easy to fall into a new routine, even with the hole that Little Man created. I was living with my anger and my sadness, as I had learned to live with everything else. My anger was so big and so deep, but I couldn't tell what in particular I was mad at, or if I was mad at everyone, Daddy and Little Man included.

I only stayed home from school one day. Then they walked me to the bus stop for a whole three weeks. Elizabeth had that duty. She walked with me in silence and waited for the bus. The whole time she would steal glances at me. I kept trying to catch her doing it. Whenever I looked at her she would look away, as if we were playing a game. But it wasn't a game; I knew she was checking me for signs of change too.

Little Man stayed gone for those three weeks. Time moved forward for everyone else, but I was frozen. The leaves fell from the trees and it got a little chilly as it usually did this time of year. I could smell the approaching winter in the air. At first I would watch the ants running around my feet while we waited at the bus stop, standing away from the other kids. The ants scurried like they were preparing for something. Then they were gone, job finished.

Daddy's schedule didn't change; I went home as usual, except I was escorted there too. I was never left alone outside the house, watched all the time. Daddy's new girlfriend came and went from our house in the evenings. She was cheery, bringing food and smiles. Daddy tried to seem cheery too. This was new. He laughed with her, making jokes that weren't funny and holding his stomach. She threw her head back and flashed her eyes that were always covered with blue eye makeup.

I asked the same thing every time I went home.

"Any news? Did we find him yet?"

"No. But we have information. He is around here somewhere, in the neighborhood. Don't worry. We'll find him soon."

Janette tried her best to be comforting, but their cheeriness made me more and more upset. *How dare they laugh when he was gone?*

After the third time I asked, Daddy snapped at me. "I will not allow you to use your brother's misfortune as an excuse to be rude, young lady. You watch the way you talk to your elders," he said.

I jumped back, surprised. My own question echoed in my head. I was surprised that he was right. I sounded rude, even to me, but I didn't know what else to do with what I felt. I was more worried about myself than I was about him. We would be silent and then they would be laughing at something again, with me sitting and watching, not saying anything else for the rest of the time I was there. I was intruding, the only one that truly cared at all. I thought about how I could "move things in my direction," like Tembo said, but remained stuck in my cocoon and at a loss for an answer.

I wanted to stomp away, but instead I just excused myself to the front yard. Janetta followed me and sat on the other half of the stoop.

"How can you laugh and joke?" My anger ignited the fuse of my words.

Janetta turned and looked at me slowly. "What would you have us do?"

I crossed my arms in front of me. "Look for Little Man."

She paused. "Your father is doing everything in his power. We both are doing our part."

"It doesn't look that way."

"It might not. To you. But I was trying to take your father's mind off of things. Relieve his stress. Seems to me you could do that too. Your attitude is just making it more stressful for everyone."

I had never thought of that. "I wasn't trying to be stressful."

"All that anger is like a big waste of energy. You might find other ways to use that. Only you can make you happy, Monica. You have to decide what you need to do about things, and then do it."

He left me alone with her in the middle of the second week. We were sitting in the living room and they were watching TV together. The one that used to sit on the floor in the corner had been replaced by a color TV, as big as they came. She was filing her nails. She moved the emery board so hard that I was surprised she had any nails left. The scraping noise she was making as she grated it back and forth over her nails was distracting me.

Daddy stood up from the couch where he had been snuggled next to her.

"I gotta go to the little boy's room." He did the same bathroom dance I did.

"Don't stay gone too long."

As soon as he left the room, her smile left her face as if it were wiped off with a rag. "Is everything okay, Sweetie?"

What kind of question was that? She obviously did not know me and I did not want her to. I looked up from my book. I was up to the fourth volume in the nature encyclopedia. Her voice was sticky sweet, like honey, but I wasn't a fly.

"Don't you want to be called Monica? You are getting so big to be called Sweetie."

"No. My mother named me that."

"Oh." She stopped filing.

I tried to resume where I left off.

"You don't like me do you?"

"It's not about you." I put the book on my lap and stared straight at her. My boldness surprised even me.

"You're right, Monica Denise. It's not." She used every

name she could, as if she wasn't what name to use. "But it's not about you either. You don't have to like me. I am here for your father and frankly I don't care if you like me." The sparkle previously in her eyes as she laughed at Daddy's jokes was nowhere to be found.

My mouth dropped open.

"I know it has been hard, but this family, your father has to move on with life. Time moves on whether you remain stuck in one place or not. We have to learn to sweep the clouds away or they stay with us forever."

Who was this woman? What did she know about moving on? "I had a mother—"

"I never said I was trying to replace your mother. No one could ever do that. I am sure she was wonderful, just from the stories your father tells me. But we all need to stop feeling sorry for ourselves, understand?"

I didn't.

Daddy thumped at the top of the stairs and we stared at each other. Daddy told her stories about Momma. I wanted him to tell me too. I wanted to remember the good things.

"It's time for us to go, Daddy." I closed my book and tucked it under my arm.

"But it's early! Don't you want to watch the Muppet Show with us? I thought it was your favorite."

"No, that was Kenny's favorite. And I am tired. Are you walking me back?"

They both did. They held hands. I guess time did move on.

THIRTY-SIX

*I*n the place between wake and sleep, I was dreaming about rain. I knew I was in Muscoda because the rain was warm. It smelled musty and fell in big drops. The wind blew, making a rasping sound. My eyes fluttered and I was drawn away from sleep, realizing that the sound I heard was not wind but heavy breathing. My eyes snapped open and focused on the fan still in the window across from me. Elizabeth's bed was long made. She was gone as usual and the room didn't even smell like her perfume anymore.

The sound of grunting wiped the grogginess from my eyes. Alarmed, I turned over. Everett was standing over the head of my bed, holding himself in his hand, rubbing back and forth. I jumped up, touching my hair at the same time. It was wet and sticky. Everett's eyes were closed and he had not noticed that I was awake. He didn't even hear my bed creak as I jumped up. I felt pressure in my chest, as if someone were sitting on me, pushing my breath out.

White liquid spewed out, and I knew immediately that it was in my hair too. He opened his eyes and tried to stop the liquid with a cloth in his other hand. He jumped when he saw I had moved, but my gaze remained fixed on his crotch. He had my soiled panties in his hand! Pressure built up in my throat, and before I knew what I was doing, I screamed.

Everett hastily finished wiping himself with my panties and leered at me. Outside my room, the steps thundered. Granny Hambay-el was coming. He zipped his pants and left my room as I stood there. My face felt hot and I wanted to shower. I screamed again.

Granny was at my door.

"What is wrong with you, gal? Why you make all this fuss, eh?"

My eyes were big. I pointed at the panties that Everett had dropped on the floor in the doorway. The front door slammed. "Everett—"

"Everett what? What you trying to say? Speak up." She sucked her teeth. "These were supposed to be buried in the yard, for good luck. What are they doing here?"

"He was rubbing himself with-- He did this. He had my panties."

Granny was silent for a minute and then a spark of understanding lit in her eyes. "I told you you was fas'! Now you here enticing me grandson! What did you do to instigate this type of t'ing? Wha's wrong with you, gal?"

I shook my head. "Nothing. I was sleeping!"

"Don't be raising your voice, gal. You hear me? You get cleaned up. Wash that hair you so dyamn proud of too! I will wait for you downstairs!"

I stomped into the bathroom and turned on the shower, making the water as hot as possible. I was not normally allowed to take showers; Granny Hambay-el allowed baths only, with as little water as possible. I stepped into the water and scrubbed my body and my hair with the black soap that was reserved for grown-up use. I could not get clean.

An arm reached in and turned off the water.

"Get out now, you wastin' watah!"

I had not even heard her come in.

"I still have soap on me!"

"You wipe it off with a towel, then. Come 'ere now."

She didn't wait for me to step out, but instead reached into the shower stall and grabbed me. She rubbed my body with the rough towel. I did not resist her. I could still smell Everett's muskiness and removing my skin might be the only way to physically remove his scent. I knew the smell would never leave my memory.

My neck began to hurt as Granny Hambay-el grabbed my hair and began to rake the comb through it. She didn't ask me to sit, instead she reached up and yanked my head down to her. I covered my face with my hands.

"You think you so pretty, gal. Don't be so proud. You know that pride is a sin, no? Pride cometh before a fall. That be in the Bible, you know."

I didn't answer. She tugged and pulled at my head with a force that I knew would leave me with a headache. My eyes stung from the remains of the soap that had run into them in the shower.

Suddenly she let me go, and I fell backwards, catching myself against the wall of the shower stall. I dropped my hands from my face, feeling lighter.

Granny Hambay-el looked at me with a strange smile on her face.

"That should teach you, no?" She waved a clump of my hair at me. "You take care! You get out of hand again and I will let the birds get this and build them nest wit' it. You see what kind of headache you get then!"

She held the scissors in her other hand, down along her leg, pointed toward the floor. She had cut my hair. Granny Hambay-el had grabbed a section of my hair, as big as she could and had cut it from my head!

Instead of reaching up for my hair, I reached for a towel. My nostrils flared. My eyes narrowed. I did not want to cry and I did not feel weakened. Instead I felt like I had gained more power and confidence than ever before. Janetta was right, I had to decide what I was going to do, then do it.

This was the first time I felt hatred for Granny Hambay-el, in addition to the anger. I realized that in her mind, this whole thing was my fault. They would say it was an accident. I had to move things in my direction. I could not stay here anymore.

THIRTY-SEVEN

No one spoke when I came downstairs. Granny Hambay-el was in the kitchen. The scowl on her face said she was still disgusted with me. She stood over the sink and poured water into a large teacup.

Elizabeth hurried into the kitchen, like she was being chased. Granny moved her teacup to the table, leaning on it as she did. The table groaned in protest, its metal legs were wobbly and some of her tea splashed from the cup into the saucer she set it into.

I stopped in my tracks. Elizabeth held Little Man's hand, towing him behind her. She was walking so fast he could barely keep up. She tripped as she stepped off the runner in the hallway and onto the kitchen linoleum.

I narrowed my eyes. No one said anything for the longest minute I had ever known. Little Man stood there, looking at his feet, his hands clasped in front of him. The position of his body screamed his defiance out loud. I thought I would be happy if he came back, but all I could feel was anger. I brushed my eyes over him; he looked clean. I didn't recognize his clothing. I felt the heat of my anger beginning in my feet, then sweeping up through my body in an arc. I was starting to shake.

Granny grabbed him by both shoulders. "Where you been, bwoy? Call his father, tell him to get here." She turned him around, checking him for damage. "Were you stolen? What happened? Tell us."

He pulled away from her, frowning.

"Tchhh! You come back 'ere now!" She reached for him again.

He slapped her hand away. My anger changed to surprise. Elizabeth dropped the phone, leaving the handset twirling in the air as the tangles in the cord unwound themselves. Granny used her hand to brace herself on the table.

"Don' you dare disrespect me dat way, no! You see me on you, you here!" she roared.

I cringed, pressing myself against the refrigerator.

Kenny seemed to have grown in an instant. He was taller, bigger. "I don't have to tell you anything. I want to talk to my father!" He crossed his arms across his chest.

Granny reached up and flew across the room so fast I almost did not see her move. She boxed his ears with her left hand. Kenny sailed to the floor.

Instead of crying, he looked up at her. His eyes were dark and smoky. Just then Everett stormed into the room. He moved faster than I had ever seen him move. He came straight to Little Man and picked him up by the neck of his shirt. He shook him hard.

I pressed myself back against the wall, out of the wall.

"If you ever disrespect my granny like that again I will—"

I was sure that his bellowing voice could be heard by the neighbors.

"Stop before you hurt him," Elizabeth pleaded.

Everett spun around and walked with Little Man still in hand. He sat him in his chair, under the steps.

"You stay right here until you calm down," he said. "A few days in the street don't make you too big for the strap."

Little Man smiled and I gasped. He looked at Everett in his face, challenging him. "What will you do? Hit me? You can't do anything else to me. Living in a stranger's garage was better than here." For a second, the room was thick with silence.

"Dat dyamn upstart chile! The boy, him cra-zee and the girl, she fas'! Call them fat'er, man! Get him on the phone now!" Granny came back to herself.

For the first time, I made eye contact with Kenny. I peeled myself off the wall and stepped to his side. We didn't speak. There would be time enough for that later. I wanted to know where he had been and what had made him so brave. He would tell me, later, on the bus when we could talk. I didn't know what it was, but I knew that if he could stand up for himself, I could too.

I went to the library during recess and wrote down my answer. I put everything in my journal, just as it happened.

The librarian walked to my desk. "Ms. Faust would like to see you in her office," she said. She tossed the hall pass onto my desk, then immediately started talking to another student.

Miss Faust sat behind her desk, writing. I stood at her door and she waved me in. I was less than a minute late and

I was in trouble anyway. Goosebumps spread over my arms and legs. I was not used to being in trouble. She pointed to a chair and I sat obediently.

She started talking to me before she finished writing, not looking up at first. "So," she said. "Your teacher says you have been distracted. Upset looking. Is there something you want to discuss?"

I shook my head.

She raised her eyebrows. "Really? I hear your brother has returned. You don't even want to talk about that?"

I didn't want to talk. I wanted things to be fixed. She raised her eyebrows. "Okay. But do you have anymore writing for me? The last piece was very...intriguing."

A small smile found its way to my lips. "Not yet."

Before she could say anything else, a loud noise erupted in the outer office. Someone was yelling.

We both jumped, and my books slid to the floor. Miss Faust stood up quickly and walked around her desk and out of the room.

"Monica, we can continue this later," she yelled over her shoulder.

I gathered my things, including my journal. I quickly glanced around the room, then opened my journal to the last entry. Gently, I placed it on Miss Faust's desk.

It was going to save me.

THIRTY-EIGHT

I could see Daddy waiting for us at the bus stop before the door opened. My heart jumped into my mouth. Had he already read my journal?

He didn't say much, he just hugged us both, then herded us into the car. He drove straight to Granny Hambay-el's house.

'Aren't we going home?" Kenny asked.

"Not yet. I have some business to take care of." His voice was gruff.

Granny looked as surprised to see Daddy at her door as I had been at the bus stop. Her mouth dropped open, but she recovered quickly, finding her daddy-smile.

"Well," she said.

"Well, indeed. Can I come in?"

"Sure, mon." She stepped aside. "Please, come. Bless the Lord. Your bwoy has returned safely, eh." She called back to Elizabeth to make tea.

Neither one of us moved to get the folding chairs. We sat on the sofa beside Daddy instead. Granny glared at us, but did not stop us.

"I have some questions." Daddy did not wait for Elizabeth to bring the tea. I watched as he reached into his jacket and removed my diary.

"Where did you get that?" I tried to sound surprised.

"Sit, Sweetie. I know it is yours. And I think you know how I got it." His voice was very calm. "Miss Faust read it because she said you have been very different over the past few weeks, which is understandable, considering all that has happened with your brother. But after she read it, she called me right away. I am so sorry. I should have listened to you."

Daddy turned to Granny Hambay-el. "I don't know what kind of house you are running, but you are crazy if you think I am going to let my children stay here and be abused by you and your crazy family. Where is your grandson, Everett?" Daddy's chest heaved. He stood up.

Granny shrank back. "I don't understand. What does he—"

She didn't have to call him. Everett appeared at the doorway.

Daddy lunged for him, grabbing him by the shirt collar. He lifted him off the ground.

Little Man grabbed my hand.

"You are some kind of pervert! You stay the hell away from my daughter or I will make sure that you spend the rest of your natural life in prison."

Elizabeth came running from the kitchen. She screamed.

Granny Hambay-el looked confused.

Daddy continued yelling, holding Everett up in the air. "I promise you they don't like child molesters in prison!"

"What yu talkin' 'bout? Dis is crazy. Let me gran go. Right now."

Daddy lowered Everett until his feet touched the ground, but he did not release him. "Your grandson is a piece of shit.

He has been sneaking into my daughter's bedroom. Isn't that right?"

Everyone in the room gasped. I looked down at the floor.

Daddy shook Everett again. "Isn't that right?" His voice rattled the china.

Elizabeth started to cry. "Please, don't hurt him."

Granny's mouth stood open for a long minute, then she rolled her eyes.

"You dyamn people! I don' know who you t'ink you are. First, your bwoy try to hit me, and den dis. You don't pay me enough to take this kind of abuse."

Granny looked less scary to me now, smaller. I searched her face. Tears streamed down her cheeks. I could find no traces of the lady who gave us fried chicken the first day, when we came here with Momma all those years ago. Where was the lady who told Momma that she would take care of us? I couldn't remember that person and I didn't know where she had gone.

Daddy cleared his throat. He shoved Everett and he fell backward onto the floor. "You won't have to worry about it anymore. I won't be paying you. And you," he pointed at Everett, "you best be glad that I am a police officer or else I'd kill you."

Daddy turned around and grabbed both of our hands. No one spoke as we left.

THIRTY-NINE

We never went back to the house. Kenny got grounded forever and Daddy cried. I was just glad to be away from there, almost happy that things happened the way they did. I never saw Granny again. I saw Elizabeth sometimes, on her way to the market, but she never spoke. I heard Daddy say that Everett moved back to Central America.

I was still angry with Little Man, but glad he had come back when he did. None of us ever called him Little Man again. He was Kenneth from that point on.

It was very different at our house, not perfect, just different. Janetta came over all the time. It turned out that she wasn't that bad after all. Together, she and Daddy cleaned up the house, vacuuming the rug and moving out all of Momma's stuff.

After a few weeks Janetta gave me a pretty perfume bottle that was Momma's, and a framed picture of her and my dad. I put in on my dresser in my new room at home that I didn't share with anyone. Pretty soon I even closed my door just because I could.

Fall turned into spring and Kenny never wet the bed. Daddy bought me clothes that were not handmade and I learned to comb my own hair.

I noticed that the grass was finally starting to sprout and went outside to sit on the brick stoop the way other kids in our neighborhood did. I used to sit and watch them run up and down, but time had moved on for them too. Instead of hide-and-go-seek, they were visiting and standing around. The yard was full of the ghosts of memories, shadows of record players and mattresses that I knew I would always remember there.

"Hey, Sweetie, long time no see. You seen Jamila?" Amy leaned on the gate the way she used to. "We supposed to go to the park and hear the deejay."

I smiled and shook my head. It struck me as funny that so much had changed but nothing had. Amy was taller and had grown the beginnings of breasts. Jamila was still leaving her behind and had probably gone on without her.

"You wanna come with us? The deejays are those *Rapper's Delight* guys. You know who I mean, right?"

I did, but I wasn't ready yet. Change was slow for me. I was just happy she asked, but I wanted to sit on the stoop in my new clothes and feel the spring breezes.

The wind blew a little harder, bringing with it the smells of cooking from the neighborhood. A flash of red caught my eye. The rose bush that Momma had planted was in full bloom, even though it was early in the season. The bush was weighed down to the ground, over-laden with roses. None of the other bushes in the neighborhood seemed to be blooming, not even the one on the other side of the yard.

It struck me that this was a sign from Momma.

Change had to come from within. No one could do it for me. Just then I felt a tickle under my left eye and I reached up. My fingers came back wet. I rubbed my fingers together, and it took a minute for me to comprehend what was on my fingers. It was tears. I was crying, for the first time I could remember.

"You go on ahead," I said, wiping my eyes. "Thanks for asking though. Maybe next time."

Amy nodded and headed toward the park. Next time she asked, I knew I would go.

I let the tears flow down my face and across my lips. I licked their salt as they clogged my nose and splashed on my lap. They left a wet spot on my bright green pants that Daddy had purchased from a store, and took with them the long-time lump in my throat.

I looked at things very differently after that. I guess we were all angry about some things. Daddy and the rest of the family had been angry when Momma died, and I was too, so much that it was keeping me locked inside. But then I woke up one day and realized that all that anger had just left me in the middle of the night. And I just couldn't remember when.

A NOTE FROM THE AUTHOR

*I*t's impossible to write a memoir. Over time, our memories fail even those of us with the clearest of faculties. Every new experience seems to change the past ones in our mind's eye, and every day in our lives brings us to new understandings of past events. We are all revisionist historians; no matter how honest and straight forward we think we are, we can't possibly get it all correct. My father used to say that there are three versions of every story depending on who was telling it, and I find this to be true. *Momma: Gone* is as much memoir as it is creative non-fiction. It is as much my memory as it is my fiction.

This is one of the first things I ever tried to write. Over the years, it took on a life of its own. As I learned more about writing and about myself, the story changed. It got pushed to the back burner as I was encouraged to write things that were more saleable, more easily. It started out as true as a child can remember and understand what was going on around them. It also started out as very boring. Over time I found that Sweetie was precocious and grown, partly because I was when I was her, but also because I had incorporated my own present-day understanding of the events that had taken place in my family. It moved from true to maybe not so much as other people gave me their version of what had happened and I folded that information into the story.

There are incidents in the book that are relayed exactly as I remember them happening. My mother died as a result of complication of breast cancer. In the end days, she drank heavily and it made my family crazy. My father loved her fiercely and my extended family argued about me and my brother in the aftermath of her impending death. I had to blend all of those protesting people into one. That character became my aunt. I cannot say I understood the motivations of all of these people when I wrote this. Because I was a child, much of it was never discussed with me. Much of my understanding was pieced together by means of conversations with and comments by various family members over the years. When I shared early versions of this manuscript with my adult family, it caused a heated discussion. Based on that, I think the story is on the right track in terms of some combined version of what actually happened.

I acknowledge that the timeline has to be off. I made changes to the story to make it feel more like a story and more like what people are used to when they read a novel. I also made changes based on what various editors and agents told me as I was writing this. What I did not do was scrap the entire story as it was suggested I do. One agent (now dead) told me that this writing was phenomenal, but she didn't feel like the readership was ready for this kind of story from a Black writer. An editor told me that no one wanted to read anything about the time period around the Vietnam War. I am still Black, but this is more than a Black story. It is an American story.

Throughout this story, music is central. Music was big in my family and in our American history and that stayed with me. There are times when I can pinpoint time for historical events and family happenings based on whatever music was popular, and I tried to weave this into the story. I wanted the readers to understand that although this happened when it did, it is a timeless story. That is why I shared the music of the day, but not the year. Certainly, there are events in the story that could only have happened in the aftermath of Vietnam, but many of them could just as easily happen in the aftermath of Desert Storm or Desert Shield. Just as families today are still torn apart by cancer, there are many mothers today who are weeping for their sons and daughters fighting a war on foreign soil and returning home to joblessness and confusion. Many of the scenes in the south may be tough to read, but even in 'post-racial' America, our history is our history and we cannot escape it. Rather than sweep it under the rug, I choose to embrace it and continue to learn from it.

Momma: Gone is about family and it is about history. It's about a woman anguishing over her impending death and what that death does to her family. It is also about a man's love for his children and a family that cannot move on until they learn to grieve for their loss. Until we understand our histories as we understand them, we cannot grow. Just as our history shapes us as a society, our families shape each one of us individually. Together, they make us strong.